Praise for

Sierra Falls

"Fans of contemporary romance will delight in Veronica Wolff's sexy, engrossing *Sierra Falls*."
—Jill Shalvis, *USA Today* bestselling author

"The first Bailey family drama is a wonderful romantic suspense that grips readers from the moment the sheriff and the hosteller meet. The charming, rugged setting, enhanced by the heroine's family, is a delightful counterpoint to a nasty predator. Still, this superserpentine, suspenseful story line belongs to the lead couple as love stuns both of them."
—*Genre Go Round Reviews*

"Tense mystery, family drama, and a rocking romance are set against a picturesque small mountain town with a seasoned history, strong memorable characters, and a tale with a twist."
—*RT Book Reviews*

"A beautifully crafted blend of compelling characters and heartwarming romance. Veronica Wolff is a breathtaking storyteller."
—Barbara Freethy, #1 *New York Times* bestselling author

"Engaging protagonists . . . Enjoyable escapism."
—*Publishers Weekly*

"A very sweet small-town romance."   —*Night Owl Reviews*

continued . . .

Praise for Veronica Wolff and her novels

"A poignant story . . . It explores family, friendship, revenge, obsession, and the power of love to heal deep wounds."
—*RT Book Reviews*

"Profoundly touching and emotionally searing!"
—*Fresh Fiction*

"Wolff writes a story that will grab you from the first word and not let go."   —*Night Owl Reviews*

"Passionate and magical."   —*Publishers Weekly*

"Refreshing and intriguing."
—*The Romance Readers Connection*

"Powerful, riveting, and vibrant. A must-read page-turner destined to be a keeper."
—Sue-Ellen Welfonder, *USA Today* bestselling author

"A rich, beautifully written love story that will haunt your heart long after you turn the last page."
—Penelope Williamson, RITA Award–winning author

Timber Creek

VERONICA WOLFF

BERKLEY SENSATION, NEW YORK

THE BERKLEY PUBLISHING GROUP
Published by the Penguin Group
Penguin Group (USA) Inc.
375 Hudson Street, New York, New York 10014, USA
Penguin Group (Canada), 90 Eglinton Avenue East, Suite 700, Toronto, Ontario M4P 2Y3, Canada
(a division of Pearson Penguin Canada Inc.) • Penguin Books Ltd., 80 Strand, London WC2R 0RL,
England • Penguin Ireland, 25 St. Stephen's Green, Dublin 2, Ireland (a division of Penguin
Books Ltd.) • Penguin Group (Australia), 707 Collins Street, Melbourne, Victoria 3008, Australia
(a division of Pearson Australia Group Pty. Ltd.) • Penguin Books India Pvt. Ltd., 11 Community
Centre, Panchsheel Park, New Delhi—110 017, India • Penguin Group (NZ), 67 Apollo Drive,
Rosedale, Auckland 0632, New Zealand (a division of Pearson New Zealand Ltd.) • Penguin Books
(South Africa) (Pty.) Ltd., Rosebank Office Park, 181 Jan Smuts Avenue, Parktown North 2193,
South Africa • Penguin China, B7 Jiaming Center, 27 East Third Ring Road North,
Chaoyang District, Beijing 100020, China

Penguin Books Ltd., Registered Offices: 80 Strand, London WC2R 0RL, England

This is a work of fiction. Names, characters, places, and incidents either are the product of the author's
imagination or are used fictitiously, and any resemblance to actual persons, living or dead, business
establishments, events, or locales is entirely coincidental. The publisher does not have any control over
and does not assume any responsibility for author or third-party websites or their content.

TIMBER CREEK

A Berkley Sensation Book / published by arrangement with the author

ISBN: 978-1-62090-832-7

BERKLEY SENSATION®
Berkley Sensation Books are published by The Berkley Publishing Group,
a division of Penguin Group (USA) Inc.,
375 Hudson Street, New York, New York 10014.
BERKLEY SENSATION® is a registered trademark of Penguin Group (USA) Inc.
The "B" design is a trademark of Penguin Group (USA) Inc.

PRINTED IN THE UNITED STATES OF AMERICA

To Joey,
with thanks for making such a beautiful
home in the mountains

Acknowledgments

I'd like to express my continuing thanks to my wonderful editor, Cindy Hwang, and the rest of the Penguin team, as well as to Robin Rue and Beth Miller at Writers House. Our collaboration makes this job a true pleasure.

I consider myself blessed that so many of my trusted friends also happen to be some of my favorite authors. I'm particularly grateful to Kate Perry, who truly is by my side every step of the way; to Christie Ridgway, for her sage advice on structure; Jami Alden, Martha Flynn, and Tracy Grant for the writing dates and pep talks; and to the rest of my beloved Bay Area crew, especially Bella Andre, Barbara Freethy, Carol Grace, Anne Mallory, and Monica McCarty. Finally, a giant thank-you to my mom for fielding my unending "so how was it?" questions— she'd deny it, but she truly has a gift for characterization.

Finally, there aren't enough words to express how deeply I appreciate my patient and supportive husband and kids. Who knew a software engineer (and original mountain man) would prove to be so masterful at brainstorming romance plots?

One

~

Laura's eyes tracked up the ladder and came to rest full stop on one of the tightest posteriors she'd ever seen. Her mind blanked. She'd been so outraged. She'd mustered up an angry speech, repeating it with increasing gusto on the car drive over. But apparently all it took was this lone example of magnificent male tushery to make her go dumb.

The ladder squeaked as the man shifted and looked down, and Laura caught sight of just whose ruggedly handsome face was attached to said magnificence.

She felt every muscle in her body stiffen. It was a Jessup. She was allergic to Jessups. Eddie Jessup, to be precise. The worst and most allergenic of them all.

He smiled broadly. "Can I help you?"

Her morning hadn't started bad like this. It'd started pretty great, actually, helping out with a bustling breakfast crowd. Her family's business was booming—visitors to the Big Bear Lodge were up, which meant diners aplenty at the tavern, and she was riding high as the new manager overseeing it all.

Over the past several months, she'd thrown herself into her work. When her sister discovered a cache of letters dating from the gold rush era, Laura had used her expertise and Bay Area contacts to capitalize on the find. They'd begun to get a little press, not to mention visits by some tweedy historical types. Which meant even more visitors and more success for their family lodge.

But not if Eddie Jessup and his cursed Jessup Brothers Construction were doing what she'd heard they were doing.

It was a clear June day, and she shielded her eyes against the glare, watching as he climbed down the ladder. She was definitely not noticing the way his white T-shirt clung in places under the hot sun.

"You got something to say, or did you just come to ogle?"

That broke her silence. "I've got better things to do than ogle you, Eddie Jessup."

He laughed, and the easy confidence of it made her cheeks burn. She shot her eyes down, making like she needed to check a text on her cell phone.

He jumped from the last few rungs, dusted off his hands, and faced her with a smile. "Well, darlin'? To what do I owe the honor?"

This particular Jessup had been getting under her skin since high school, but she was past that now. Back then, she'd looked only ahead, longing for the day she could hightail it out of Sierra Falls. Somehow Eddie had sensed it, and he'd upped his torment, always coaxing, teasing, and challenging her. It was a habit he'd never gotten over.

But she was over it. Big-time.

In fact, she liked to consider herself Jessup-proof. She was a college-educated, formerly incredibly successful Silicon Valley marketing professional who'd moved back home as a full-grown woman simply to get some perspective. She wanted only a change of scenery. No men—Jessup or otherwise.

She'd sworn off dating, just as she'd sworn off her old

life in the city. She had an ex-fiancé she didn't miss and an old job she'd pushed from her mind, and yet she'd once spent so much time chasing both. But why and for what?

She'd come home to figure out the answers. To determine what it was she wanted from life, what made her happy. Because she'd learned the hard way that a man and a successful career didn't always go together in harmony.

She reminded herself that she was self-assured. Self-reliant. Self-made. She put her hands on her hips. "I'm not your darlin'."

He gave her an assessing look. "More's the pity."

She resisted the urge to adjust her clothes under the intensity of that stare. "So don't call me that."

"Yes, ma'am." He'd said it with mock gravity, touching a finger to an imaginary hat. Before she could demand that he not *ma'am* her, either, he continued, "So what would bring a fine, not-your-darlin' city girl like you to a construction site? Because I can see on that pretty face of yours— you've got something to say."

Fine . . . pretty. She refused to register the comments. Eddie probably spoke like that to every female within a ten-mile radius. And what had she come to say? It was in her brain somewhere.

It took a moment for the arguments she'd rehearsed in the car to shoot to the forefront of her mind, but then she demanded, "What are you doing here?"

He got an innocent look on his face. "I'm fixing a storm drain."

"I can see that. I mean, what are you *doing*?" She swept her arm, taking in the abandoned house and surrounding ranch property. "Here."

"Ah." He met her eyes, and for once he looked serious. "You heard the news."

"Yeah, I heard about your Golden Slumbers Ranchlandia."

He laughed. "It's Sleepy Hills Resort and Spa."

"Whatever." She waved an impatient hand. "Sounds like a cemetery to me. Fitting, seeing as you're about to bury the Bailey family business."

"We have no intention of burying your business," he said, his tone annoyingly kind. "It'll be good for the whole town. Fairview Properties contracted the Jessups. We buy our supplies from Tom's hardware store. Soon we'll hire local workers. Workers who'll then go eat at your tavern. An influx of money all around."

She tapped a finger on her chin. "And hmm . . . let's see. Who do you think the big winners are in this whole thing? Fairview, that's who. Because apparently they can just go wherever they want and install their giant resorts, meanwhile mowing down whatever stands in their way." Mowing down *her family's* lodge. "What's next, another Trump Tower?"

"Easy, Laura. I'm not the bad guy here."

His soothing tone had the opposite effect on her—it always did—and she stabbed her finger into his chest. "How about we kick the Kidd sisters out of their house and turn it into a Holiday Inn?"

"Nobody was kicked out. You know full well how those dot-com people abandoned this place for a swanky Sausalito condo years ago. It'll be good to fix it up." He took and held her finger, giving it a soft squeeze. "Look, Laura. I run a small business. We're working hard to get by, just like the rest of the town. We've got to take our jobs as we get them." Eddie's hand was callused, and warm, and aggravatingly gentle.

She pulled her finger free. "How about our business? The lodge will never be able to compete with this." She glared at the traditional ranch house. It was a rambling one-story affair, with several timber beams in need of patching, and electrical and plumbing systems that probably needed replacing. "It's a dump, by the way."

"Nothing the Jessup boys can't fix."

"I hope you get overrun by raccoons."

"Don't get any ideas." He stood behind her, putting his hands on her shoulders, staring at the property with her. "Look, you see the size of the place. It's smaller than a regular hotel. The Fairview guys want it to be a boutique spa resort. High-end, aimed at people who like to think they hike but wouldn't know a day pack from a day planner." He gave her shoulders a squeeze. "But you guys, your lodge is authentic. Tourists will always love it. You'll be fine."

She stiffened, stepping away before he had a chance to reach out and touch her again. The last time a man had told her *you'll be fine*, she'd ended up losing her job. "Eternal Slumbers here could put us out of business, and you know it."

Eddie's face fell. His expression looked like he was genuinely considering it, and she didn't trust it for an instant. "What do you want me to do?" he asked.

"I want you to get back into that ridiculous vehicle of yours, and call Fairview, and send them back to wherever it is they came from. Then they can go menace some other small town instead, and you can slide back under whatever rock you crawled from."

Instead of rising to the bait, he smiled an exasperating smile. "Not a fan of the pickup, are you?"

"You're compensating."

His expression softened. "Look, Laura. I'm sorry. I really am. But if we hadn't been the ones hired for the job, it would've been someone else. Probably some out-of-town development company."

"At least they would've needed a place to stay."

"Mm-hm." He checked his watch, looking distracted.

"Am I boring you?"

His eyes shot up, and he gave her that cocky grin she hated. "Never you. I've gotta run, though."

"Are the bars opening soon?"

"You know me better than that," he said, sounding oddly serious.

"Well, what if I'm not done talking?"

"Then we can take it up later," he said suggestively.

"You're maddening." She stormed past him, back to her car. He probably had a mistress out there waiting for him. Some noontime booty call.

"You can't really be angry," he said, following her.

"Can't I?" No matter how quickly she walked, his long strides kept up.

"I really believe this'll be good for the town. More rooms can accommodate more visitors. More visitors means more diners—"

"Spare me." She hopped into a half jog, annoyed that he was following, and without so much as breaking a sweat. "I'm going to stop you."

He slowed, and if she didn't know his type better, she'd have thought she heard actual sympathy in his voice. "Come on, Laura. Let's discuss this."

She'd messed up a job before, and she wouldn't fail again. She would show her family that she could be trusted with the business. Better than that, she'd be more successful than they'd ever dreamed. Which meant she needed to stop Fairview Properties from building a competing hotel. And it all began with Eddie.

She flung open the door to her little BMW sedan. "Oh, I'll be back all right. I'm about to become your worst nightmare."

Two

Eddie watched Laura drive away. When she'd first arrived, silently assessing him, he'd had a moment's fantasy that maybe she'd come to see him. That maybe he could take her hand, haul her into the empty house, and have her in one of the many thousands of ways he'd fantasized about since their high school days.

But Laura Bailey wasn't for having. She was cold and prickly and focused on only one thing: herself.

But she was also smart and funny, always surprising him, catching him off guard since they'd been kids. And now she'd grown up so fine, into this sexy woman with a tight-as-hell body that taunted him.

He scraped his hand through his hair, cooling the dampness. Where the hell had those Sierra breezes gone?

"Damn," he muttered. It wasn't just that sexy tank top with the pink bra straps peeping out that had him bothered. What she'd said niggled at the back of his mind. Would the Sleepy Hills project put the Big Bear Lodge under? He had no doubts that a big conglomerate like Fairview would happily watch as they drove a family-owned enterprise out of business.

But then again, Laura was probably just being Laura. Needing to be in control. The Expert. Truth of it was, they *needed* this—the future of his own family business was at stake. This job brought Jessup Brothers Construction onto the brink of something bigger. They could continue as they'd been, doing handyman work and the occasional bigger job around Sierra Falls, or they could grow into the construction company developers called to build things in Silver City, or Reno even.

His cell buzzed, pulling him from his thoughts. He looked at the screen. It was Hunter Fox, aka Mister Fairview himself. He wasn't the CEO, but he was close—he was the one who'd contracted Jessup Brothers Construction in the first place. Hunter was the man who signed Eddie's paychecks, and in this economy, that was all that mattered.

Eddie wandered under the awning to take the call. Sierra days never got too hot, but it was a clear June afternoon, and hard work, the hot sun—and one hot Bailey sister—had him eager to seek out a shady breeze. "Mister Fox."

"Eddie," a jovial voice greeted him. Hunter Fox might have been built like a refrigerator, but he was probably greasy enough to slip through the eye of a keyhole. "I've told you a thousand times, it's Hunter. Fairview might be a big company, but we've got small-town spirit. That's why I hired you boys."

Sure it was. Sure, it had nothing to do with the fact that a town as close-knit as Sierra Falls would look skeptically at a bunch of strangers coming in and bulldozing their land.

But Eddie wasn't stupid enough to say any of that. He might've sometimes played up that good-old-boy vibe, but it was because it made work easier—it was what people expected of him.

People. He blew out a sigh. People underestimated him.

People like Laura. What was the word she liked to call him . . . *Neanderthal?* She saw him as nothing more than a hick in a red truck, ready for Miller time. It'd gotten to the point where it was easier just to let her believe that clichéd idea of him. It was all she was willing to see, anyway.

"I appreciate that," Eddie said with forced ease. He'd rely on the easygoing good-guy voice for the Fairview suits, too. "The Jessups welcome Fairview to Sierra Falls."

"So, young man, when are we gonna break ground?"

Ah, the royal *we*. But Eddie knew how to play the game, and it was time to get his head in it. "I'm here now, taking a look around the property. She's an old girl, this ranch house, but nothing we Jessups can't handle. Outside is mostly cosmetic stuff—weather, wear and tear, that sort of thing. But the rest of it"—he stepped inside to get a better look—"I'm afraid we'll need to go down to the studs. Replace the old plumbing with copper. And then there's the electric. She's still got the old knob-and-tube wiring that'll—"

"That's why I'm calling," Hunter interrupted. "There's been a slight change in plans."

Eddie went on alert. "What sort of change?"

The man's rolling laugh reached him over the cell. "Don't get scared off, Edward."

"Mm-hm." It was *Edwin*, but Eddie never told anyone that. He was sure it was a fine name for some other guy, but he was just plain *Eddie*. The last person to call him Edwin had been his kindergarten teacher, and even then, he'd so hated it, the epic silent treatment he'd given the woman had made it just *Eddie* ever since. Only his family knew, and his brothers understood that spilling the beans brought with it pain of death. "Jessups don't scare easy, so all due respect, just spit it out, sir."

Hunter laughed again, only this time it had a canny edge to it. "I get it. You've got mettle. I like that. So I'll shoot straight. With the town's proximity to Sacramento and the Bay Area, we need to be thinking bigger. There are a lot of deep pockets in San Francisco. Those city folk do like their mud baths and salt scrubs."

Eddie bristled at the man's folksy way of talking—it was too contrived—but he played along nonetheless. "Bigger, sure. We can think bigger." Here came the trickiest part of his job: translating client-speak. "But . . . bigger *how*?"

"Pop on another story. Add a solarium. That sort of thing."

Solarium? He nudged a loose floorboard with his boot. Damned if Laura's concerns didn't jump back into his head. "I thought you wanted a traditional ranch house. *Boutique spa experience*—weren't those your words? Boutiques and ranch properties tend to be single stories."

"Single story. Did I hear you right, Edward?"

Edwin. "Edward" was a teenybopper vampire.

"Yes, sir. You wanted an authentic ranch experience." He stepped outside to look at the façade. It was an old building, dating to the late 1800s. Hell, it was probably on some historical register somewhere. And even though it had only one floor, it wasn't short on space. "I think we can expand, while keeping to the original spirit of the plan." *I think we can do this without crushing the Baileys in the process.* "This place is sprawling, as is. Adding another floor will double the work time. Change your bottom line. We'll need a whole new set of plans. And the engineer will need to come back out, recheck the foundation, that sort of thing."

"I had our architect do up another set of drawings. Permits are a go." There was a moment's silence on the other end of the line. "My only obstacle now is you. Are you able to do the work?"

Life shot into his veins. "Of course we can do the work." They couldn't lose this job. Not only did they need the money, but he was sure Fairview could have some big-city builder out tomorrow, razing the building to the ground, and probably for twice the money. "I just want to make sure I understand what you want."

"What I want, Edward, is to be *the* destination resort of the Sierra Nevada."

Those grand words were echoing in Eddie's mind as he hopped into his truck. His family business needed to prosper. He could be responsible and do the work without crushing the rest of Sierra Falls in the process. He and his brother were the best men for the job—in fact, it was a boon that they had the work and not some uncaring out-of-town operation.

A new hotel wouldn't put Bear out of business—his lodge was only so big, anyway, able to take in only so many visitors. Besides, a big-time resort and spa might attract even more tourists to the lodge and tavern. Not that he'd ever say any of that to Laura. Not that he'd even try.

He was being a smart businessman. He wasn't being a jerk.

So why'd he feel like one?

Eddie revved the engine and took off to his favorite trailhead. Nothing like a hilly run to clear the mind of everything—and everyone.

Three

~

"I need to look at the registry," Laura said before the Town Hall door had even clicked shut. She'd been sitting in her car, waiting. The place wasn't exactly run like a Swiss watch and was open only according to a bewildering schedule of bimonthly evening meetings, alternate Tuesday mornings, first and third Monday and Wednesday afternoons, and whichever Friday hours the community volunteers could make.

She eyed those two volunteers now: Ruby and Pearl Kidd, the elderly doyennes of Sierra Falls. They'd been in the process of settling in for the day when she'd burst in. They gaped at her, looking alarmingly startled by her sudden appearance.

What was wrong with her? The Kidd sisters were in their eighties. Laura wanted information, not heart attacks.

She took a deep breath to steady herself. She wasn't in the city anymore, and *sudden* was not the way to get things done around Sierra Falls. "I mean, *hi*," she said, smiling and trying not to look quite so much like a madwoman. "How are things with you two?"

"Not as exciting as it seems to be for you, I fear." Ruby took Pearl's purse to stash with the rest of their things beneath the reception desk.

Pearl's eyes were a little more judgmental when she said, "I know Edith taught you better manners than that, dear." They were both spinsters who'd been raised by a fire-and-brimstone father and didn't hold back when it came to sharp-tongued censure.

"You're right," she replied with a sigh. "I apologize. It's just . . . I'm a little . . . upset." She suddenly felt choked up in front of these two women she'd grown up with, and she gritted her teeth. She was an adult now, taking charge. Take-charge women didn't break down.

But Ruby sensed it and told her gently, "Sit for a while."

Laura was pressed for time but decided that taking a minute would be a necessary means to an end. Pearl began to teeter to standing, but she beat the woman to it, hopping up and grabbing an old ladder-back chair from the corner.

Pearl smiled and patted her hand. "Tell us what's on your mind."

She dove right in. "Have you heard what the Jessups are doing to the old ranch?"

"Which ranch?" Pearl directed the question at her sister instead of to Laura.

"She'll mean that old place on Timber Creek, I imagine." Ruby's voice wavered with age.

Pearl's eyes widened with recognition. "The old Wexler homestead?"

"Is that who—" Laura began.

"Those Interweb people let it go to pot," Ruby interrupted, and both sisters scowled with distaste and mistrust.

"They bought it and then just left it with a never-you-mind."

"I heard they paid cash."

Laura scooted forward in her chair. "The thing is—"

"And now it's abandoned." Pearl shook her head in dismay.

"All sorts of critters running around in there."

"A shame." Pearl tsked.

"It'll attract drifters, if they're not careful."

Finally, Laura just decided to let the women's conversation peter out.

Ruby was the first to bring her attention back. "What are our grandnephews up to, then?"

"They've got plans to—"

"Oh, I do hope they fix it up," Pearl said brightly.

"They're good at that. Eddie and Jack. They have their own business, you know."

"Are they going to fix it?" Pearl asked. "We can't allow drifters into Sierra Falls."

"That's what I came to talk—"

"Or vagrants," Ruby said with a gasp under her breath.

"A big hotel hired them," Laura interjected quickly and loudly. She was trying to keep her cool, but she felt like she'd burst from frustration.

"Isn't that exciting?" Pearl cooed. "Big-city types coming all the way out here to vacation."

Ruby agreed. "Exciting."

"No," Laura snapped. "It's *not* exciting." She softened her tone. "That's what I've been trying to say. I mean, tourists are good, but they're going to put *our* lodge out of business."

The ladies' expressions grew grim. "Ohh," they said in tandem.

Ruby wrung her hands. "Surely our boys don't mean to do that."

Laura breathed a quick sigh. They'd finally heard her. "Whether they mean to or not, it's happening."

Pearl frowned and looked at Ruby as she said, "Our Eddie and Jack would never try to put Bear out of business."

Laura sensed their bias wavering and was quick to amend, "They wouldn't, no, of course not. But this big corporation is powerful—they're the ones who'll put us under. They're making it a resort and could add, well, anything. A pool, greenhouse, gym, spa . . ." She racked her brain for what might most horrify ladies of the historical society. "It'll probably be new, modern construction. All steel and glass."

That got the sisters, and they frowned, aghast.

"How can *we* help?" Pearl asked.

"The historical society keeps the town records, right?" At their nod, Laura continued, "I thought maybe if the ranch was on the registry, we could halt construction."

"The registry?" Pearl asked Ruby.

Ruby looked to Laura. "Which registry?"

She forced a calm smile. Patience. "You know, the *historic* registry."

Understanding dawned on their faces. "I'm sorry, dear. That ranch is old, but it's not historic."

"Not precisely."

"Well, could you check maybe?" Laura's jaw was beginning to ache from forcing the pleasant smile.

The sisters disappeared into the records room, and she fought her impatience. She really should've been home, working. Discreetly, she checked the time on her phone. She could make a call to the California Historical Society—*that* was where she should've started, not here.

Just as she began to debate whether it'd be rude to find the number while she waited, the women reemerged with a tattered manila folder.

"Wow." Laura shoved her cell back in her purse. "That was fast."

"The records were pulled recently." Ruby settled back in her chair and began to riffle through the stacks of paper. There were yellowed photographs, old survey maps, and notes on scraps from a steno pad that looked to be older than Laura.

She felt a knot in her shoulders begin to release. "So it *is* on the registry."

Pearl reached over her sister's shoulder and plucked a fresher-looking page from the pile. She shook her head, tsking. "Adaptive reuse."

"What?" She scooted to the edge of her chair to get a look at the paper in Pearl's hand. It was on Fairview letterhead and bore an official-looking stamp with a signature scrawled over the blurred purple ink. "What do you mean? What is that?"

"Can't fight that," Ruby said.

Pearl nodded. "Happened in South Lake."

"The old Valhalla boathouse."

Laura interjected, "What did?"

"I hear they put on shows there now."

"What?" Laura looked from one to the other. "What shows?"

"Plays, dear. In South Lake. One of these days we'll get out there."

The sisters shared a smile. "Emerald would've loved to see it."

"We're not talking about South Lake," Laura said.

Pearl's eyes got misty. "There's no tomorrow. Only today."

"We'll go and think of our Emmy." Ruby reached over and patted her sister's hand.

"What is adaptive reuse?" Laura's voice came out louder than she'd anticipated, and the older women flinched.

Ruby sat up rigidly, looking offended by the interruption. "Your ranch *is* historic."

"But they've got a permit," Pearl added, beginning another back-and-forth between sisters.

"Adaptive reuse they call it."

"As long as the builders keep the character of the building—"

"Then they can change it and use it for something else."

Dead end. Laura's throat tightened, and she went into autopilot, thanking the women, wishing them well, inviting them out to the tavern, all the while barely holding herself together.

This was it. Failure. Again. There'd be no fighting it.

She was halfway out the door, convulsively swallowing back the emotion, when she felt a gentle hand on her arm.

"Wait, dear." It was Pearl. "If there are any problems with the permit, any problems at all," she added meaningfully, "they'll need to go back to square one."

"What do you mean?" She looked from Pearl to Ruby, who'd appeared at her shoulder. "Are there problems with the permit?"

The other sister leaned in, a conspiratorial gleam in her eyes, and whispered, "Make our boys double-check the property lines."

Four

It was the annual Fourth of July bash, and Laura should've been excited. This year, the Baileys had been hired to cater. This year, it was the Big Bear Lodge that was hosting the chili cook-off, with the Thirsty Bear Tavern providing bottles of beer, soda, and water from several ice chests they'd set up under a tent. Her sister, Sorrow, was a master of comfort foods like four-cheese mac and cheese, grilled corn on the cob, and homemade apple pie. The mouthwatering food was bringing in hungry revelers—and with hungry revelers came cash. Lots of it.

She smoothed some of that cash, shoving the growing pile of ones into the cash box.

No, Laura should've been happy, but instead all she could do was think about how next year, it'd probably be *Fairview* setting up shop on the picnic grounds. Their tent would be giant, some air-conditioned outdoor pavilion that'd dwarf the Bailey family setup and draw all their patrons, too.

"Earth to Laura," said the kid in front of her, and she

tuned in to see the line that'd appeared in the several seconds it'd taken for her to zone out. "Come in, Laura," his small, dirt-encrusted companion shouted.

"You're Helen's kids, right?" She handed the older one a few bottles of water and took his money with narrowed eyes. "Okay, smarty-pants. Just because your mom works at the tavern doesn't mean you can sass me."

"A little help here?" Sorrow said from behind her. She was balancing a foil-covered tray of corn, hot off the grill, and a handful of cold beers, the bottles sweating with condensation. "I'm losing it."

Billy swept into the tent, snagging the bottles and hot tray before it all crashed to the dirt. "That's what fiancés are for."

Sorrow wiped her hands on her shorts, a broad grin instantly brightening her face. "Hey, Sheriff. Where'd you come from?"

"I sensed a maiden in peril." He peeked under the foil and smiled. "I thought Sierra Falls was all about barbecue."

"That's what we serve at the spring festival," Laura said distractedly. Though next year, Fairview would probably have something fancy, like . . . quiches or something.

Sorrow tucked the foil back in place. "For Independence Day, it's all chili, all the time."

"Babe, if you're the one working the magic, it's all good." He planted a firm kiss on Sorrow's cheek and a loving pat on her rump.

Laura turned away. She was happy for her sister, really she was. Not jealous at all. She'd sworn off men. Men were a recipe for disaster and failure.

So why the pang in her chest?

"I've come to rescue you," Billy said, then smiled Laura's way. "Both of you. I brought backup."

Helen Haskell, their tavern waitress and bartender, ducked into the tent, slinging her purse atop one of the coolers.

"Hey, Helen." Sorrow greeted her with a smile.

Laura, though, was feeling a little more impatient. "That's not a great spot for your bag."

She credited her mom with keeping the woman employed despite the fact that she was an inveterate flirt who was a bit scatterbrained, with a cranky attitude that was sometimes only thinly veiled.

It was clear Helen had more problems than she let on. But Laura didn't want to hear it—work was work. Her mom disagreed, though. Edith Bailey wasn't one to judge, nor would she stand by as another woman struggled alone.

Helen ignored the comment and shouldered her way behind the folding table. "I got it, I got it," she said, snatching the quarters from Laura's hand to make change for a young couple grabbing some Sprites.

Laura stepped back, sharing a quick look with her sister. Helen wasn't generally warm with her, but this was a new low. "You sure you're up for this?"

Helen watched as the couple felt their tepid cans. "That's as cold as they get," she said flatly. "Take it or leave it." Then she dismissed them with a brittle smile and turned to the Baileys. "I'm here, aren't I? Though I'm still not quite sure how your sheriff convinced me to take an extra shift." She'd grumbled the words but pasted a smile on her face, and it struck Laura as only half-playful.

It was good enough for Billy, though. He stood tall, straightening his shirt. "It's the uniform," he said proudly. They were playing the nearby town of Paley Pines in their annual softball game, and this year Up Country Hardware had sprung for team shirts emblazoned with a hideous royal-blue version of the Up Country logo on garish yellow. "It gets the ladies every time."

"Gets them what?" Laura asked. "Blinded?"

Helen's attention was in the distance, pinned on two of her three kids, roughhousing. "Where's your sister?" she shouted. "I told you to feed her." She and her husband had still been teens when she'd gotten pregnant. They'd married, and two more kids had followed, though lately Helen was always grumbling how she might as well have been a single mom.

It gave Laura chills. There'd be no men for her, she resolved. No way, nohow.

Just then a dirt-scuffed little girl appeared, waving her corncob like a greasy baton. "I *am* eating, Mama."

Laura didn't know kids well, but she had a feeling they were supposed to be cleaner than this. "Are you sure you're up for working the tent? If you need to watch your kids, really, I don't care about the stupid softball game."

Helen swung on her. "Are you kidding? Working the tent *is* a break for me."

"Stupid?" Billy exclaimed, still hung up on her dissing the big game. "Softball is a sport of great consequence."

"C'mon, Laura." Sorrow gave her a nudge, moving her along. "We'll keep an eye on the kids, Helen."

"All right, troops." Billy swung the little girl onto his shoulders, grease and all. "Let's go kick some butt."

The man was a natural with kids—and of course he was. He'd bought her sister a ring, had just bought her a house, and Laura was sure it'd only be a matter of time before Sorrow popped out a whole softball team of children, probably all strapping dark-eyed boys like their father.

The pang returned to Laura's chest, sharper now. She wasn't jealous, she told herself, not even a little. She didn't want a man, and she definitely didn't want a passel of dirty kids.

Billy walked ahead, and Laura wondered just who was going to watch said kids while he was in the outfield. The prospect of serving a bunch of hungry picnickers in the hot sun suddenly seemed preferable. She turned back to Helen, calling, "You sure you want to miss the game? Isn't Rob playing shortstop this year?"

"You got me," Helen said bitterly, suddenly intent on

counting the ones in the cash box. "I don't know where my husband has got to."

Feeling a stab of sympathy and womanly fellowship, she walked closer, asking quietly, "You sure you don't need me to stay?"

"No," Helen shot back. "I don't need you to stay." Her mimicking tone was as flat as her eyes.

She took a step back. "All righty then. Don't say I didn't offer."

The baseball diamond was at the far end of the picnic grounds, and as they headed there, Sorrow and Billy entertained the kids while Laura trailed behind, trying to turn her mood around. Watching all these smiling faces, Sierra Falls felt more like home than ever. And yet she'd fought it for so long, fantasizing about any place but here.

It hadn't been easy weathering her teen years in a small boondock town in the foothills of the Sierra Nevada—particularly as she'd had to do it in the shadow of a sports-star brother and the family-pet little sister. She'd grown up feeling underestimated, underappreciated, and overlooked and had taken off for San Francisco the moment she graduated high school. At the time, she'd vowed not to return until she had a fast car, a killer body, and lots of money—anything to finally get some attention.

But the trouble with chasing those sorts of goals was that, for years, she'd only looked outward to feel good about herself. A high-paying marketing job had bought her that car, a personal trainer, and all the respect she'd craved, but it hadn't been enough to fulfill her. When she hit her twenty-eighth birthday, she'd panicked. Her fiancé had dumped her and she'd lost her job because of that same man, and yet, once she recovered from the blows to her pride, it was a shock to realize how little she missed either of them.

She'd been going through the motions, and it was time to look inward and figure out why her life felt so empty. She knew she could find another fiancé and another job, but she

was terrified that if she did, she'd wake up ten years later
and still feel unfulfilled. She was tired of pretending she
was someone she wasn't.

She needed to unlock the clues to herself and track down
how and why things began to go wrong. What did she really
want from life? And why did she always feel like she had
something to prove? She knew the answers waited for her
in Sierra Falls.

So she'd returned home, and she wanted it to be for good,
too. She was done with the city and done with men—the
two went hand-in-hand, anyway, seeing as she had no interest in the guys of Sierra Falls, lawmen and laborers all of
them.

Laura was surprised to be discovering a friendship with
her formerly estranged baby sister, and getting respect from
her normally crotchety dad. They'd handed her management
of the lodge, and she wanted to do everyone proud. Wanted
to turn the place around, to have her family business
succeed.

And, more than wanting it, she *needed* it, with a despera-
tion that surprised her. She'd had so many personal failures,
but this would be her chance at redemption.

She knew she could do it, too. She was no good at the
great outdoors, but the fact that their home was out in the
middle of nowhere was just an added challenge. She wasn't
a big hiker and definitely had no interest in fishing, but there
was one thing she was good at, and it was business. Marketing, to be specific. And she had big plans about how to use
those talents and turn the Big Bear Lodge into a quaint
destination resort. Besides, having spent the past several
years test-driving every spa, winery, and B&B in Northern
California, Laura considered herself something of an expert.

Miraculously, her dad was staying out of her hair, too.
He'd been walking on air ever since they discovered gold
on Bailey family land. Not that it was going to make them
rich or anything—the vein wasn't easily accessible and

would cost too much to mine. But still, as a family, it felt like they were at a turning point. Everyone was putting their trust in her—eyes were on her for what felt like the first time—and she couldn't fail.

Which made Eddie's development project all the more infuriating.

She wasn't dumb—she knew that if it hadn't been the Jessups, Fairview would've hired some other construction outfit to do the work. But it was Jack and Eddie who'd been hired, and it should've been a stroke of luck. They were born and raised in Sierra Falls. They had the ears of the Fairview execs—they should've been talking sense into them. Finding a way to persuade them to leave the town and take their soulless hotel conglomerate elsewhere. But instead, Eddie was acting the yes man and going ahead with construction, without asking a single question.

Boutique spa resort. She scowled. *As if.* Fairview marketed themselves as some community-oriented, eco-friendly company, but really she knew they'd bulldoze the whole town if they thought it'd make them a buck.

She would *not* stand by as the Jessup brothers helped nurture to life a competing business. And Fairview wasn't just friendly competition—they had bottomless pockets, and she was sure they'd use them to either absorb or squash the Baileys.

A man had stood in her way once before. She wouldn't let it happen again. *Never again* was her mantra as she rounded the back of the bleachers. *Never again*, she repeated over and over in her head, and she was so caught up in her thoughts, she nearly stormed right into her sister.

She caught herself on Sorrow's back and walked around, and who was standing there with a grin on his face? *Eddie.*

A wicked glint darkened his eyes. "She's coming in hot."

Five

Laura put her hands on her hips, looking ready to do battle. "What's that supposed to mean?"

Eddie had seen the fury on her face. He knew why she was upset. He knew he should leave well enough alone. But knowing and doing were two different things.

"Well, let's think about that." He tilted his head, admiring her. "*Comin' in hot.* Lots of levels at work there, I think. You're hot. You're clearly on a rampage. As for coming—"

"Jessups," she said with disgust as she shouldered by him.

"Lovers' quarrel?" his brother Jack muttered, and Laura shot him a look that could kill.

"Shut it." Eddie punched his brother on the arm, then jogged to catch up to her on the bleachers. "You sure are pretty when you're wound up," he said to her back. He couldn't help it—he loved nothing more than to bait Laura Bailey.

"Then don't wind me up."

He grinned, a thousand one-liners popping into his head.

She put up a hand. "Don't go there."

"Can't help it." He'd been going there with her for as long as he could remember.

"Just naturally repellent?"

"Only trying to make you smile."

She paused, turning slowly. "Honestly?" A wicked gleam had appeared in her eyes. "You really want me to smile?"

"Oh, yes." He put his hand up in a vow. He was dying to know where she was headed. "Scout's honor."

"Then I want you to remeasure the property line."

"You want me to . . . *what*?" It'd taken him a moment to register what she'd said.

"You heard me."

"This again?" He should've known that hoping for anything else would've been in vain.

"Yes, *this* again. This is far from over."

What did she care about the property line, of all things? "Jack will think I've lost it."

"That's your problem."

"Fine. You want me to measure, I'll come out Saturday with my survey gear." That property was gorgeous—he dreamed of owning land just like it someday. He'd be happy to spend a summer afternoon trekking in the woods, measuring. "No skin off my back."

She looked taken aback, and it gave him a flash of satisfaction. "You'll do it?"

"Happy to. Want to join me? We could take a little skinny-dip in the creek after."

Her eyes went flat. "What do *you* think?"

He smirked. "I think I'll be measuring alone this weekend."

"That's right, you will be."

"Fine, I'll do it, but it won't make any difference."

She huffed—the girl actually huffed—and spun to find a seat in the stands.

"Hey, I was promised a smile." He took the bleachers two at a time to catch up—the girl had long legs—but he was enjoying the view all the same. "You gonna choose a seat, 'cause I could chase you all day."

It was true. Ever since high school, she'd been his catnip. And just as in high school, the girl still thought she was better than the rest of them. She had the fancy car, the gym body, and the designer clothes to prove it. He happened to be an accomplished businessman, but she was too caught up in her prejudices ever to see that.

Finally she stopped and sat. "I wish you wouldn't."

"No chasing, huh?" He cracked a grin. "I'll do whatever you say. Just give me that smile."

What she flashed him was more a teeth-baring than a genuine smile.

He laughed. "Bigger," he insisted, and she tried to glare, but he saw it wavering.

"I'll smile as big as you want if you tell me you're stopping your stupid Fairview project."

He sighed. "You know I can't do that." He plopped next to her and scooted close.

She scooted away. "What are you doing?"

"Sitting," he said with a smile.

She gestured to the field. "Just go play your game, why don't you?"

"Seems like you're the one playing games." An idea hit him, and before she could snap back, he said, "Funny you should mention playing." He peered at her feet. "Because I see you've got your running shoes on."

"And?"

His brother Scott shouted at him from the field. "You ask her?"

She inched farther away, looking wary. "Is he talking about me?"

"You're all I talk about."

She rolled her eyes. "Spare me."

He watched her, waiting for her to look back at him. He was a patient man.

Finally she gave him a tentative glance. "Okay, what?"

"We need another player." He wasn't lying—they were short a man. Or rather, short a *woman*. The league had rules about how many women and men there were per team, and Rob Haskell wasn't the only person who'd bailed on the game; a couple of girls from his nephew's high school had skipped out as well.

Her eyes widened. "You're not asking *me* to play."

"That's exactly what I'm doing."

"I'm not on the team."

His team had all assembled on the bench below, and they were clearly growing antsy. Shielding his eyes from the sun, Mike Haskell found him and shouted, "C'mon, Jessup. Batter up!"

He glanced at Laura, amused by her look of terror. "Whaddya think?"

She was staring at the field, aghast. "You want me to play softball?" She gave him an incredulous look. "That's a horrible idea."

"It's an inspired idea. Just think, you can work out all your anger on the field."

"Anger." She huffed. "You're the reason I'm angry."

"Then you can show me what-for on the field."

"I haven't played softball since eighth grade."

"Good. Then you'll be like a fresh lump of clay." He couldn't stop himself from wrapping his arm around her shoulders to give her a squeeze. "All the better to mold you."

She flinched away. "You are not molding me, Eddie Jessup. Why don't you ask Sorrow?"

They scanned the field at the same time, finding the youngest Bailey sister. She'd just bought Helen's kids snow cones, and they were already covered in sugary streaks of electric blue.

He bit back a smile, knowing he had her. "Cool," he said with a straight face. "You're right. We'll have Sorrow play instead, and *you* can watch Helen's brood."

Her flat look told him he had her. "You wouldn't."

"Tell you what," he said seriously. "You play, then tomorrow you come by the job site, and we'll discuss this problem of yours."

"Problem of *mine*? If Sierra Falls is destroyed by some international corporation, it'll be more than just *my* problem."

"Is it really that bad?" He shrugged. "You taking my offer or what?"

When she didn't answer, he leaned forward, resting his elbows on his thighs, watching the other players warm up, making like he didn't care. He let Laura have her tense few moments of silence.

"Fine," she said finally. She stood, but instead of edging by him, she made her way down the center of the bleachers. "I'll play," she called over her shoulder, "but you'll pay."

And pay he did, but not in the way she imagined.

Playing with Laura would be the death of him.

And he wasn't the only person who'd noticed her in her sassy little short-shorts. After the third inning, he caught up to Jack as they walked from the outfield. Snagging the collar of his brother's shirt, he said, "Need I remind you, you're a married man?"

Jack flinched away. "Easy, little brother. I'm married, not blind. Your woman's something else to look at."

Eddie grinned—he liked the sound of *his woman*. He wished. It wasn't like she was consciously putting on a show or anything, but she was so cute out there, so into the game, jumping up and down as she cheered. He kept catching glimpses of pale belly as she reached her arms up to stretch, her face lit by the sort of smiles he longed to tease from her himself. It was killing him.

And then, after he'd gotten a base hit, he'd caught her staring at him. She'd glanced away quickly, but it'd been enough to tell him that she was as curious about him as he was about her.

It was enough to drive a man to distraction.

To complicate matters was the fact that Eddie was a competitive guy, and their new sheriff, Billy Preston, was turning out to be a surprisingly good athlete. Eddie was determined to be the best man on the field, but it was hard to keep his mind in the game when his eyes kept drifting to Laura.

Paley Pines was at bat, and he forced himself to pay attention. Billy was manning second, and he'd just turned a double play. One more out was all they needed, and Eddie was determined it'd be *his* out.

He was playing shortstop, and they'd parked Laura in left field—the Paley players weren't exactly sluggers, and the outfield seemed a safe enough spot for someone who wasn't dying for action—but that meant he couldn't watch her. He'd turned once to steal a glimpse, and she'd looked bored out of her mind. She caught him looking immediately, and he swung his head back around, forcing himself to keep his gaze pinned straight ahead.

Was she bored out there? Would she occupy her time by watching him? They sure did seem to catch each other looking a lot. Not that it was anything new—they'd been catching each other looking since puberty. Remembering it now, he wondered how much of his adolescent acting-out had actually been to get Laura's attention. He readjusted his ball cap, forcing himself not to think about it.

The sharp crack of bat on ball shocked him back into the moment. A hit. He shaded his eyes, jogging backward. It was a pop fly . . . headed right for Laura. Her expression of sheer terror told him she wasn't pleased about the development.

Eddie spun and hauled ass into left field.

Laura was backing up, her wide, panicked eyes glued on the ball coming straight for her. She put up her hands, looking like she wanted to duck but was too proud. "Can you—?"

"Heads up." He flung himself toward her, his body slamming into the dirt, and grinned to feel the satisfyingly sharp slap of the ball in his mitt. He rolled to his feet, certain he'd finally be greeted by her smile. And with the ridiculously athletic maneuver he'd just pulled, he hoped it might even be a fawning and appreciative one.

But when their eyes met, she was colder than ever. "Thanks," was all she said, and then she strode past him back to the bleachers.

How was it possible she'd gotten even angrier in the past thirty minutes? He hadn't done anything.

He pulled off his cap, raked a hand through his sweat-dampened hair, then settled the cap firmly back on his head. Softball wasn't the only game he refused to lose. He jogged to catch up to her. "Why so angry, pretty lady?"

"You know why." She took off her mitt and tucked it firmly into her crossed arms as though it might act as a shield.

He saw it as an invitation to goad her. "You mad I caught the ball?"

"I didn't know men like you had balls."

A laugh exploded from him. She always had known how to catch him off guard. "If you're trying to get the one-up on me, it's not working. But if this is your way of flirting . . ."

She upped her pace before he could finish, making a beeline for the bleachers, where she squished between two other players. "I was not flirting," she muttered angrily. She kept her arms tightly crossed as she glowered straight ahead.

With one look from Eddie, the other players instantly scooted, making room for him to sit next to her. He chuckled as he settled beside her. "Whatever you say."

"Hey, Billy," he called. "My bag?"

The sheriff tossed Eddie his duffel, and he dug through for his bottle of water. He cracked it open and offered it to Laura first.

"No, thank you," she said primly.

"Whatever." He guzzled the whole thing down and caught her glimpsing him out of the corner of her eye. It was a hot day, and the girl was bound to be thirsty. He unzipped the side pocket and pulled out his stuff until he found another bottle to hand to her. "Just in case."

She took it, but her focus was on the contents of his bag. It was the usual gym bag assortment—car keys, towel, fresh shirt—but she smirked when she spotted his book. *The Rise of Theodore Roosevelt*, by Edmund Morris. It'd won a Pulitzer. Not exactly smirkworthy. He raised his brows, giving her a challenging look. "What?"

"I didn't know Neanderthals could read."

He looked down, tucking everything back in the bag, feeling suddenly tired. She really refused to see him.

Fine, then. If Laura thought he was nothing more than an oversexed, sports-playing, joke-cracking townie, then that was how he'd show himself to her. She wanted Neanderthal; he'd give her Neanderthal.

He raised his eyes to hers, raking her body with a slow, sizzling look. "I've got a brain, darlin'. I just prefer to use my body."

She gaped, and for a satisfying moment, her shocked eyes remained locked with his. He was the first to look away, making like he was watching their teammates up at bat. He shifted, making sure his thigh brushed against hers, even though he kept his eyes glued to home plate.

He felt her tense and fidget in a way that told him she was mustering a response. Finally she found her voice and whispered angrily, "You can do whatever you want with your body. I'm sure you're as much of a womanizer as you've always been. Just keep away from me."

"Womanizer?" he exclaimed, unthinking. It was the last word he'd use to describe himself.

But then he thought about how he must seem. He flirted, sure. And he dated. He was easy and fun, and women always liked that. So what if he was a ladies' man—it wasn't that he didn't respect them. Quite the opposite.

His problem was, he was holding out for the full package, waiting for The One. He wanted true love, a wife to grow old with, a bunch of kids, and the white picket fence, too. But guys didn't go around bragging about stuff like that. And so he bided his time, flirting and having fun.

"I'm no womanizer," he grumbled, unable to muster a more clever response than that.

He wondered what it was *Laura* wanted out of life—aside from him and Fairview disappearing off the face of the earth.

Fairview. They were a wily bunch. Secretly, he'd done as she'd asked and triple-checked their paperwork—not that he'd give Laura the satisfaction of telling her as much. He'd reviewed their permits, combed through the building plans. It was all clear. They had a green light to begin work. It was time to break ground.

So why was he still delaying? He'd been postponing, finding little things to hold them up, telling Hunter and the suits how their fixtures were back-ordered, how his subs were tied up till next week. All true, of course. Only normally, Eddie would've kicked some ass and gotten the fixtures elsewhere or told his subcontractors it was now or never. Workers, sadly, were easy to find in this economy.

But he was up against it now. There was no more delaying. Come Monday, it'd be time to get going. He hated the thought that he wouldn't just be building a second story onto the old rancher—he'd be building a wedge that would permanently separate him from Laura.

Billy was up at bat, and Eddie made himself focus. The sheriff was obviously close to the Bailey family—being engaged to the youngest daughter had a way of doing that—and he found himself oddly competitive, oddly jealous.

Preston hit a grounder in the gap to right and ran to first. Nice and solid. Eddie flexed his hands, scrutinizing every

move the pitcher made. He wanted to do better than nice
and solid.

Meantime, it was Laura's turn. "You're up."

"Me?" Suddenly, she looked stricken.

He'd never seen her appear anything but confident and
on top of her world. "Am I seeing what I think I'm seeing?
The Laura Bailey, nervous?"

But she didn't laugh. Instead, she just looked ill. "I
haven't batted since eighth-grade gym class."

She really was having trouble. Without thinking, he put
a hand on her knee. "Hey, it's just a game, okay? Nothing
to make yourself sick over."

"Easy for you to say. Can't you . . . what is it . . . pinch-hit
for me?"

"That's not how we play." He nudged her. "Just give it a
shot. This can't be your first real softball game." He peered
at her, and when she didn't respond, he exclaimed, "It *is*.
City girl's never played ball before."

"Shut up." She stood abruptly, and damn if he hadn't
spotted a flash of genuine hurt in her eyes.

He stood and, with a hand on her lower back, led her to
the plate. "C'mon. I'll help you. It's easy. Just gotta keep
your eye on the ball."

They reached the plate, and she hesitated, like she was
unsure she even knew where to stand.

"You really don't know how to do this, do you?" He
guided her shoulders, and her feet followed. "That's it. Now
bend your knees."

"Just play the damn game," someone shouted from the
stands.

"C'mon," Sorrow shouted back, "let him help her."

"Hey, Taylor," Billy called from first base. "If you don't
want me to write you up for public intoxication, you'll give
the lady a moment."

Sorrow came to stand behind the catcher, her fingers

twined in the chain-link fence. "Don't mind him," she told her sister quietly. "Take your time."

Seeing how Laura's hands were all wrong, Eddie said, "You almost got it. Now just choke up on the bat a little." When she did the opposite, he simply wrapped his arms around her, nestling her body snug against his. He'd have sworn the touch of her skin on his brought an electric shock. She must've felt it, too, because she sucked in a breath that reverberated through his chest. He'd have liked to find a million different ways to take her breath away, and in that moment, he fantasized about a good half dozen.

"Get a room," Scott shouted.

She stiffened, and he made a mental note to strangle his brother later.

"He's an ass. Ignore him." He bobbed his arms gently, trying to get her shoulders to loosen.

Women in the crowd began to cheer her on. "Come on, Laura!"

Bringing his mouth to her ear, he whispered, "Relax. Nice and easy."

"I *am* relaxed," she said, sounding far from it.

He pressed more closely against her. "Do I make you uncomfortable?"

"Not at all!" Her overly chirpy tone told him otherwise. "I got it from here. Thanks!"

He stepped back and made like he was simply studying her form as he let his eyes linger over those sleek, tanned legs and that tight butt, sticking out in the most adorable batting stance ever.

"You look great," he said, meaning every word. "Eyes on the ball and swing."

And God love her, but she swung and she hit that damned ball. The pitcher was too surprised to catch it, and it barreled to his right, and by the time the shortstop scooped it up, Laura had made it to first.

Eddie punched a fist in the air, whooping for her. Laura looked his way, and that beautiful face was beaming . . . right at him.

His heart swelled in his chest. Finally, finally, he'd won a smile. He grinned back, giving her a big thumbs-up.

She did a cute little bounce and wave, but it was that smile.

Her smile did him in.

Six

Helen was running late, and of course she was. She did this drill every morning. It would've been easier to herd cats than get her kids into the car on time. She'd wrangled the two youngest outside, but her oldest was still missing. With a quick check to her watch, she opened the screen door and leaned back inside.

"Luke," she shouted. "Get down here right now. I'm gonna be late for work." She waited. "Do you hear me? I'm leaving." She pretended to shut the door, then paused. Nothing. She didn't know why she even tried that one anymore—it never worked. She had a better idea. "Get down here this instant or I'll tell Bear that it's your fault I'm late. Maybe *he* can scold you instead of me."

That brought his feet galloping down the stairs.

Luke appeared, and Helen's breath caught. Though her oldest was only fifteen, something had happened in the past year. Where once there was a boy, she now saw the shadow of the man he'd be. And that man would be the spitting image of his father. She felt a pang, realizing their son wasn't too much younger than Rob had been when they'd first met.

"Sorry, Mom. Ellie stopped up the toilet."

She scowled and tossed down her purse. If she told that girl once, she'd told her a thousand times: not too much paper. "You get in the car. I'll go take a look." The last thing she needed was coming home to an overflowed toilet and flooded bathroom.

"Don't worry, Mom. I dealt." He shuddered. "I would've come down, but I wanted to fix it for you."

"You're too much," she said, suddenly choked with emotion. Her boy might've looked like his dad, but he sure didn't act like him, and thank heaven for that. Her Luke was always the caretaker, the peacekeeper, though sometimes it made her heart ache. She wanted him to be a *boy*—to have fun and get dirty. "You didn't have to do that."

"Sorry I made us late."

She grabbed her purse. "Are you kidding? Don't you give it a second thought."

"You won't really tell Bear on me, will you?"

She had to reach up to scruff his hair. "If Bear doesn't like it, he can lump it."

It saddened her, knowing how hard it was to focus on being just a boy when you had a no-good absentee dad. As the oldest, he saw more, noticed more. He remembered more, too, from before, when Rob had actually spent time around the house. When he'd been a real father. A real husband.

Her other boy, Emmett, pushed inside. "I forgot something."

She caught his collar, stopping him. Her stern-mom tone came back with a vengeance. "Oh, no you don't. We're almost out of here. Get back in the car."

Emmett flinched free, and she could see the machinations clear on his face. He'd just turned eleven, and there was something about that age that had him trying rebellion on for size. "But I wanted to bring my canteen."

"I've got a water bottle already packed for you." She aimed him back in the direction of the minivan. "Now go."

She followed him outside, and just as she was about to lock up, she got a good look at her youngest. Helen cursed under her breath. "Ellie Lynn Haskell, stop right there. Where are your shoes?"

Her daughter waggled her foot, showing off a strappy Cinderella sandal with a big Lucite heel covered in silver glitter. "I've got shoes."

"Those are *dress-up* shoes. Go inside and get your sneakers on." With a quick check over her shoulder to make sure the boys were getting in the car, she pointed Ellie inside. "You know Uncle Mike is taking you for a hike. There's no way you can trek to the falls in those."

The little girl dug in her heels. "He puts me on his shoulders when I don't feel like walking."

Helen's response was instant. "I am *not* raising myself any princesses." She prodded her daughter back inside. "You're a strong girl, and you're going to walk on your own two feet if I have tell your Uncle Mike myself."

As Ellie slipped on her sneakers, Helen fumed. It was hard enough watching the Bailey sisters live out their fairy-tale lives every day; she was not raising herself a girl who expected to be carried by a man. She knew the truth—there were no such thing as princes, and she'd not raise Ellie to have any delusions.

Finally, the girl sprang out, sneakers on, and Helen locked the door behind them. "Hallelujah."

She dropped the kids off, thanking heaven for her in-laws. It wasn't the first time she'd mused how she'd married the wrong brother. But Mike was a good ten years older and hadn't been nearly as cute as Rob, and when you were seventeen as she'd been, not much had mattered more than cute.

Mike was happily married now, though there'd been some tough times when he and Judy had been unable to have kids of their own. Eventually, they'd stopped trying, but

Helen still caught the wistful looks the couple shot her own kids, and it was always a reminder—in the worst of times and during the hardest of days, she had to thank heaven she had three beautiful children. And God bless Judy and Mike, for there wasn't a resentful bone in either of their bodies. Instead, they'd spelled her more than the average uncle and aunt would. Maybe Mike felt guilty about his no-good baby brother, but he especially looked out for the kids, taking them on hikes, for bike rides, or to ice cream.

Things their own father should've been doing.

But how could Rob be there for their kids when he hadn't even come home last night?

It'd been happening more and more lately. When he pulled stunts like that, she had no clue where he slept. Maybe he had a hottie on the side—who knew? All she knew was that most nights, by the time her shift ended, he was gone from the house. He'd always leave clues to his existence behind—a plate in the sink, mussed pillows on the couch— and it was those little signs of life that were the hardest to take.

She was pensive as she pulled into the lot of the Thirsty Bear Tavern, and once she slammed the minivan into park, she couldn't help but peek at her cell, even though she knew what she'd find: nothing. No calls from her husband. No texts, no voice mails. But still, she always checked. And damn her soul for trying.

She tossed the silly thing back into her purse, unbuckled, and sneaked a peek at herself in the rearview mirror. At least she still had her looks, not that anyone cared. The good men of Sierra Falls wouldn't touch her with a ten-foot pole, and she had no use for the bad ones—not that she'd let anyone touch her, not really. She had some fool notion that her husband might wake up one day and decide he liked her enough to want to start showing up to their marriage every now and again.

And so she kept on trying, just in case. If she kept up her

looks, maybe Rob would stop looking for whatever it was he thought he was missing. She flipped the visor mirror shut, feeling an inexplicable flicker of hope. She was looking *good*, if she did say so herself. Her red hair was saucy as ever and still free of gray—thank you, Grandma's good genes. Plus, she'd saved up her tips and splurged on the Victoria's Secret catalog, buying a sexy little bra that did wonders for her sagging, mother-of-three assets.

What the hell, she thought, as she dug back in her purse for her phone.

Maybe this would be the day Robbie would answer. Sometimes he did. Maybe this time something had happened, and maybe he was worried she was mad and was too nervous to call. Maybe he needed *her* to make the first move. She dialed.

It went straight to voice mail.

"Stupid." She blew out a breath. "No princes in my world."

Holding her purse on her lap, she stared at the tavern's front door, gathering herself. Forget her favorite new bra—some days she wished she had a full suit of armor to face the place. It was getting to feel like a real love nest.

The new sheriff was so smitten with Sorrow, you'd have thought she was the only woman on earth. And then, just a couple of weeks ago, Sully had taken off with Marlene, though Helen had a hard time resenting that. She didn't know Marlene well, and the woman hadn't always been exactly warm with her, but it was hard to resent someone whose husband had ditched her for his mistress.

Though, maybe if Rob ditched *her*, she could get on with her life. She was only thirty-two, after all.

She frowned. What was she thinking? She was stuck. As stuck as stuck could be.

And now Laura Bailey was back in town, acting bossier than ever, making her life a nightmare. Control freak, exercise freak, diet freak . . . the girl was wound up tight, not that anyone judged those things. If anything, every man in a sixty-mile radius was coming by to ogle her, though Laura probably had her head so far up her own butt she didn't even register the attention.

What *Helen* wouldn't do to be noticed. She didn't want any of those other men, though. She just wanted her husband to step up. She'd been a hot number in her day—not that she was so ancient now—and Rob had once looked at her like that, with all those hungry, lusty looks. All she wanted was for him to be there, with her, just once in a while.

Nobody knew where he went when he disappeared, or if anybody did, they weren't telling. He still had his job at the hardware store, miracle of miracles, but the paycheck was erratic at best. It seemed the man showed up for work even less frequently than he showed up in their bed.

It certainly didn't make him enough to be able to provide alimony. Not enough cushion for her to break out and support the kids on her own.

Someone rapped on her hood, and she startled. It was Bear, the tavern owner. She glowered at him through the windshield.

"Gotta work to earn that break time," he hollered from outside.

With a roll of her eyes and one last sigh, she got out. "Easy, boss." She made an elaborate show of checking the time on her cell. "I've still got two minutes before I have to clock in."

"This always happens on the holiday weekends," he said, beginning the same rant she'd heard a dozen times over the years. "All those fireworks and beers. People get too loose."

"I did two things yesterday." She held up a hand to count it out for him. "One: I minded my kids. And two: I minded *your* tent. So don't talk to me about beers. And anyway, maybe *you* should try a little loosening up. Might do you some good." She passed him, headed into the tavern, and didn't need to look back to imagine the scowl on his face.

She tucked her purse behind the bar, doing a quick scan of the place. A few men sipped coffee at the counter. An elderly couple sat in one of the booths, working on their breakfast specials. Eddie Jessup was there, too, taking up a whole booth himself, sipping coffee, reading some book— and wasn't that odd?

The clattering of pans got her attention, and she peeked at the pass-through window, into the kitchen. Glimpses of two blond heads told her she had both Bailey sisters to contend with today.

Helen snagged her apron, tying it on with a sigh. Catching the eye of one of the men at the bar, she said, "Another day, another dollar, huh?"

Her autopilot kicked on, and she did her usual morning jobs—refilling coffees, putting up a fresh pot of decaf and one regular, wiping down the bar, filling a pitcher of water and topping off the tables—eventually making her way into the kitchen to continue her routine in there.

The Bailey sisters spoke over each other, saying, "Morning, Helen." And, "Hi, Helen."

"Morning yourselves." She emptied a fresh bag of English muffins into the bread bin.

Sorrow stood at the stove, frying up hash browns. She might've had a talent for making fancy gourmet stuff, but sometimes people just wanted good, old-fashioned home cooking—especially at breakfast.

"That for Eddie?" Helen asked, with a nod toward the frying pan.

Laura narrowed her eyes. "How did you know?"

"Easy. He's a man. Men like big breakfasts. Especially the Jessups." She couldn't help goading the girl and smiled to herself as she ducked into the fridge to snag a jug of OJ. "He'll be having a large juice, too, if I know our Eddie."

"*Our* Eddie. Whatever."

Helen smirked. "You sure seem prickly on the topic of Jessups. Especially the youngest one."

She and Laura weren't too far apart in age, but while Laura drove a fancy car and wore fancy clothes, *she* spent her days dealing with stubborn kids and stopped-up toilets. The girl was acting like a child. It was a wonder how she'd ever gotten so successful.

Laura grabbed the sponge and attacked the counter with aggressive strokes. "I am not prickly."

She nodded at the spray cleaner in Laura's hand. "That counter's cleaned already."

"Not cleaned enough."

"Those stains are permanent." There were a million things that needed doing, not to mention several customers who needed attending, and here was Laura, wasting her energy on counters nobody could see. "You don't like it, tell your dad to refinish the kitchen."

Sorrow took the spray from her sister and put it back below the counter, giving her a gentle hint. "What are you up to today?" she asked brightly, in a blatant effort to change the subject.

"I need to make some calls to the El Dorado Hills City Council."

Helen stopped what she was doing to gape. "El Dorado Hills?"

"Yes. El Dorado Hills. I have a question about building codes." Laura gave her a quick side-eyed look, apparently deciding she wasn't good enough to hear details. "It's nothing."

Calls. All the girl had to do today was *make calls.*

She had to bite her tongue. She'd always thought of herself as a can-do woman, but maybe she should've acted needier. It sure worked for Laura, who did as she pleased. Would that *she* could've stayed home today, sitting around, gabbing on the phone, making calls. Instead, here she was, filling a dozen tiny white ceramic pitchers with half-and-half.

Laura shouldered in to scrutinize. "What are you doing? Wouldn't regular milk be cheaper?"

"They *are* called *creamers*," she said, not stopping her task for a moment.

"Well, I think it's a waste." Laura turned to Sorrow. "Does she do this every morning?"

"That's enough, Laura." Sorrow scraped the hash browns onto the plate, slid the whole thing under the warmer, and quickly set to scrambling up three eggs in the leftover oil. "*I* like to serve real cream for the coffee. Now, Helen, would you please pop one of those English muffins in the toaster for me?"

"The maple syrups also need topping off," Laura said with an edge in her voice.

Helen froze. Slowly she faced the oldest Bailey sister. "My job is out there on the floor. The manager's job is back here. Seems to me, the maple syrup is back here, too."

"Jeez, ladies." Sorrow made a little chuffing sound as she used her sleeve to wipe the sweat from her brow. "In case you haven't noticed, we've got customers out there." She slid the eggs onto the plate. "Helen, order up. You know who gets it."

As Helen brought Eddie his breakfast, she tried not to fume. Laura had returned from the big city, and she'd brought a pile of Louis Vuitton bags and loads of attitude with her. Word had it, she was here to stay. Helen hoped the attitude wasn't.

She didn't know what'd brought the girl back. Didn't care to know, frankly. She'd never had much interaction with Laura, anyway, but Bear had anointed her manager, and like that, the woman was acting like she owned the place—though Helen supposed she sort of did own it—partly, at least. "It's no excuse to act like a know-it-all," she muttered to herself.

Eddie looked up from his book. "What's that?"

Her frown flipped into a smile. That Eddie Jessup sure was easy on the eyes. "I said, eggs like you like them, Eddie. Scrambled *hard*." Her smile turned flirty.

Not that she'd ever pursue anything with a man other than her husband. Sometimes it just felt good to remember how it felt to be noticed.

He lifted his book, making room for the plate. "Thanks, Helen," he said, ignoring her saucy innuendo.

"There's nothing sexier than a man who reads," she said, trying even harder, bringing her smile up a notch. Though she was unclear why she made the effort. Eddie was a good-looking guy, a guy's guy. He'd have no interest in a married woman like her. She was all used up. Too many kids, too many bills, and one husband too many.

But still, she tried—she always tried. It was all perfectly innocent. Mostly, she craved the attention. She longed for someone, some man, some *adult*, to give her a friendly smile and a pat on the back every once in a while.

And maybe someday her flirting would capture the attention of the man she craved most of all: her husband.

"I don't get why you women are all so surprised to see a guy with a book," Eddie said, laughing off her comment. And of course he did—a guy like him would be used to flirty comments. "We can read, you know. It's not all *SportsCenter* and Skinemax."

She laughed. She hadn't made him uncomfortable at all, and he hadn't blown her off like some men did, either. He was friendly and normal, and it made her feel friendly and normal, too. The whole exchange put a temporary patch on the giant hole in her heart.

But then he met her eyes and asked, "How are you doing, Helen, really?" His tone was overly earnest, and she suddenly felt pathetic.

Everybody knew her situation. She supposed that, around town, she'd become either a butt of jokes, an object of gossip, or both. Hell, she supposed maybe she *was* pathetic.

That hole in her chest tore right back open.

Her smile felt stiff, and she went back into automatic. "Doing fine, doing fine," she said, feeling brittle enough to shatter. "Nine-to-five, gotta survive, right?"

Embarrassment was burning through her. She wanted to walk away, to forget who she was, but Eddie wouldn't let her walk away.

Instead he said, "You got that right," and he was smiling and shaking his head with the neighborly wisdom of it. "Those kids of yours can't be cheap." His complete attention was on his food as he squirted a big glop of ketchup on his plate and dragged a forkful of hash browns through it. "How's Luke? He playing fall ball this year?" He shoveled the bite into his mouth.

Helen might not be proud of herself, but she sure was proud of her son. Her oldest boy had quite the pitching arm, and it made her smile. "Yeah. You know he wouldn't miss it. The kid thinks the major league will be calling any day now."

She'd scoffed, but Eddie only shrugged. "Who knows?" he mused. "Someday, maybe they will."

It was a charitable and generous thing to say. Oddly, although the comment made Eddie soar in her estimation, the fact of it made her feel lonelier than ever. He was a good man, and what she wouldn't do for a good man.

"That boy's got an arm on him," he went on. "You let me know if you want me to throw the ball around with him. I'd be happy to teach him my fastball. I call it the Jessup Special." Eddie mimicked a slow pitch with an elaborate flourish to his wrist. "It's all in the release."

She gave him a sad smile. Ball practice was supposed to be for dads. But she gave him an appreciative nod. "I'll do that, Eddie. Thanks."

Laura practically leapt on her the moment she returned to the kitchen. "He still out there?" she demanded in an angry whisper.

Something about it annoyed Helen, and she intentionally answered in a normal volume, "Who, *Eddie*?"

"Shhh!" Laura stole a peek through the pass-through, staring in his direction for more than a few seconds. "Good Lord, how many coffees can one man drink?"

Helen took a step toward the door. "Want me to go ask?"

Laura swung to face her, pinning her with a flat stare. "Do you have a problem?"

Helen feigned confusion. "What do you mean?"

"I thought we girls were supposed to stick together."

She laughed at the concept as she went to unload the industrial dishwasher. "I didn't realize we were on the same team." She had to step back to avoid the cloud of scalding hot steam—some women went to the spa for facials; Helen unloaded dishes.

Laura looked momentarily flustered. "Well . . . we are. On the same team."

Sorrow chimed in, "Give him a break. I'm pretty sure Eddie's bad-boy days are way behind him."

"Still," Laura said, "I try to steer clear of men like that."

"Mm-hm," Helen acknowledged, but it was mostly to be polite. She didn't look away from the sturdy white dinner plates as she got into a rhythm, systematically drying and stacking them in the cabinet. "I'm sure you do."

"What does that mean?" Laura's voice came out a squeak.

Helen thought on it a moment. She was concentrating on her work. The comment hadn't meant anything, not really. And anyway, since when did what she thought matter one bit to Laura Bailey? Helen was way too tired and full of her own problems to craft double meanings or spend her time psychoanalyzing the girl. Seemed like Laura made drama for herself, while there *she* was, drowning in crises not of her own making.

Stay away from men like that. Eddie was a good and simple man, and just then, good and simple seemed like heaven. She put down her dishrag, and, letting out a gusty sigh, she met Laura's eyes. "Honey, what I wouldn't do for a man like Eddie." When the Bailey girl shuddered, she gave her a wicked smile. "Come on. He's cute."

"He's *not* cute," Laura said vehemently.

She raised her brows and gave the girl a pointed look. "Come. On."

"All right," Laura relented. "*Fine.* Eddie's cute, okay? But he's, like, twelve."

"He's your age." She swallowed her real comment, which went a little something like, *You might be special, but the clock ticks for you as much as it does for the rest of us.* The whole thing made her want to needle the girl, so she added in a feminine purr, "Plus, he's some ball player. Did you see the home run yesterday?"

Laura took over dish duty, which spoke volumes to Helen. If the older Bailey girl was resorting to manual labor without being asked, she really was troubled by something. "Yes, I saw that home run," she said tightly.

Helen couldn't help it; she decided to bait her. "Of course you did. It took them five minutes to find the ball in the bushes. He's so good at all the outdoor sports."

"Some people call that a ski bum."

"He has his own business."

"Yeah, one that's trying to take us down."

"Seems like your mind's made up," Helen said, but what she thought was, what *she* wouldn't do for a ski bum.

Forget cute. If she could find herself a bum half as reliable as Eddie Jessup, she'd be on him like white on rice.

Seven

Crossing the border into Nevada, a man didn't need to travel far till he spotted his first casino. They were everywhere, especially once you hit the bigger towns, a common sight on street corners, with signs that cried LOOSEST SLOTS IN NEVADA! and TEN DOLLAR PRIME RIB. Those slot machines were as prevalent as ATMs—in grocery stores, motel lounges, strip malls.

There was no end of ways to lose money in Nevada, and Rob Haskell had tried every one.

He sat at the table at one of the seedier joints outside Reno. Usually his game was Texas Hold 'Em, but he'd gotten a feeling about Seven Stud, and the Seven Stud table was where he'd sat since nine o'clock the night before. The last time he checked his watch it'd been two A.M. It was when he'd gotten his thousand-dollar marker. Actually, not a marker—an investment. His luck was just that close, he could taste it.

Going home hadn't even occurred to him.

Oddly, home was what drove him. His wife was such a hot number—always had been. And somehow, even after all these years, he'd never felt good enough for her. He'd seen how the men at the tavern flirted with her. Even that Damien Simmons did double takes whenever she was around. Some day *he'd* be as rich as Damien. *He'd* be the one driving around in the hot car, wearing the nice suits, not the crappy Up Country Hardware apron he had to put on for work.

Smoke choked the room. He thought he was probably hungry. Thirsty, too. He'd finished his last Scotch and soda hours ago—he'd nursed four of them over several hours, having calibrated his exact tolerance through the years. But these things registered only at a distance. Mostly he was aware of one thing and one thing only: the cards in his hands.

Dealers and players came and went around him, but they were also a blur, a parade of cowboy hats, cigars, toothpicks, and garish pinky rings on beefy fingers. There were women, too, in a procession of faces and ages and races, manicured fingers glittering with overlarge gemstones, hair sprayed into perfectly dyed helmets, and eyes schooled into careful blanks behind large-framed glasses.

He shifted in his chair. He sensed it was morning, and it was hard to ignore his fatigue. Distantly, he thought of Helen, and shoved her image from his mind. It just made him feel like a failure, and there was no room for failure. He had to imagine himself a winner. And so, although he knew in his head he should've been getting on home, he sat in that chair, and if something didn't happen for him in the next hand, it'd be coffee for him till something did.

It'd been this same Seven Stud table all night, and with his blurring vision, the cards swam over green felt. But he couldn't leave now—he was still riding that hunch.

Plus there was the marker to consider. One G. That was one thousand dollars that needed to go to the mortgage. To food. To whatever it was Helen spent their money on. As it was, they'd needed to deal with the unexpected expense that was her new minivan when she'd totaled the Dodge by slamming it into Phoebe Simmons's Mercedes on a patch of black ice.

That was his luck these days—a big, dead patch of black ice.

But not tonight. Tonight, when he'd gotten in the car, the clock had read 7:07, and it was a sign. *Sevens.* He'd been itching for some Seven Stud, and this would be the night he'd come away a big winner.

The game was dealt two cards down, four up, and the last one down, and it was time for that last card. Everyone but him and some woman had folded. It'd been an epic game, and there had to be at least a thousand in the pot, probably closer to two. After he paid his marker, it'd be a tidy chunk of change. He'd had better nights, but there'd been much worse, too.

It was time to bet. He eyed the woman's hand. She had a pair of eights showing, but he had no clue what else she might be hiding. He knew what he had, though—he had a winner. He was sitting on the proverbial ace in the hole, working an inside straight. Not much beat a straight, ace-high.

The woman eyed his cards, eyed him, then put a blue hundred-dollar chip in the pot.

With a silent nod, he called her bet, put in his own chip. He was in. He hesitated a moment, then raised her a hundred.

As he always did, he slid his hand in his pocket and rubbed his old buffalo nickel between thumb and finger. Forget rabbit's feet or lucky pennies—his lucky charm was a nickel, the same one he'd had in his pocket the day he met Helen.

The dealer kept up a monotone patter as he doled out the last card. Rob had a ten hiding next to his ace, plus a queen, a pair of twos, and a king showing. All he needed was a jack, and that pot would be his. That pile of chips was a car payment. Maybe he'd even take Helen out to celebrate. All that money could be a leg up to a fresh start.

The dealer eyed his hand, drawing out the moment. "The man's got a lady, a pair of deuces, and one cowboy showing." He dealt the final card, and it made a crisp flick sound as it was placed before him. It was the sound of hope. "Down and dirty. Good luck, people."

He put his fingers atop the card, rubbing it on the felt, willing it to be *the* card. He'd seen only one other jack, and he liked his odds. He peeled up the corner, peeking.

A seven. A damned seven. Was that what all those signs had meant? That he'd be screwed by a seven? All he had was a pair of twos, and he wasn't beating anyone with a pair of damned twos.

He kept his poker face but wanted to scream. He wanted to punch a hole in the table. To collapse onto the felt, hiding his face in his hands.

He was desperate. He owed a thousand-dollar marker. He had no choice. He had to bluff. He wouldn't be scaring anybody with a pair of twos, but if he bluffed well enough . . . Maybe the woman didn't get her card, either. Maybe if he went balls-out, bluffing with a pair of deuces, she'd fold. Maybe.

He shoved the rest of his chips to the center of the table and gave her a slow nod, thinking maybe it'd scare her off. *All in.* She met him there.

"Time to show me what you've got," the dealer said.

The woman flipped over her cards. It was a full house—three eights and two sixes. And all he had was a pair of damned twos.

"Eights over sixes," the dealer said in his monotone, sweeping the chips her way. "The boat wins it."

She grinned a yellow tobacco smile as she began to stack Rob's chips into neat, color-coded piles.

He was bust. It hadn't been luck he'd had a premonition of—it was disaster. He was done. Nothing left. As it was, he'd need to figure out how to talk his way into a credit for that marker. He calculated his next paycheck—one week till he could pay it all back. What would he do in the meantime? Maybe dip into Helen's purse—he'd done it before, God help him.

He checked his watch. Ten A.M. *Damn*. How had that happened?

The kids would be in school. Or would they? No, it was summer. His oldest would be home doing whatever he did, while Emmett and Ellie Lynn would be at daycare.

Was that right? He tracked his mind back to yesterday. He'd had his shift at the hardware store till seven, which meant it'd been Friday, which made today Saturday—Helen would be working at the tavern, and the kids would be . . . somewhere.

It meant he needed to get home and get to sleep before she got off her shift and the rest of them returned, one loud bunch, clueless to his crisis. He couldn't bear to face any of them, and sweet sleep was the easiest road away from the shame. He'd go home and strip and crawl into bed, where he could fall into blackness.

Someday he'd hit his big pot, and then he'd stop. Someday he'd show Helen he was a winner.

Eight

❧

Laura reached the parking lot, panting hard. She'd pushed herself that morning, doing a hilly seven-mile run rather than her usual leisurely four, but not even the scenic route to the old fire road and down around Granite Lake was enough to clear her mind. She slammed her heel onto one of the posts that lined the driveway and leaned over to stretch out her hamstrings.

Eddie. Cute, cocky Eddie. His face swam in her vision, making it go red.

He'd been getting the best of her since they were kids, and here he was again. Him and his construction project. It would put her family's business under. He claimed it wouldn't, but she wasn't stupid. Sure, it might bring new people at first, but eventually Fairview would add a darling gift shop, and then would come the old-timey saloon, and finally they'd build a folksy little diner that felt homey but was really run by the corporation, and eventually tourists would forget the Big Bear Lodge even existed.

But would Eddie listen? No. He only laughed it off. He had that attitude, that *guy* attitude, the kind that came with being easy and well-liked and hot.

Damn his hot.

She stood tall and grabbed her foot, stretching it behind her to get her quads. Her muscles trembled, and still it wasn't enough. Because, in addition to her worries about the family business, it was Eddie's *hot* she couldn't get out of her head.

It'd been like that for as long as she could remember. Him flirting with her—*flustering* her.

The stupid softball game had only reminded her. She hadn't wanted to play in the first place, and she definitely hadn't planned on watching *him* play. What a mistake that had been. She should've stayed in the tent, serving beers and slopping out helpings of chili. Helen was a pain, but she was better than Eddie.

He'd always been cute in his bad-boy way, but something had happened on that field, like light shifting through a prism, and all of a sudden there he was . . . hot. Disarmingly so.

Athletic guys weren't supposed to be her thing. If she were going to have a man in her life—which she wasn't—it'd be a millionaire software engineer. Or maybe a high-powered business exec in an Armani suit. Not Eddie in his tool belt.

After all these years, she hadn't expected to still find him so attractive, but now she couldn't stop thinking about him, and it annoyed her. It was the last thing she needed. She'd tried to blow it off, thinking how it was just one of those phenomena—put a guy on a field with a ball, or on a stage with a guitar, or in a uniform with pretty much anything, and *boom* . . . instant hot.

But then he'd stood behind her at bat.

Her breath hitched at the memory. She did *not* still feel those solid legs cradling hers, and she definitely didn't feel that hard stomach at her back, or the tickle of his breath in her ear, his voice a low and sexy rasp . . .

"Aw, hell." She squatted and rose and squatted and rose, feeling the burn in her butt. *Exercise* was what she needed. It'd been forever and a day since she'd been with a man, and that was the only reason remembering his touch made her feel this strange . . . tug.

He'd wrapped his hands around hers as she'd held the bat. They were large and tanned and strong and callused from laboring on houses all day. "Dammit." There it was again . . . the *tug*.

She straightened her legs and flopped in half to touch her toes. With a sharp exhale, she fought to reach her palms all the way to the ground. The stretch danced on the edge of painful, but she pushed it—all she needed was to work out her muscles harder than before and she'd get these traitorous urges out of her system.

A guy was the last thing she needed—especially this guy. She'd put the softball game behind her. She was playing a different game now, and she needed to get her head in it. She'd messed up a job before, and she wouldn't make that mistake again.

"Who am I kidding?" she muttered, thinking she hadn't just *messed up* in San Francisco, she'd screwed up royally. And it'd all been because of a man.

Against her better judgment, she'd hooked up with a guy from work. Before she knew it, he had a set of her keys and she had a carat on her finger. But then the job had gotten in the way. She'd been the acting interim vice president, and when a prized client came their way, she'd let her fiancé talk her into letting him take the account. She'd wanted it, but he claimed to have wanted it more.

Then promotion time came and he was the one given the permanent VP position, not her. She'd thought she was a shoo-in for the job and still wondered if it'd been their

CEO's way of punishing her for having a work relationship. Not that *Patrick* had gotten in trouble for it. Rather, it was almost like he'd been rewarded instead.

But her fiancé had tried to make it okay for her, kind of. He'd said he needed money to take her on the honeymoon of her dreams. But then the economy busted, and layoffs came, and guess whose name was on the list? *Hers.*

She got fired, and her fiancé didn't go to bat for her. That was when she'd begun to doubt whether he'd ever really respected her at all. Professionally, at least. It also marked the end of their engagement.

"No more men." She stretched an arm across her chest, tugging at her triceps. "No more screw ups. No do-overs." In managing the lodge and tavern, she had a second chance to earn people's respect, and she was going to get it right. "No third chances."

"Don't tell me the zombie hordes have finally arrived." It was Sorrow, heading from the lodge to her shift at the tavern. At Laura's perplexed look, she clarified, "You're bathed in sweat, looking like you just outran an angry mob, that's all."

"I went for a run."

"Uh-oh." Sorrow stopped at the door, peering hard at her. "What happened?"

"Nothing happened."

"*Something* happened. Look at you. You're wearing one of my scrunchies in your hair. If you're preoccupied enough to wear a scrunchie, the apocalypse truly is nigh."

She put a hand to the back of her head. "Am I that predictable?"

"It's only because I love you." Sorrow stepped closer, giving her a bolstering smile. "Now tell old Doc Sorrow what's up."

"I guess I am a little out of it."

"A little? I haven't seen you this sweaty since Chip Merriweather asked that Sandra girl to the prom instead of you."

"That Sandra girl was a—"

Sorrow put up a hand, cutting her off. "That Sandra girl had her own problems—and *there but for the grace of God go I*, as the Kidd ladies would say." She added mischievously, "You know you were always cuter, anyway."

She smirked—her sister was good medicine.

Sorrow took her arm and steered her toward the door. "Now you need to take a breather. Come in, hang out with me a while. I'll make you a coffee."

"A real one?"

"The coffee we brew *is* real, dummy. But yes, I'll make you one of your fancy-shmancy French press coffees."

"Okay, okay," Laura said, sounding more resigned than she felt. A coffee would be good, and some talk, too. This thing with Eddie and the hotel was feeling big, and it was time to confide in her family about it. "We need to talk, anyway. I've got news."

She'd been putting off telling them about the construction project, hoping she could deal with it herself. Though they'd probably already gotten wind of it—after all, their tavern was ground zero for Sierra Falls gossip. But she was sure they had yet to understand the full extent.

She sat on the kitchen counter, sipping her French press coffee, watching her kid sister work. She'd just finished telling Sorrow the full story, and the girl looked thoughtful as she was systematically chopping veggies and sweeping them into a big soup pot . . . chopping and sweeping, chopping and sweeping.

"You look so Zen," Laura told her, "doing what you do. I'm jealous."

"You mean because I'm good at chopping onions? Believe me, more than once I've regretted how my therapy is cooking and eating." She put down her knife. "You want jealous? If I could've gotten *your* genes instead, using running to get my mind off things"—she patted at her waist—"then maybe I wouldn't have these."

Laura had always envied how content her sister seemed with her body. To hear this now was a surprise. "What do you mean . . . *these*?"

"You know, love handles."

"Doesn't seem like your sheriff has a single problem with your love handles."

Sorrow blushed as a knowing and secret pleasure flashed in her eyes. "I guess you're right."

Laura felt a flicker of envy and put down her mug with a sharp clack. "Okay, back to business. What are we going to do?"

"About?"

"What do you mean, *about*? Get your mind off your fiancé. We were talking about what we're going to do about that, that . . . Eternal Rest Hotel and Spa."

Sorrow laughed. "Oh, Laura. Is it that bad? Maybe Eddie's right. Maybe a fancy spa could bring in more business for us."

"Thanks for the support, but yes, it *is* so bad." Her throat clenched a little as she said it.

Sorrow paused to look—really look—at her. "You're really upset. All right. I hear you. Tell you what. I need to finish up here, and the lunch crowd will be here soon, but once it thins out there, we can talk, okay? Make a plan." She grabbed another handful of veggies from the fridge and began to wash them. "When times get rough, I recommend soup. Go take a hot shower. This'll be done in an hour. You'll think better with a full stomach."

She looked longingly at the pot. "You know I can't." When things felt out of control like they did now, she always liked to be extra careful of her diet.

"Give it a rest, Laura. You can. Soup and salad can't be more than, what, five hundred calories, max."

Bear burst into the kitchen, the door swinging on its hinges. "What's keeping you girls?"

Sorrow didn't even pause what she was doing. "I'm doing

my job, Dad. You know, making lunch?" How her sister had become so bulletproof to the man's moods was a wonder.

Unable to get a rise from Sorrow, their father swung his gaze her way. He eyed her with a frown. "What happened to *you*?"

Her shirt was still damp and cool with sweat, and she peeled it from her body to air it out. "What's with you people? Can't a girl go for a run without getting the third degree?"

"You're dripping on the counter."

"I am *not* dripping on the counter." She hopped down.

Bear's eyes narrowed to tiny slits. "Ain't those shorts a little . . . *short*?"

"Yeah, Dad," Sorrow said blandly, coming to her rescue. "It's why they call them *shorts*."

"Well, dry yourself off before you get out there," he said with a wave to the pass-through window. The low hum of chatter had already begun, diners come early for lunch. Some liked to bring the newspaper and park at the counter for hours.

Laura gave him an incredulous look. "Who says I'm going out there?"

"Somebody needs to man the tables."

Sorrow met her eyes with a mischievous twinkle. "Don't you mean *woman* the tables, Dad?"

"I don't care who does it. All I know is Helen's not here yet."

"Helen needs to step up," Laura said at once. Their waitress fought her on everything, and while she didn't need her employees to bow at her feet, Helen's attitude verged on downright disrespectful. "We pay her good money. If she's not going to work for it, then we should find someone who will."

"I know you're not exactly friends," Sorrow began.

"Not friends? Not hardly. Does she even have any friends?"

"We can't just fire her," Sorrow said. "She's got kids."

Bear shrugged. "Your mother won't hear of it anyhow."

"Well, she needs to at least *attempt* to be on time."

"I'll talk to her," Sorrow said. "Try to give her a break. I feel bad for the woman. Her husband's never around."

Laura did a mental scan. "She's married to that Rob guy, from the hardware store, right?"

"Yeah." Dad nodded. "Real piece of work, that one."

Women too hung up on their men . . . as far as Laura was concerned, everyone should take a page from her book and swear off the male sex completely. "Not my problem." She went to put her coffee cup in the sink. "All I know is, business is up, and we're relying on her more than ever."

"Hey," Sorrow exclaimed, and her knife froze midchop, "what's up with hiring another person? Dad, didn't you say we could get some more help around here?"

"Did I?" he asked, looking a little like a trapped animal.

Sorrow smiled. "Oh, you did. You told Billy, remember? How we could get someone to help with the cleaning and front desk stuff."

"Seriously? Hired help?" Laura perked up, joining her sister. "That'd be awesome. I totally need help managing reservations."

"I don't know about any hiring." Their father looked panicked. "Don't be getting ahead of yourselves."

She'd been momentarily light-headed with excitement, and then her mood dipped lower than ever. "Doesn't matter, anyway. We won't even be able to afford Helen once we go under."

Dad swung to face her. "What kind of nonsense are you talking, girl?"

"Have you heard about Eddie's construction project?"

"Sure." He shrugged. "You mean that rundown ranch what's on the old logging creek?"

"That's the one."

He waved it off. "Yeah, Jessup told me about it. He says

sprucing it up could be good for the town. Damned if those dot-commers ever did anything with the place. Fat waste that was. Good people could've been living there all this time."

"Nobody is going to *live* there," Laura said. "His project is to turn it into a hotel."

"What of it?"

"What of it?" She looked to her sister for support.

Sorrow took over in more even tones, telling him, "Laura's worried because of who the developer is. Fairview Properties isn't exactly small potatoes. They've got plans to turn the ranch into a resort."

"But they mostly run those little hippie places, where they charge rich people an arm and a leg to eat nuts and berries, that sort of thing."

"They run world-class resorts," she protested. "They'll be touting *this* as a world-class resort."

Bear looked back and forth between the two of them, clearly not getting it. "That little place?"

"They're building up *that little place*," Laura said. "They're turning it into a spa thing, like *Forever Sleepy Resort* or something ridiculous like that. Whatever. What I do know is that once they finish, it'll be just a matter of time before they put us out of business."

Their dad thought on that for a moment but finally brushed it off. "I don't care how big they are, that old ranch is small potatoes, and small potatoes ain't gonna bring us down. Not with Sorrow in the kitchen now." He gave his youngest a wink.

"How times change," Sorrow murmured with a smirk. Just a year ago, Sully had been in charge of the food, and it was meat loafs and meat pies all around.

"Well, some things don't change," Bear asserted. "I've seen that old rancher go from hand to hand since I was a kid. Trust me. Nobody's gonna bend over backward to stay there."

The girls' eyes met. There was no convincing Dad when he didn't want to be convinced. At least her sister would be able to enjoy several months of cooking before they went under.

"It'll be okay," Sorrow mouthed to her as she went to the sink to fill the pot with water.

Bear followed and peered over her shoulder. "What the heck are you making?" Suspicion was thick in his voice.

"She's just busting out her famous toxic witch's brew," Laura deadpanned.

"Jeez, Dad, it's soup." Sorrow gave a swirl to the water with her spoon.

"Looks watery."

"This is how it's done," she said matter-of-factly.

He peered closer, picking up a particularly long leaf. "What the heck is this?"

"A leek."

"Sounds like a plumbing problem, not a vegetable."

"That's it." Sorrow spun and waggled her fingers at him. "Shoo! Out of my kitchen."

"Come on, Dad." Laura put her arm through his. "I hear zombie hordes might be coming to the tavern today."

"What on earth?" her father exclaimed as she ushered him into the dining room. "Zombie-whats? What are you talking about?"

But she barely heard him. All she registered was the sight of Eddie, folding his long, strong body into a booth. "Apocalypse," he said in his deep voice. "Sounds bad. Should I go get my gun?"

She stopped short, glaring. *Eddie.*

"In the flesh, tiger." He gave her a slow smile. "Just in time, too. You'll need somebody around to help propagate the species."

Nine

Bear looked his way. "We were just talking about you."

"Yeah," Laura said in a flat voice. "Speak of the devil." The way it came out, one would have thought he was actual evil-spawn.

Eddie touched a hand to his forehead. "What? Are my horns showing?"

She bustled by without sparing him another glance, headed behind the bar. "Shouldn't you be at your job site? You know, sawing, hammering, crushing the hopes of others, that sort of thing."

Bear sauntered over to join him in his the booth. "I got something to ask you."

"Shoot." He kept the easy smile on his face, but inside he braced. Laura looked ready to snap, and it gave him an inkling of what her father wanted to discuss.

"I hear you're trying to put us out of business."

"No such thing, Bear. I regret your daughter has a problem—"

"Problem?" Laura exclaimed.

Here it came.

He ignored her to lean forward and talk fast. "With respect, sir, so long as Fairview plays by the rules—and I've got a permit in my truck that says they are—then I've got a responsibility to grow my business."

Bear liked the *sir*. He gave a gruff nod. "A man's got to look out for his business."

"I believe this'll only bring more tourists to Sierra Falls. That rancher can only hold so many guests." It'd be more guests once they added a second story, but he'd work up to that part. "People coming to visit the spa will need some-place to stay . . ." He cocked his head in the direction of the lodge, letting Bear do the math. And he honestly believed it, too. A night at the Fairview property would probably run about four times what a night at the lodge cost.

Sure enough, the man gave him a slow smile as he rose from his seat. "That was my notion exactly. I like how you think." He went to the bar, pausing to smack a hand on the counter. "Can't fight progress, girl."

Laura looked unusually deflated. Quietly, she said, "They'll put us out of business, Dad."

"No prissy health farm is going to put us Baileys out of business. Seems to me you've got enough to fret about, so get back to it." Bear shook his head as he settled onto a far stool, muttering, "Spa Jacuzzi city folk prissiness."

Laura automatically poured her dad a cup of coffee. Eddie had known the man for years, and he knew to let him sip and sit with this latest development for a while before he broke the rest of his news. It took baby steps with Bear Bailey.

And besides, something else was demanding his attention at the moment. Laura had begun to crash around behind the bar, slamming the coffeemaker open and shut, rattling cups in the bus tray, breaking up the ice in the freezer bin. To someone else, she might've looked angry, but Eddie saw something in the way her mouth was drawn. A pinched look to her eyes that made it seem like she was damming back some emotion.

He hated it. Hated to be the bad guy in those eyes.

He popped up from the booth and joined her behind the bar.

She grew utterly still, watching as he poured himself a cup of coffee. "What are you doing?"

"I came for coffee, so I'm getting myself some."

"I can see that. You know what I mean."

He could tell she wanted to tear into him, but how could she fault his helping himself? Their waitress wasn't in yet, so serving fell to the family. "Just trying to help a pretty lady."

"Then rip up Fairview's check."

He topped off Bear's cup, then walked back around and grabbed a stool at the bar. "Seems our goals are mutually exclusive." As he leaned his elbows on the counter, he couldn't help but eye her tight body in that skimpy workout getup. "Although . . ."

"Although, what?"

He shot a glance at Bear, chin-deep in a copy of yesterday's paper, and whispered, "Although it seems like one of your goals is a good workout. I could always help by racing you around in those little hot pants of yours."

Abruptly, she stood erect, putting her hands on her hips, doing her best to look put out. "They are not hot pants. They're running shorts."

He let his gaze rove along those sleek thighs, and when he brought his eyes back to hers, something gratifying awaited him there. "You're blushing," he said with genuine surprise.

"I am not blushing." She turned her back on him to wipe down a part of the bar that didn't need wiping. "I'm just flushed from my workout."

"Next time, you let me know if you need a running partner. Because seriously, I'm available for chasing."

"Dream on, Jessup." She threw the rag into a bin under the counter. "Now, do you have a reason to be here, or is it just to plague me?"

He was working up the guts to break it to her about the rancher's second story, so for now it was pretty much the plague-her thing. He had an appointment to keep in Reno, but instead he found himself reaching for a menu. "What's today's special?"

"Soup, but it won't be ready for an hour."

"Forget the soup," Bear said. He put his paper down and shot a thumb in the direction of the windows. "You've gotta finish the screens."

Eddie popped up to take a look. "I did finish, good and solid." He helped the Baileys out with small jobs, and it wasn't like him to mess something up. "Here's your problem," he said, seeing it immediately. One of the pegs holding the screen in place had broken, leaving a gap wide enough to let bugs in. "I told you, Bear, you get what you pay for."

"They told me these were perfectly good."

"And I told you they're perfect crap. These cheap ones can't take any wear." He wedged the screen back into place. "Hey, sugar," he called to Laura, "you got a toothpick behind that bar?" She gave him a frosty look in reply, so he added, "I need something tiny to pick out the broken bit."

"These things came with a bag of extra parts," Bear said, headed to the door. "I'll go to the garage, see if I can find them."

Laura brought him a few plastic cocktail spears, and instead of returning to the bar, she stayed to watch as he used a toothpick to jiggle the piece free. "How'd that happen?" she asked.

He found her interest oddly gratifying. "It was probably some little kid, sitting in the booth, fiddling with it. Snapped the head of it right off."

"Well, can't you just snap it back on again? It's letting in a ton of mosquitoes." She put a knee on the bench of the booth to get a closer look, and the fake leather upholstery crunched as she leaned in.

The piece popped free, and he dropped it into her hand. "Got it."

"Good. I worked the evening shift yesterday and was practically nibbled to death."

Her thigh was tanned and smooth, and he had a good idea of what *he'd* like a nibble of. "I'll bet you taste mighty good, too."

Too good. He had to turn his back to her, giving himself a second to cool it.

But then she made an exasperated sound, and he just had to get a look at her expression, so he stood. He moved sooner than she'd expected, though, because as he did he practically bumped into her.

Stepping back, she made a little "Oh" sound. Her eyes were wide and lips parted, making her look as heated as he felt.

"Is there something the matter?" He stepped closer, touching a finger to her chin. "Because, sweet thing, you're looking flushed."

"Just fix it and be done, Jessup." She shifted her chin, evading his touch, but she didn't move outright, which he took as an excellent sign.

He inched even closer to her. "You want me to fix it?"

She took another step backward, looking a little unsteady. "Please."

"Well, then. All you had to do was say *please*."

Bear reappeared with a tiny, clear plastic bag. "Got 'em."

"Maybe if you'd installed it right the first time," Laura said flatly.

He smirked to himself, wondering if she was this saucy in all areas of her life. "I did install it right the first time." He emptied the parts into his palm, looking for the right little black peg. "Maybe if the manager of this place hadn't been so stingy . . ."

"I am not stingy," Laura said.

"Whatever you say." It took Eddie just a second to click the part into place.

Bear hooted a laugh as he headed to the bar, mumbling, "I need coffee for this." The man walked slowly since a stroke had left him with a bum leg, but damned if he hadn't been moving around better ever since Sorrow'd had her emergency down at the old mine.

Bear gave the coffee a sniff, and, despite his grimace, he poured himself a mug. "Well, kids, if that's it on this whole ranch nonsense—"

"Actually," Eddie interrupted, "there's one other thing." It was now or never. He settled on a stool, bracing himself for the fight he knew was coming.

Laura froze. "I knew it." She looked at her father. "Here it comes. The part about how he's going to destroy Sierra Falls and all the rest of us with it."

"Let's hear the man out," Bear said. He turned to Eddie, adding, "Ignore her. I told my girl it's just a little rancher."

"Sure," Laura muttered. "Ignore the girl."

Her dad pretended not to hear as he stirred a couple of spoonfuls of sugar into his coffee. "No old, beat-up one-story hotel is gonna put the Big Bear Lodge out of business. Ain't that right, Jessup?"

Eddie didn't smile along, though. The churn in his gut made such a thing impossible. "Well, funny thing that. It turns out Fairview wants more than just a one-story rancher."

Laura's expression shattered—it was what he had been dreading most. "What did you say?" she asked, her voice gone hushed.

His attention was only on her as he said, "I'm sorry, Laura. I tried. They want to build up, not just out. We've got to take the place up a floor. But," he quickly added, "what I said still stands. They're building a spa in there, too, and once they add things like treatment rooms, there won't be all that much space left for guest rooms. I honestly can't see how it'll put you guys under."

"Build up?" she exclaimed, clearly not agreeing with his assessment. "How can they do that?" The hollow look in her eyes gutted him. But then her pain sharpened to fury. "How can *you* do that?"

Everything about her—her tone, her words, and the accusation in those eyes—put him on the defensive. "Because I need to put food on the table, Laura. Forget me, how about Jack? He's got Craig and Tina to think about. If it hadn't been us hired to do the job, it would've been some other outfit. Think about it."

"No, *you* think about it. Your swanky new hotel isn't just going to put the Bailey family out of business—it'll change everything about Sierra Falls. Corporations who don't give a damn about the town or the people who live here, they'll come in and build their big chain stores and chain hotels and chain restaurants, and it'll put the rest of us—the residents, the heart and soul of this town—out of business."

He scrubbed a hand through his hair. Did she think these things hadn't occurred to him? All he could do was try to remain optimistic. "I can't stop it," he said tiredly.

He checked his watch. His other commitment was calling him. Construction wasn't the only thing in his life—not by a long shot—and it was a long drive to Reno.

"Are we keeping you?" she asked in a voice like acid.

He slid from his stool in answer.

She glared. "Where do *you* have to go?"

"Reno." Like she cared.

"Hitting the strip?"

With a roll of his eyes, he got back on topic. "Look, Fairview has the permits ready to go. Neither of us can stop them."

"Oh, I'll stop them all right." She stormed from behind the bar. "Think about it, Eddie. The former owners had a ton of dot-com money. If they could've made that stupid property into something bigger, or better, or somehow more than just a little old ranch house, they would have. No, there's something fishy about your *permits*," she spat, "and I'm gonna get to the bottom of it." She looked at her dad. "Tell Sorrow I'm taking a rain check on lunch."

She stormed out. The door slammed behind her, leaving a deafening silence, with just the sound of Bear's spoon clinking against his mug to be heard in the tavern.

"Building up, huh?"

Eddie sighed and leaned against the dinged-up counter. "If it weren't us on the job, it would've been someone else. There's no stopping those people."

"I always figured that was some sort of historic property. You know, the sort of thing you can't change, just restore." Bear shrugged. "I'm assuming you're not doing anything illegal."

"Fairview got special permission. Some *adaptive reuse* thing."

"Never heard of it."

"We've got the permits."

"I heard you the first time."

"Look, Bear. This is my livelihood we're talking about. In this economy, Jessup Brothers Construction can continue to scrape by with odd jobs, or we can go big-time. Fairview is big-time."

"It's our livelihood, too, boy. The livelihood of the whole Bailey family." He stood and patted a definitive hand on the counter. "But Marlene raised you well. I'm sure you'll do the right thing."

Eddie headed back out to his truck, evading the nosy stares of the other diners. Screw the soup. His appetite was gone anyhow.

What Laura had said nagged him. What if there *was* something fishy about that permit?

A quick phone call to Hunter Fox was supposed to put

his mind at ease, but the man's smooth-talking protests weren't as easy to swallow as they'd once been. Eddie snapped his phone shut and pulled the permits from the glove compartment. All neat and tidy, just as Fox had said. He shoved them back in and slammed it shut.

Laura was just being her old self. Self-involved, self-absorbed, and snotty.

He needed to stop being distracted by things like smooth legs and teensy-tiny running shorts. What he needed was to start construction once and for all. Get this thing built and finished—the future of his family business relied on it. That was all he could afford to think about.

And if it meant the total ruination of his relationship with Laura, well, he never stood a chance with that kind of woman anyhow.

Ten

Laura startled, hearing the creak of the attic steps. She gave a sharp sniff and scrubbed a quick hand over her face.

"Are you up here again? I can't find the—" Sorrow's head popped into view and she paused, taking in the scene. "Hey, you okay?"

"Yeah, fine." Laura turned her back on her sister. She'd allowed herself a mini-breakdown in what she thought would've been the solitude of the attic. "Got some dust in my eyes. What are you doing?"

"I'm looking for the dustpan." Sorrow's eyes swept the room. "What are *you* doing?"

"Organizing." She gave a sharp sniffle and got back to rifling through an open trunk. "Ditching some of this old stuff."

"Don't throw away too much. I already went through it when the roof caved."

"There's still a ton of junk." She shrugged. "It's bad feng shui."

"Okay . . ." Sorrow said warily. "Don't tell me the dustpan was bad feng shui, too?"

"I threw it away." She began to refold and smooth a stack of old linen napkins.

"You threw away the *dustpan*?"

"I bought a Swiffer to use instead. I cleared out the pantry; it's hanging in there on its own hook."

Sorrow clomped the rest of the way up the stairs. "What do you mean, you *cleared out the pantry*?"

She didn't have the energy to get into it with her little sister. Cleaning was therapeutic, and she'd just as soon continue in peace. "There was stuff in there that didn't belong," she said dismissively.

"Like what kind of stuff?"

"Like . . . duct tape. And envelopes. Stuff that belongs in the garage. Or the office." She slammed the trunk lid down. "Look, I'm not up for this right now, okay?"

"Easy, Laura." Sorrow put up a quelling hand that, at the moment, felt patronizing.

"Don't tell me to take it easy. Who do you think will get the blame if we go out of business? *Me*, that's who." She smooshed the lid all the way closed and clicked the hasps shut.

"We're not going to go out of business because there's duct tape in the pantry."

Laura felt the emotion clawing at her throat again. Controlling her environment helped her feel in control of her destiny—why was that so hard to understand? "I need to get this place in better order."

"Hey," Sorrow said, "don't forget I'm here, too. Just because you're the manager doesn't mean you're in this alone."

Her sister had obviously sensed her distress, but instead of comforting her, the sympathy only made her feel teary again. "Thanks," she said tightly. "But I like chores like this." And she did. Dealing with practicalities kept the demons at bay.

Sorrow knelt to her eye level. "I want you to be able to focus on business stuff, remember?"

"*Do I remember?* I was up all night with business stuff." She leaned an elbow on the trunk, suddenly heavy with exhaustion. She'd spent hours pulling together a hard-core, bulleted presentation outlining the next steps for confronting the Jessups' treachery. There was so much to consider: budget, publicity, outreach, growth estimates. She was approaching the management of her family business no less seriously than she had in her job as interim vice president. Though look how *that* had turned out.

"Just . . . don't forget I'm here to help. I can totally deal with stupid stuff like cleaning out the pantry."

"You don't always know where everything goes."

She realized how bratty that'd sounded and waited for Sorrow to take the bait, but her sister just sighed, telling her gently, "You can't control everything."

Couldn't she?

But she didn't say that. Her sister would never understand. Sweet, loving Sorrow had always been everyone's favorite. Lately, Dad was always going on about his talented chef daughter, or his brave Marine son. But when it came to Laura, the only praise she ever got was how on top of things she was. On it.

Our Laura's on it.

And now that the welfare of the entire family business rested on her shoulders, she dared not consider what would happen if, for once, she wasn't *on it.*

But she wasn't about to go there with Sorrow, so instead she told her, "Look, I think I put the dustpan in a charity box in the garage." She turned away, scooting in front of the next trunk, effectively ending the conversation.

She heard her sister sigh, pause, then head back down the stairs.

Laura didn't have a shrink, but at the moment, this kind

of therapy would have to be enough. After two more trunks, it was.

Until Helen tracked her down later, shattering her hard-won calm.

Laura had gone into the tavern kitchen to hide out—anyone who knew her knew she didn't hang in the kitchen if she could help it, but she was craving some of Sorrow's homemade hummus, so she'd given herself a moment to sit on the counter, crunch on carrots and dip, and scan the seventy e-mail messages visible on her cell.

Sorrow had sensed her state of mind and given her a wide berth for the rest of the afternoon, but Billy had no such clue. "How's the new phone?" he asked. He was spending his lunch break as usual, stealing some time with her sister as she did her advance dinner prep.

Laura frowned at the thing. "Jury's still out." She'd splurged on a new smart phone, but so far it just showed her all the work she had to do, and yet the tiny screen made it barely possible to do anything about it. "Can you believe . . . thirty-two new e-mails in just the past three hours?"

"Thirty-two?" Sorrow stowed a platter of chicken breasts in the fridge to marinate. "Who's sending all the e-mail?"

Laura shrugged. "Reservations. Lodge inquiries. Spam. Plus I'm working on some other stuff. I'm in touch with the California Office of Historic Preservation." She caught the look that shot between Billy and her sister and quickly added, "If there's some error in Eddie's building plans, any technicality at all, it'll void the whole permit and they'll need to start over."

She'd learned that trick from Ruby and Pearl when she'd gone down to the Town Hall to investigate the historic registry. She still needed to stop by with some flowers to thank them.

"Start over?" asked Sorrow.

Laura braced for the speech that was to come, about how it wasn't a big deal, the Jessups wouldn't do anything illegal, there was no fighting the system. Increasingly she felt like Don Quixote, tilting at windmills.

But then Helen burst into the kitchen, interrupting, which meant for once she was happy to see the woman. "Hey, Helen."

"I see you're all hiding in the kitchen while some of us are out on the floor, hustling our butts off." Their waitress thrust the tavern phone at her.

She gave the phone a wary eye, making sure to keep her tone exaggeratedly even. "Is this your way of saying the phone is for me?"

"It's my way of saying I need more help out there."

Laura put her ear to the phone. "Hello?" She waited a second, then rolled her eyes. As far as she was concerned, Helen's days were numbered. She'd even begun to keep a list of the woman's transgressions, remembering from her office days how the two most important things in any employee termination were to keep calm and to keep documentation. "There's nobody there."

"So sorry," Helen snapped. "Maybe if I had more help I could've run back here sooner."

"Hey, I could use more help, too." Laura was more committed than anyone and could school the lot of them in what it meant to work hard. "But my hands are tied. Consider yourself lucky you even have a job." She was speaking from experience, as someone who'd recently been fired, but the way Helen bristled, she'd clearly taken it as a threat.

Whatever. She glared at the phone instead, putting it back up to her ear. "Who was it?"

"Did the call get transferred to the other line?" Billy asked.

Helen ignored them, looking to Sorrow. "We've got more business than ever, and I just can't handle it."

Laura switched to the other line, only half listening to Helen's griping—she had neither the time nor the patience—but there was silence on the line. "Nope, that's dead, too."

Helen finally tuned in, and, shooting a quick glance Laura's way, she said, "They must've hung up."

"Gee, thanks," she grumbled.

"Well, if I hadn't had a dozen other things to do at the same time, maybe I'd have found you." Helen angrily crossed her arms, and the gesture plumped her already ample chest—did she purposely flaunt her assets at any given opportunity? "But can I say one word to complain? No. I do much of the work yet have none of the say in how things go around here."

"You have a say." Sorrow tapped her spoon on the edge of her frying pan and gave Helen her full attention. "We're listening."

"Go on," Billy said. "They won't bite." Then he pointed to Laura and added with a smile, "Well, *she* might." He placed his hands on his fiancée's shoulders. It seemed he was always touching Sorrow with those affectionate, automatic gestures.

Helen only glared.

The chatter from the other room swelled with the sound of new patrons. It was time to defuse the situation and get back to work. Helen had diners to serve, and *she* had a certain construction worker to confront. Even if nothing came of things like forcing Eddie to remeasure the property lines, it'd still provide nice little setbacks for him.

She hopped from the counter, pocketing her cell phone with one hand and holding the tavern phone in the other. "We're all overwhelmed, Helen. Our marketing efforts have begun to pay off, and it just means we all have to work extra hard."

"It's a case of be careful what you wish for," Billy said wryly.

Helen stiffened. "Well, it's become too much. I can't keep running between tables, back to the bar, back here, back to the tables—"

"Okay." Sorrow smiled. "Okay."

"Okay?" Laura gaped at her sister. *Okay* was not the way to manage people. The situation had been in hand before Sorrow had interrupted. "What do you mean, *okay*?"

"Okay, we've hired someone to help."

Laura almost dropped the phone, not believing her ears. "Since when?"

"Since Dad finally relented."

Annoyance quickly followed her relief. "When exactly were you planning on telling me? I *am* the manager."

"Chill out," Sorrow said. "We just finalized it today. You were hiding in the attic, remember? Hey, if you looked up from that cell phone every once in a while, I could've told you sooner."

She shut her eyes for a second, regrouping. "All right. You're right."

"I am?" Sorrow grinned.

"Don't let it go to your head. Now tell me how you finally convinced the old man. He's been all talk, promising help for ages."

"I did it with a little help from this guy." She leaned back into Billy, and he cradled his arms around her waist.

Helen snapped, "Shouldn't you two be on a honeymoon somewhere?"

"We're having a long engagement."

Laura had to agree with Helen on that point—those two were a bit much to watch sometimes. "You can honeymoon all you want if you're telling me someone else is showing up to help around here."

"Believe it," Sorrow said.

As Helen began to rail in detail about all the various skills their new employee would require, Laura considered the Caller ID on the tavern phone. It was a 212 area code. *Manhattan?* "Hey, Helen. You never said who called."

The woman looked annoyed to be interrupted. "He said he was from the History Network."

"He said *what*?" Laura exploded into action, seeing in a flash a whole new world of possibilities.

Eleven

By the time Laura took the turnoff to Timber Road, her mind was going a million miles a minute, and unfortunately the car was going a little faster than it should've been, too. Gravel spat under her tires as she brought the Beemer to an abrupt stop in the ranch's parking lot.

A couple of the construction workers hooted at her daredevil entrance. She really should sell the thing and buy something much more practical for mountain living—a nice SUV, or a Jeep maybe—but she was having a hard time parting with the thing. She'd left San Francisco with her tail between her legs, but she'd bought that sedan fair and square, working her butt off for every last payment. It was a symbol of her meager successes, and she wasn't ready to part with it yet. Other successes had been just too hard to come by.

But then she caught sight of Eddie's ridiculously giant pickup—it was a godawful vehicle. Maybe the BMW *was* just the thing.

Eddie. She shaded her eyes, looking for him among the other workers.

She bit her cheek not to grin—she felt like she'd already won the battle. It *had* been the History Network who'd called. The execs had raved about Sierra Falls, the lodge, and the discovery of letters from her three-times-great-grandmother that'd uncovered much about the famous California figure Buck Larsen.

They were interested in *her* family's lodge. Not Eddie's Slumber Ranch.

She squinted, trying to make sense of what she was seeing. Workmen roved the rooftop of the ranch house. It'd been only a few days since her last argument with Eddie—surely she wasn't too late. Had they begun building another story already?

She peered harder, shading her eyes from the sun. The home really was a beautiful old girl—like something from one of those aged sepia photos of the Wild West. It had a low, flat roof, with no-nonsense posts and pillars hammered together at right angles. A porch wrapped around the front, adorned with old wagon wheels in various states of decay. Part of the façade had been torn away, and though she was sure it'd been necessary to repair the extensive damage years of snow and ice would've done, still, the sight sickened her. She was protective of her town, and nothing more symbolized the heart of Sierra Falls than a turn-of-the-century building like this.

"What can I do you for?" a friendly voice shouted from above.

"Hey, Jack." She knew she could take her issues up with Eddie's brother—after all, it was Jessup Brothers, plural—but she found she mostly wanted to continue the conversation with Eddie. "Where's—"

"My little brother? He's off in the woods, no thanks to you."

"To me?"

"You're making the man nuts. He's somewhere out there now, with his surveying equipment." Jack gestured into the distance. "Got it in his head to check all the property lines. Again. Said we have you to thank for it."

"Don't thank me yet," she muttered.

"What's that?" He began to make his way toward the ladder. "You need me to come down?"

"No, no need. Thanks, Jack. I'll go find him."

"You do that. He's been making stupid mistakes, distracted. Doesn't help with that phone of his buzzing every two minutes, and don't think I don't know it's you hounding him. He said you're in a lather about something." Jack gestured into the distance. "I told him to stay out there and take a long lunch."

Distracted. She didn't realize guys like Eddie had a conscience. Did it mean she'd begun to get through to him after all?

As she wandered away from the house toward the tree line, the beauty of the place struck her. She didn't consider herself a big outdoorsy woman—she must've driven by the place thousands of times, but never once had she explored beyond what was visible from the road—but the property really was quite pretty. A creek curved over the land like a ribbon, sparkling in the sunlight. Summer had coaxed every color of the rainbow, and a carpet of green, red, and yellow grasses lined its banks, dotted with blue, pink, purple, and white Sierra wildflowers. Scattered pine trees in a deep green flanked the water on either side, and the mountains rose in the far distance, feeling ancient and wise. Thin veins of white dappled a few of the peaks—snow that had yet to melt.

The closer she got to the water, the more distant the construction became. Instead of the sounds of sawing and shouts, she heard only the lazy splash of slow-moving creek water, the sound of tall summer grasses swaying, birds chirping. She might not've been a nature girl, but even she couldn't deny how idyllic it all was. She stopped to take a

moment, shutting her eyes and inhaling deeply. Feeling the
sun on her face was both the simplest and the most profound
of pleasures.

"Lovely, huh?"

Her breath caught. Eddie's voice was a low rasp, and her
skin beaded at the sound of it. Bracing herself, she opened
her eyes. He'd appeared next to her, standing in his jeans,
dirt-smudged T-shirt, and old work boots, looking as rugged
as the land. Momentarily speechless, she stood there, inadvertently sharing this quiet with him. She had the odd
thought that the blood in her veins felt as enlivened as that
babbling water.

She cleared her throat, looking away to stare at the creek
instead. "It is."

"And you're here to tell me to stop."

"I am."

"You're here to tell me if we develop any further we'll
be invaded by people come to cut all the flowers and fish
out the creek."

"That's about the size of it."

"I tried, Laura." He took off his ball cap, scraped his
hand through his hair, then adjusted it back on his head.
Despite the shade it provided, sun marked his face, in faint
lines around his eyes and mouth. He'd clearly spent a lot of
time outdoors, squinting and smiling—smiles that, lately,
were rarely directed at her.

She glanced away, gathering herself. "Not very hard, I
imagine."

"I measured and remeasured the property line. I even
looked into rules about building near conservancy land. I'm
listening, Laura. What else do you want me to do?"

That took her aback. She finally looked, really looked
him in the eyes. They were a sparkling blue in the sunlight,
looking even bluer for his tanned skin and brown hair. In
that instant, her traitorous mind came up with one answer.
Kiss me.

"I—" She gathered herself, and standing rigidly upright, looked away. "I've got news, Eddie. Big news."

"I'm all ears."

"I got a call earlier. From the History Network."

He looked momentarily baffled. "You mean, like on cable TV?"

"Yes, you know, *the History Network*. 'Bringing the past to life,' that one?" This was her big moment, the most success she'd had since losing her job, and she found she wanted it—needed it—more than ever.

"Hey, cool. What'd they want?" Something about the surprise on his face was deeply gratifying.

"They found out about all the Buck Larsen stuff," she said, referring to the letters Sorrow had found, revealing the secret affair between their ancestor and one of the most famous figures from California history. "They're talking about doing a documentary on the town."

There was nothing like the interest of a television network to feel like validation. She'd been working her fingers to the bone—it was what the Baileys did—and her efforts had brought their family business to the brink of real success. Finally, she'd have her chance to make up for her past failures. She could prove to herself, prove to the world, just how talented she could be.

"That's great news," he said, sounding actually genuine. "Sorrow might've found those letters, but the rest is all you, you know that, right?"

Taken aback, she stammered, "I . . . yeah . . . thanks."

"Seriously, Laura, congrats. I hope Bear understands what he has in you."

The unexpected warmth broke down a wall she'd had erected since junior high. No longer able to monitor her excitement, she found herself revealing more. "We've been booked solid ever since the call. Film types are flying out from LA, if you can believe it. Dad even let us hire someone to help around the place. We're on the brink of something real, with the lodge, I mean. We're so close to becoming something big, or at least, you know, bigger than just a run-down family operation. This would really put us on the map. So now you really do have a reason to call it off with Fairview."

"That's all awesome," he said, but his voice sounded suddenly strained. "I'm excited for you." He grew quiet and stared at the ground, kicking at a rock.

If he was so excited, then why couldn't he look her in the eye? She pressed him. "But?"

"But I don't see how it affects this project."

Embarrassment choked her, a pained, self-consciousness that sizzled through her till her cheeks burned with it. Why had she just told him all that stuff? Why had she thought *he'd* understand?

"Don't you get it?" She turned and stabbed a finger back in the direction of the ranch house. Distance made it seem even older—but for the men swarming the roof, she might've been looking through a window back in time. "You can't change something that's historic, you know, when *the History Network* is coming."

"I've got permits," he said. "I signed a contract. We're all buttoned up, no matter how many times I remeasure the place. Look, I'm glad things are turning around for you. People will always want to stay at the Big Bear. I genuinely hope this Fairview thing doesn't hurt you. I really do believe that maybe it'll even bring in more business for you."

"You can't really believe that," she cut in. With a sharp exhale, she took a few steps closer to the water. Stupid Fairview would probably build a little bridge over the creek—a silly-looking faux Japanese Zen thing, that people would stand on and flick their cigarette butts from.

How could the sight of all this nature make her feel better and so much worse at the same time? The low, loud rumble of a saw cut through the air, followed by a sharp crack. It galvanized her.

Everything she'd worked so hard for was falling apart. *She* was falling apart. Just when she'd made peace with Sierra Falls, it would be taken from her.

She burst forward, needing to be closer to the creek, to touch it for herself. Fed by the snowmelt, it would be cold, and she wanted to dip her hand in and pluck out a stone to skip across its surface. Why had she once resented all this so much? Why had it taken her so long to see how these mountains brought her such peace? She'd fled for the city, but it was here that she knew herself. Her throat burned with emotion, but she refused to get emotional in front of *Eddie Jessup*. She put more distance between them, wandering closer to the banks, walking in among the thigh-high grasses.

"Laura," he shouted.

She spun a slow circle. "How can you build on this?"

"Watch it."

"What? Am I trespassing now?"

He laughed, and it was an aggravating sound. "Not hardly. I just want you to watch where you're going."

"What is your problem?" she demanded. "You refuse to see what's in front of you."

He approached. "Believe me, I see." There was a husky, suggestive note in his voice, and it made her defiant.

The damned man—why did he have to *do* that? She whirled around and plunged deeper into the grass. This time, when he called for her to stop, she ignored it. Instead, she challenged over her shoulder, "When was the last time you really saw how pretty this all is?"

It was so exhilarating to reconnect with the land she'd known as a child. She'd spent so many years chasing other things—how had she forgotten *this*? She plunged into the waist-high grass, stroking her hand along the tips of leaves.

His hands were hard, grabbing her shoulders. "Jesus, Laura. Stop."

She flinched away. "You're an ass."

He began to walk backward, pulling her with him. "And you're in a field of poison oak."

"I . . ." She stopped her struggling and froze. "What?"

"Poison oak."

"I thought it was red."

"Sure. In the *fall*." He scooped her up and simply carried her out.

She stiffened in his arms, shoving against him. He was hard and strong, and the heat of his body burned through his T-shirt. She fought dueling urges, wanting to either shove away from that hard chest or simply give up and curl into it. "Put me down."

Why did she keep feeling embarrassed in front of him? Exposed? She had the stupidest urge to cry, and she *never* cried in front of people.

Eddie ignored her and instead calmly said, "For the record, I see how pretty this place is every day. Almost as pretty as you," he added, a hot whisper in her ear. "Come on." His voice was gentle as he put her down, but he didn't take his arm from her shoulders. "I've got some stuff back at the house that'll wash off the worst of it. But we've only got about twenty minutes before you start to have a reaction."

As they emerged from the grass, she looked down at her clothes in dismay—a pair of khaki shorts and flip-flops. Was it her imagination, or was her skin already crawling with itchiness? She realized he'd been eyeing her, too, and she gave him her best glare.

He laughed, damn him. "I don't know what were you thinking, city girl . . . wandering into a patch of poison oak."

"How would I know that was poison oak?"

"Don't you know the saying?"

She tried to storm ahead, but he kept pace. "I thought it was 'leaves of three, okay for me.'"

"No, goof. 'Leaves of three, let it be.'" He opened the passenger door of his truck. "Get in. I'll drive you."

She hesitated, and he simply took her waist and hoisted her high onto the seat. She had to shove a couple of rain jackets and a pile of blankets out of the way. "What do you need all this stuff for?"

"The great outdoors, darlin'."

"Can't you stow it in the back?"

"It'd get wet."

"It's rain gear."

"Mm-hm," was his only, maddening reply before shutting her door and walking around to the driver's side.

She craned around, peering out the little rear window, and saw that there already was gear in the back. A toolbox, some tent poles, and a giant set of waders.

"You're trusting," she told him the moment he got in. "That stuff would last twenty seconds parked in San Francisco."

"I've been meaning to get a lid for the truck bed."

He turned the ignition, and the truck rumbled to life. He put it in gear, and they bounced and jostled out of the rocky lot.

She braced a hand on the dash. "This thing is ridiculous."

"She's got a V-8 engine. Over four hundred horses under the hood."

"Whatever," she grumbled. She'd have protested more, but already she felt a prickling sensation. It was probably just adrenaline, but her legs were shaky with it.

When he pulled onto the main road, she demanded, "Where are you taking me?"

"I told you. I'm taking you to my place." He reached across the bench, and with a casual confidence that rattled her, he swept the hair from her face. "Don't worry, beautiful. I'll take care of your legs."

Twelve

~

He pulled into his driveway and hopped out of the truck, headed to the passenger side. He felt intensely self-conscious that she was seeing his cabin for the first time. He wished for her to like it but braced for some sassy comment to spill from her pretty mouth instead. Preoccupied, he plucked her down from the high bench seat.

She twisted in his arms to give him a funny look. "You don't need to carry me, you know."

He put her down with a laugh he hoped didn't sound nervous. Why was he so uncomfortable all of a sudden? He'd had scads of women at his cabin, so why was this one any different? "Yeah, sorry."

Who was he kidding? He knew why he was self-conscious. It was because the girl was so damned judgmental. He took the porch stairs in two quick steps, unlocking the front door. "It's not much."

When she didn't follow him in, he peeked back out to find her staring at the cabin, an unreadable look on her face.

Here it came. "What, Laura? Did you think I lived in a cave?"

"Kind of." The smile she gave him made it impossible to get too mad. Then she shocked him by saying, "It's actually kind of . . . darling."

"Oh. Seriously?" He joined her on the porch. It was a small thing, just one bedroom, one bath, a small kitchen and living area, with a wall of windows and a panoramic mountain view to knock your socks off. It wasn't anything good for raising a family, but just right for a confirmed bachelor like him. "I built it myself."

"Get out." She stepped away to get a better look at his face. "Seriously? You built this?"

"Yeah, sure." He laughed at her dumbstruck expression. "Where do you think homes come from, sugar? Men build them."

"You did it all by yourself?"

"Jack and Scott helped."

"You're close with your brothers," she said. "It's nice."

"I guess it is." He nodded thoughtfully. It wasn't something he thought about much, but his brothers were part of who he was. "The four of us, we're tight. Though we don't see Doctor Mark nearly enough—he spends most of his time in his condo in Silver City. And then there's Jack . . . working with him every day, well, we do our share of bickering."

"Like fighting about whether you should remeasure the property line?" Something in her eyes had shuttered as she said it.

They'd had a moment where they'd actually connected, but that was it. Just a moment was all it would ever be with Laura, and it was too bad. He headed inside. "Come on. We don't have much time. If you're going to have a reaction, it'll set in quick."

He felt her follow him into the bathroom and grabbed the special scrub from the cabinet. When she didn't say anything, he gave her an urging look, gesturing toward the tub. "Go ahead. Sit on the edge there." She looked like a trapped animal, so he clarified, "I promise this isn't some elaborate way to get in your shorts."

Wasn't it?

She sat warily on the edge of the tub, and those shorts tugged higher than should've been legal. Suddenly, his tiny bathroom wasn't nearly big enough to contain him, her, and those mile-long legs. He went and ran the bathwater, shoving his whole arm into the cold stream as he waited for it to warm up. It didn't help.

He opened the tube and rubbed the gritty cream between his hands. At her questioning look, he said, "This breaks up the oil. We've got only a few minutes before it sinks in for good. If you scrub with this stuff before the poison soaks in, sometimes it can minimize the allergic reaction."

"How do you know?"

"I've had poison oak more times than I can count," he said, happy to have something he could reasonably answer.

She smiled wickedly, asking in a singsong voice, "Don't you know the saying?" Mimicking his words from earlier.

"City girl visits one creek bank and suddenly she's an expert." The cream was warmed in his palms. He held his hands out. "You ready?"

"Don't call me that," she said quietly.

"What?" He replayed his words in his head. "What did I do wrong now?"

" 'City girl.' " She wore a peculiarly bereft look on her face. "Please don't call me that."

"Okay," he told her cautiously. He took a calf in his hands and began to rub. "I won't."

It took every effort of concentration to keep his face a careful blank. With the cream in his hands, his touch slid up those tight calves, and he fantasized what might happen in another lifetime, if Laura didn't hate him, if he were the sort of man she'd let slide his hands up her legs, to get a peek at what she hid under that cute little outfit.

"Mmm," she moaned, and thank God she'd shut her eyes, because his jeans just pulled way tighter than usual. "That feels great."

He managed some sort of grunt in response, but clearly she wasn't aware of his situation, because she blithely continued, "So, you never answered my question."

"Question?" With her eyes shut, he could stare unabashedly, and *damn*, she was pretty. So pretty. Normally her hair was done to perfection, but the wind had blown it into sexy wisps framing her face, with errant strands on her forehead and tucked behind her ears. It was a little darker than Sorrow's, with brown streaks among the yellow. He imagined gently twining his fingers through it. He'd cup her cheeks and kiss her, long and slow.

"How come you've gotten so much poison oak?"

"What?" He came to, registering her question. "Oh, that. Well, sometimes, hiking, you know, you miss it. Or, if I'm on my mountain bike and hit a patch, I can't help it." He rubbed the cream over her knee, on up to her thigh. It was as smooth and sleek and taut as it looked. "Damn," he whispered, then caught himself.

He hadn't meant to say it, and it'd been under his breath, but she'd heard. She opened her eyes, focusing instantly on him. "What?"

"I said, uh, damn, because . . ." Meeting her gaze like that, he realized just how close he'd edged to her. He glanced down and smudged aside a bit of the cream, revealing a swatch of skin. It already looked an angry red. "Aw, damn, darlin'. A rash is appearing."

"Oh." She slouched forward for a peek, looking defeated. "Damn is right."

He wanted to kiss her forehead and tell her she'd be okay. He'd put her on his bed, and bring her a tray of food, and ice her skin, and massage her with creams, and keep her company, taking care of her till she was better.

His cell buzzed, and he quickly washed off his hands, happy for an excuse to grab a little air. "Keep rubbing. We've got to break down the oil."

He gave a quick check to the Caller ID. Hell. It was Hunter Fox, with impeccable timing. "Mister Fox," he answered quietly.

He was painfully aware of Laura's eyes on him, and how the one-sided conversation would've sounded to her:

"A what?

"In the Sierras?

"No, sir, I don't—

"Don't you mean a hot tub?"

As the conversation progressed, the clouds in Laura's expression grew darker. She was rinsing off her legs, looking angry as a wet cat.

"That, too?

"Yes, sir.

"Yeah, I suppose we can dig for a pool."

He flipped the phone shut, silently cursing those stupid dot-com people who'd sold to Fairview in the first place. There was a ton of young Internet money in the foothills, parcels of land owned by people who didn't remember how many houses they owned or where. Why couldn't Fairview have pursued them instead? Why'd they have to come sniffing around Sierra Falls?

Laura verbally accosted him the moment he'd clicked off. She'd clearly understood the gist of the call. "They want you to add a *pool*? Who swims in a pool in the Sierras? They'll be able to use it, what, one, maybe two months a year? Have they ever been here in the winter? It's *cold*."

And so was the tone of her voice. Cold enough to chill him to his bones.

He sighed heavily, back to square one. "Then it doesn't matter if there's a pool, now does it, Laura?"

But when he dared risk meeting her eyes, what he saw

there speared him. Laura stood, a towel clenched in her hands, visibly holding herself together. She looked so sad, so alone in her despair.

"Don't you see?" she pleaded. "I can't lose. I need this. The past few years have been such a mess. I need to succeed. For once."

"Laura, you have a TV network coming to film here. If that's not success, then I don't know what is."

"But Fairview has all the money in the world to throw at this project. Whatever I do, they'll come in and do better. Bigger. How can I ever compete?"

He didn't know the answer. There was no beating a competitor like Fairview. He just wished he could make her see how, to him, whether she was wildly successful didn't matter. "You're a winner, Laura. You always have been. Losing against Fairview won't change that."

His intentions had been good, but it was obvious his words weren't.

She bristled. "A *winner*? Seriously? What are you, a motivational speaker? You don't get it, Eddie. I can't lose." She tossed the towel on the bathroom floor and strode down the hall to the front door. "Take me back to my car."

He checked the time on his cell. "I gotta go, anyway."

"What? Back to Reno for you? You're always running off. The mistress getting impatient?"

"There's no mistress, Laura." Was that really what she thought of him? The only thing she'd ever think of him? He met her at the door with a tired sigh. "Maybe one of these days you'll open your eyes and see things for how they really are."

Thirteen

Laura was driving probably a little faster than she should've been, but she knew these roads as only a local would, anticipating the exact moment to downshift to second for the turn, when to pop it back to third, and smoothly into fourth.

The scent of grocery store flowers overpowered the car and made her nose twinge. She cracked a window. She was anxious, at sea, over her head, not to mention ready to crawl out of her skin. She was too proud to admit the full extent of her despair to her family, and yet she craved comfort. She longed to be someplace she could feel like a kid again. A safe place.

Lately, with Eddie sniffing around, and Helen having tantrums, and Dad hassling her, and Sorrow and Billy taking every spare moment to play kissy-face, the lodge and tavern felt far from safe. But she did know one place she could find it.

Finally she slowed way down to pull into the Kidds' driveway—it'd do no good to shock the sisters with peeling tires and spitting gravel. As it was, the last time she'd seen them, she'd been agitated and impatient, and she regretted it. She owed them an apology, and a thanks, too.

Though nothing had come from having Eddie remeasure the property line, it'd stalled him a little, and for that she was grateful. The idea had come from Ruby and Pearl. She got the feeling that despite the fact Eddie was their grand-nephew, they didn't look askance at badgering a man every once in a while.

Girl power, the old-fashioned way.

Ruby had heard her drive up and came to stand on the front porch to greet her. She clutched the zippered front of her pastel blue seersucker housedress as if bracing a winter's chill instead of a pleasant July morning. "Laura Bailey, you tell me everything's okay with your poppa."

It took her a second to understand, and then she quickly put the woman's mind at ease. "Of course. We're all fine. I just wanted to stop by and say hi."

The way the woman looked at her made Laura wonder, was the friendly gesture such a shock?

She went around to the passenger side and grabbed the bouquet of flowers she'd brought. There wasn't a florist around for miles, so the daisy-carnation mix from the Raley's in Silver City would have to do. "You and Pearl were so sweet, and I was such a crazy woman when I came to see you at the hall."

Pearl appeared behind her sister. "Is that Edith?" She adjusted her glasses.

"Laura Bailey's come to pay us a visit." Ruby gave her sister a weighty look.

She kept the smile pasted on her face. This was getting ridiculous. Really, it couldn't have been so very shocking to see her pay a friendly visit, could it?

"Flowers?" Pearl stepped forward, and the screen door slammed behind her.

"For us?" asked Ruby.

"Of course. I wanted to thank you for helping me with the building stuff."

"Oh, dear," Pearl exclaimed.

Ruby looked too nervous to accept. "But you shouldn't have."

"Well, I did." When neither sister took the flowers, Laura simply walked inside and brought them to the kitchen to snip the stems and put them in water.

Sunlight shone through the curtains, and though the yellow gingham was faded with age, it was no less cheery. She let go a breath she didn't know she was holding. "It's good to be here."

"You're just in time," Pearl told her as she led them into the sunroom.

"Just in time," Ruby repeated. "We were sitting down to tea." She pointed to the side table, which bore a plate of sweets and a teapot that probably contained the same Lipton they'd been serving since she was a kid. "Pearl even made a plate of fancies."

"You made these?" She studied the homemade petit fours, momentarily tempted. There were several of them, each a tiny little cake with a hard frosting shell in pale pink or white. They were a bit lumpy and uneven but looked yummy nonetheless.

"Pearl did."

"How?" She took one for her plate to be polite, choosing a white one with an uneven pink bow.

"It's a simple pound cake," Pearl said proudly.

Ruby beamed. "But it looks like more, doesn't it?"

"I used to use almond cake."

"But the taste was too much."

"Almonds are a flavor best reserved for liqueur," Pearl finished, and the ladies tittered.

It was the Kidd sisters in a new light. She made a note to bring a bottle of Amaretto instead of flowers next time.

As Ruby poured their tea, Pearl leaned forward and put

her hand on Laura's knee. "You tell us. That old Wexler ranch still giving you trouble?"

She plucked a few packets of Sweet'N Low from a decorative dish. "How'd you guess?"

"Your brows." Ruby offered her the cup. "You keep frowning like that and you'll get wrinkles."

"You've got to mind the elevens," Pearl said, rubbing between her eyebrows to explain. She turned to her sister. "Remember how Emerald used to use those things at night?"

"Frownies," Ruby exclaimed. "Our Laura could use some Frownies."

Pearl nodded. "Look into it, dear."

"I will." She consciously tried to smooth her brow and relax as she blew on her tea.

"You need another." Pearl plucked a pink petit four and put it on Laura's plate. "Nothing like a little sugar to soothe the soul."

"Try it," Ruby urged. "You've got to have fancies for your tea."

"I've asked it once, I've asked a thousand times, how do you women not weigh a thousand pounds?" She let herself take the tiniest nibble and for a moment was transported to another place, one that was sweet and innocent, that allowed time for cakes and tea. Her next breath was deeper, her shoulders easing just a bit. "Oh, that is good."

They were light and sweet and airy, and she wanted more. A lot like Eddie's smiles.

She scrunched her face against the sudden and treasonous thought.

The sisters nodded as though witnessing some essential truth coming to light. "You see?"

"Now tell us what's wrong."

"Is our Eddie still giving you trouble?"

"What's that boy done now?"

She decided another bite wouldn't hurt. "It's what he hasn't done," she said, swallowing. "Namely, he hasn't told those Fairview people where they can . . ." She stopped herself, hearing Sorrow's warning in her head. *Language.* "Where they can build their ridiculous resort instead of Sierra Falls."

The women *hmm*'ed thoughtfully. Ruby dunked a corner of her petit four into her teacup and took a delicate bite. "Did you check the work permits like we said?"

"And have him remeasure the property?" chimed Pearl.

"I've got it." Ruby snapped her fingers. "Conservancy land."

"You're right," Pearl said with widened eyes. "That property backs up onto conservancy land, I'll bet."

But Laura didn't get excited. "Nope, I looked into that. I looked into all of it. There's no stopping them."

"But I heard television people were coming out," Ruby said. "That's something."

"That's what *he* says. But it's not enough."

"Maybe you're not looking at the big picture."

"Now you sound like *him*." Eddie, Eddie, Eddie . . . she heard his voice everywhere.

She'd gone in there having sworn to avoid their sweets but decided this particular topic called for another. Besides, chewing gave her extra time to think.

The sisters exchanged a look that wasn't lost on Laura.

She swallowed. "What?"

"Well . . ." Pearl began, and Ruby finished, "Why don't you tell us what our nephew said."

"He told me I don't see things how they really are. Can you believe it?" She took another petit four and popped the whole thing in her mouth.

"Maybe he has a point, dear," Pearl said kindly.

What? Sudden emotion clutched her throat, and she had to swallow twice to get the little cake down. "I know how things really are."

The sisters nodded knowingly. Ruby said, "There was a day when I thought so, too."

"Both of us," added Pearl.

"We were real firecrackers."

"Knew better than anyone."

Ruby clucked. "How to do things. How not to do things."

"Not Emmy, though."

They sighed in unison, remembering their sister, who'd recently passed. "Emerald was never afraid to be soft," Ruby said. "To be . . . what's the word?"

"Vulnerable," Pearl said.

Ruby nodded. "*Vulnerable.* Emerald let herself need people. And look. Of the three of us, she's the only one who found love."

Laura refused to accept that she was destined to live a loveless life. "Yeah, but then Emerald was alone."

"That's a different story," Pearl said. "She knew love, though. Once."

"And what we wouldn't give to say the same."

Pearl reached out and took her sister's trembling hand. "To have a child like she had. Emerald had Marlene. Had four strapping grandsons."

She focused on her tea. "I'm not interested in men right now."

"If you're not careful, you'll wake up one day and find that you're eighty years old."

"Trust us," Pearl said. "It happens."

"I just can't seem to . . . balance it all."

"Oh dear." Ruby spotted it instantly.

She blinked hard. She *never* cried in public, and now she'd been caught twice in one week. "I'm sorry. I don't know what my problem is."

"There, there." Pearl leaned over to pat her knee. "The problem is, you're too much like that petit four."

A disbelieving laugh burst from her. "What?"

Cute pink teacakes with bows pretty much summed up everything she wasn't. She was strong and in control of her destiny . . . not fluffy and crumbly.

"It's true," Ruby insisted. "Hard and pretty on the outside, but soft on the inside."

"Surprisingly sweet, too," Pearl added with a smile.

"I don't know about *that*." She felt the tears burn and blinked hard to stop them. *Dammit.*

"You work so hard," Ruby said.

Pearl interjected, "But you have to take care not to *become* hard."

"I have to act hard to do what I do." She'd let herself go soft before, and it'd only brought hurt.

Ruby handed her a clean but rumpled handkerchief. "Don't let our boy make you cry."

"Eddie? Eddie is *not* making me cry."

Pearl gave a decisive nod and turned to her sister. "Sparks."

Ruby hummed. "Definitely sparks."

"Sparks?" Laura's voice came out a sharp squeak. She blotted her eyes, the tears gone as fast as they'd come. "Please tell me you're referring to the ranch's electrical system."

"You silly goose," Ruby said. "Sparks between you two kids."

When he'd touched her, there sure *had* been sparks. Forget poison oak, the way his strong hands had moved surely along her thighs, she'd have overlooked a case of leprosy. She blushed, remembering it.

"See!" Pearl exclaimed. "I told you."

"You did. Sister, you always see."

"There are definitely no sparks between me and Eddie," she lied.

"Eddie and *me*," Ruby corrected.

"There's a simple trick to remember the grammar."

"*Me first is the worst*," Ruby explained. "Never put yourself first."

"In all things," Pearl said, nodding. "Scripture says, 'Let each of you look out for the interests of others.' "

Her sister frowned. "Are you certain that's how it goes?"

"Of course. It's Philippians, dear."

Laura flopped back in the chair, waiting for the women to peter out.

"I know it's Philippians," Ruby said. "I think the quote is longer than that."

"Don't tell me how to quote Scripture."

Their fire-and-brimstone preacher daddy had schooled them well, but Laura was anxious to get back on track. She put down her saucer, letting it clink louder than necessary on the table.

"I'm sorry, dear," Ruby said.

Pearl shrugged. "I forgive you."

Her sister frowned. "I was talking to Laura."

Laura waved it off. "Either way, I promise you, there's nothing between Eddie *and me*." But suddenly, a question niggled in the back of her head. She hated it, but she needed to know. She took a nonchalant sip of her tea. "I think he has a girlfriend, anyway."

"Eddie?" they exclaimed in unison.

Ruby shook her head. "Not our Eddie."

"We'd know," Pearl agreed.

She nodded, though she doubted it. Eddie had probably had hundreds of girlfriends—if you could call them that— since junior high.

Pearl shook her head. "Our Eddie's a good boy."

Sure he is.

"A good egg," Ruby agreed.

A Neanderthal.

"See." Ruby nudged her sister as they studied her expression.

Pearl grinned. "She likes him, I think."

Laura sat up straight. "I do not. I was just thinking."

"About Eddie." Pearl tittered.

Ruby tried to hide her grin. "Last time I saw sparks like that, Bear and Edith got engaged."

"I do love a wedding."

"Promise you'll have it in spring," Ruby cooed.

Pearl gasped. "The waterfall is so pretty in spring."

Laura gave it up. As the sisters smiled and nodded, she considered *sparks*. Well, of course there were *some* sparks between them. There always had been. The only thing was, while once Eddie had been just the sexy bad boy, now he was tanned and strong and all man. He looked more delicious than any cake.

And he wasn't her type.

Right?

Fourteen

Helen cleared her last table of the lunch rush. "Thanks," she muttered, seeing the tip. Two dollars on a twenty-dollar check. She pocketed it with a frown. "Ten percent. That'll pay the gas bill, for sure."

She carried the dishes into the kitchen, and Billy and Sorrow snapped apart when they saw her. There wouldn't be many more patrons till dinner, and they'd been taking advantage of the lull by doing some canoodling, Sorrow's untouched sandwich beside her on the counter.

"You could get a room," she said with a smirk. "It is a lodge, after all."

But then her gut churned. Her husband was out there, somewhere. Maybe *he'd* gotten a room—some seedy place to share with a girlfriend.

Because there had to be a girlfriend. Why else hadn't he come home again last night?

She kept herself looking good, and when that hadn't worked, she flirted with other men to show him proof of how desirable she could be, but that hadn't worked, either. She didn't know what else she could do to make herself attractive to him.

Billy laughed at her comment, clueless to her turmoil. "A room? Now there's an idea." He never took anything personally—he'd been wearing a permanent ear-to-ear grin ever since he and Sorrow had become engaged. He stood behind her now, nibbling her neck as she attacked her sandwich. "Whaddya say? We could get started on that basketball team."

Helen loaded up the dishes as quickly as she could. "I'll give you some space," she muttered, getting out of there.

The two of them . . . it was too hard to watch sometimes. Had she and Rob ever been like that? She thought maybe so, in the early days. They'd ended up with three kids somehow.

The jokes about Billy and Sorrow's future kids began after he'd bought her that big Excursion, when Laura wrecked the old car. Helen was happy for them—really she was—but it sure was hard to watch the carefree way Sorrow had taken to that fancy new SUV. The Baileys griped about money, but the way the girl had slid into that new Ford, it seemed like it was nothing for her to have a brand-spanking-new car, like she was entitled to such a thing.

But then there'd been her own accident around the same time. She'd hit a patch of black ice and slid into another car, and like that, the hood of her old Dodge had folded up like an accordion, no good to nobody. But had Robbie gone out and gotten *her* the keys to some fancy new car, crowing about how he needed her safe at all costs? No, the man had snapped at her, some distant look on his face, his eyes empty but for an anger she'd begun to see more and more frequently.

So she'd taken on an extra shift, carrying her own anger, lodged in her heart like a splinter she couldn't pluck free.

She grabbed the carafe and made a pass through the

dining room, refilling coffees, all the while surreptitiously taking stock of the few women in the room. *Are you her?* she wondered, studying each face. *Are you the woman my Rob is sleeping with?*

The bell on the door dinged, and in walked Damien Simmons. He was unaware of her eyes on him as he scanned the room and chose a booth.

It was a surprise how he hadn't stopped coming to the tavern after all that'd passed between his family and the Baileys. She guessed he needed this community more than he let on. He'd taken his breakup with Sorrow better than anyone had expected, though she supposed it was easy not to be too proud when you were as handsome and as rich as Damien.

His eyes met hers, lasering in like he'd known all along she'd been watching. "Hey, Helen, you all right?"

She caught herself just standing there and jumped into action. "Yeah, sorry." She scampered over to hand him a menu.

She grabbed the pitcher of ice water and filled his glass. "Do you need to take a look, or is it the usual?" The guy was a fitness freak, and it was always a chef's salad, hold the bread, and the day's meat special on the side. "The dinner special's not up yet, but we've got some pot roast from last night I could serve up."

"Sounds perfect." He gave the menu a quick glance, then handed it back to her. "You sure you're okay?"

"Of course." She brightened her smile—it was what men wanted, wasn't it? Pretty, smiling faces? And Damien was an especially good tipper, so best not to jeopardize that. "I am, now that you're here." She winked.

The bell on the front door rang, then rang again, but she kept her attention on Damien.

He shook his head, tsking. "Too bad you're a married woman, Helen. You and me could run away together."

Married . . . *barely.* "Maybe in the next life, hon."

There was only one man she cared about, and it was her husband, though she could flirt with other men until she was blue in the face and it wouldn't get him to notice her. Rob knew how chatty she could be with men, and he didn't care. She imagined that not even the attentions of Damien Simmons, basically the prince of Sierra Falls, would make him jealous.

"I think those people need menus, Helen." It was Laura, using her boss voice.

She hadn't heard her come in and felt a spurt of panic. "Of course," she said, trying not to sound too tart about it.

More and more, she sensed Laura's critical eye on her. The older Bailey girl was a control freak, and losing this job was the last thing she needed.

Edith came over to smooth her daughter's ruffled feathers. "I'm sure Helen's got it." She gave a gentle pat to Laura's shoulder.

God bless the woman. Sometimes it felt like Edith Bailey was the only reason she still had this job.

With a last stiff smile to Damien, she said, "I'll go put in your order."

She had to brace herself to face the love nest in the kitchen. She was lonely—so lonely her heart ached with it. But as she felt Laura's eyes bore into her back, she reminded herself this wasn't her time. Someday down the road she'd figure things out for herself, but for now, she had three kids she needed to take care of. Which meant she had a paycheck to earn.

She wouldn't give Laura any excuses to fire her.

She came back out to wipe down tables that didn't need wiping, and as she worked, she felt Edith approach. Tucking the rag in her apron, she turned to express a quick thanks for earlier, and was surprised to be greeted by a positively gleeful expression on the other woman's face.

"Have you heard?" Edith asked, excitement clear in her voice. "The History Network is coming to film here. Us!"

"Oh." She pasted a smile on her face. "Congratulations."
Wasn't *that* just exciting, how life was starting to happen
for everyone but her?

Laura said from across the room, "Easy, Mom. They're
here to film the town. But yeah, they'll be staying here. And
who knows, maybe they'll get a little footage of the lodge,
too." She came closer, directing her next words at Helen.
"Which means we need to be extra on top of things."

What was that supposed to mean? "I always am," she
said tightly.

Laura waved a hand. "Well, you know what I mean."

But Helen wouldn't let her blow it off. "I don't, actually."

"Fine, then. Like your purse," Laura said, pointing to a
cubby under the bar. "It doesn't belong out here. You know
I hate when you put your stuff behind the bar."

She forced herself to stay calm. Laura had been away for
years, living it up or doing whatever she did in the big city,
while Helen had been *here*, helping the Baileys and stashing
her bag in that very cubby. "I'll move my purse. That's it?"

"It also means that now, more than ever, it's important
for all of us to be on time." Laura gave her an insincere
smile—in a few short months, the woman really had mas-
tered the passive-aggressive boss tone. "That sort of thing."

Inside, she fumed. *All of us*. She was always on time, and
those few times she wasn't had to do with her kids, not
because she was out gallivanting around town.

Edith hated conflict and piped in cheerily, "Helen's
always on top of things. Don't you worry."

"Actually, I'm glad you're here," Laura told her. "We just
have one other problem."

She braced, but Bear barked a laugh from the end of
the bar. "Just the one?" He rustled his newspaper, folding it
to the next page. "You ladies let me know when it's all
worked out."

With a moan, Laura limped toward a booth. "I've gotta
sit down."

Only then did Helen spot the angry patches of red along the woman's legs. Momentarily forgetting her irritation, she asked, "What happened to you?"

"Poison oak." Laura gingerly sat down, sticking her feet out so as not to touch her skin to the seat.

Helen fought not to roll her eyes. *That* was her problem? That she'd been out hiking and having fun, and she'd gotten a little poison oak? Poor thing.

Not.

"Is that the *one other problem*?" Because if it was, boy could she tell Laura about *problems*.

People who had family didn't get it. They talked about troubles, but how bad could it be if you had family around to share it with? People who loved you and could catch you if you fell.

She wanted to smack the girl upside her head, to make Laura wake up and appreciate what she had. Because all *she* had was a no-good, no-show of a husband and a mom who got in touch only when she needed cash.

She had her beautiful kids, sure, but she refused to share her burdens with them. If anything, she protected them more than ever. Especially Luke—as her eldest, he was trying to act like the man of the house, and rather than comfort her, mostly it made her feel shame. Her children should've been able to act like children, not taking on adult concerns before their time.

That there was a problem. Not an itchy rash that'd pass in a few days.

"I need you to do my shift," Laura said. "I can barely move with these legs."

Edith's face pinched with concern. "You need calamine, honey."

Laura nodded. "I'm going to put some on and get back in bed."

What Helen wouldn't do for a day in bed. Instead she said, "Sure thing. I'm happy to pick up an extra shift." What

else did she have to do, anyway? She didn't need to rest.
Unable to look at Laura anymore, she went to her station at
the end of the bar and began to refill the ketchups.

"Cool, you can just stay on." Laura glanced at the clock
over the bar. "The early birds should start trickling in soon."

"Actually, I'll need to run out and get the kids. Drop them
at home." She *hated* leaving them to fend alone for dinner.
Hated leaving them alone at night. But she knew Luke would
hold down the fort. He'd make sure everyone took their baths
and did their homework. She'd splurge and give him cash
enough to order a pizza.

"That reminds me," Laura said. "I made flyers." She
caught her mom's eye. "Would you grab them? I think I left
them in the house kitchen."

"Flyers?"

"Yeah, I've got a petition going to stop construction at
the old ranch. I'd love it if you put them up at your kids'
school. Or, wait, they're in two schools, right?"

"Day camp for summer."

"Same thing, right?"

She nodded tightly. Why explain?

But it did put her in mind of the fall. Two schools meant
twice the work. Until next year, when Emmett would start
middle school, and she'd need to figure out how to get them
to *three* different schools.

She supposed she could put them on the bus, though in
a rural school district as sparsely populated and far-reaching
as theirs, it'd mean getting out the door a full hour and a
half earlier each morning.

Either way, soon they'd need to scrap all their extracur-
ricular stuff until Luke was old enough to get his learner's
permit. Just the thought of that gave her chills.

"Even better. Thanks, Helen."

She didn't recall saying yes, but she didn't see as she had
any other choice. But that was how Helen operated. She was
a hard worker—always had been.

Unlike Laura, who was a wuss. Laura, who'd been taken care of her whole life. Laura couldn't deal with a little itchy skin. A week off in bed, well good for her.

The bell dinged as a good-looking stranger walked in. What *she* wouldn't do for a week in bed with a fine man like this.

With her husband.

She gulped back the pang and greeted him, grabbing a menu and gesturing to a booth in the corner. Helen gave him her biggest smile, thinking she knew all about itches she couldn't scratch.

Fifteen

Laura had spent the past couple of weeks scratching, writing, fuming, but mostly she'd been hiding. Not that she couldn't deal with a stupid thing like poison oak, but she couldn't bear to see Eddie—at least not until she could wear shorts again without worrying that she resembled a leper.

She'd felt a nightmarish riot of feelings last time she'd seen him. First, there'd been embarrassment at the whole wandering-through-a-field-of-poisonous-weeds thing—she'd felt so stupid. But Eddie's tender ministrations had somehow pierced the guard she usually erected whenever he was around. Sitting on the edge of the tub, hearing the genuine concern in his voice, she'd thought for a moment that maybe she'd been wrong about him. Maybe they could find common ground.

And then he'd touched her. *How* he'd touched her. The man worked with his hands, and wow, did he know how to use them. Her face flushed hot at the memory.

Under the touch of those hands, all broad and strong,

she'd instantly forgotten her nervousness, her aggrava-
tion . . . as one itchy sensation was replaced by a whole other
itch.

One that she hadn't had scratched in far too long.

Her chat with the Kidd sisters had haunted her. There
were sparks, sure enough. The old attraction between them
was stronger than ever. His touch on her had been too hot.
He'd had the upper hand—literally—and she'd almost forgotten why she'd gone to his work site in the first place.

But then he'd gotten that phone call, and overhearing his
conversation had instantly pulled her back to reality. *A pool?*
Whose bright idea was it to put an outdoor pool in the mountains? Though she was sure Fairview would figure out a way
to heat the thing. More than that, they'd probably install hot
tubs, a slide, diving boards . . . her imagination had gone
wild in the days since. How could their family lodge ever
compete with a *diving board*?

When he'd hung up, she could tell he felt guilty. She'd
seen in it his eyes. It was the look of a dog who'd known
he'd done something wrong.

"Dog," she grumbled. He was a dog just like the rest of
them. She had plans, and never again would she let a guy
get in the way.

Unfortunately, there was no denying those sparks. Her
chat with the sisters had planted a seed she hadn't wanted
to consider, though she found she wanted to poke at it, anyway. To tease and test, seeing just how far she could push
these sparks. To use them to her benefit.

She studied herself in the mirror. Her rash had faded into
faint pink swatches, her legs once more ready for prime
time. She stepped into her lucky skirt—she was off to battle,
and her hot little denim mini was her secret weapon.

The skirt had gone out of style a few years ago, but Eddie
wouldn't know fashion if it hit him over the head. Men had
always responded well to the way the jeans skirt clung to
her hard-earned shape, and she donned it like armor.

She had her petition in one hand—it'd garnered dozens of signatures—and grabbed her strappiest sandals in the other. She was off to work it.

Eddie would be open to seeing her, too. She'd heard reports of how he'd come around the tavern looking for her. As if. He'd probably come around to rub her nose in his triumph. Well, after she was done with him, he wouldn't know what hit him.

"Dirty, no-good dog," she said with a smile, eyeing her backside one last time in the mirror.

"You okay in there?" Sorrow knocked on her bedroom door. "Laura?"

She swung open the door, a general ready for assault. "I'm *good*."

"Wow." Sorrow took a step back. "You *are* good." She glanced down at Laura's freshly shaved legs. "Your legs look great. But why so dolled up? You headed out?"

"Yup, errands." She breezed to the stairs, and Sorrow followed her down. "I've got some business." She waved several pages of signatures triumphantly. "*Jessup* business."

"You go, girl." Sorrow paused on the landing. "But . . ."

"But?"

"Do you think you could help out in the tavern today? Helen is starting to pull some attitude about you taking time off."

"What is with her?" Laura had worked hard all her life—was the woman going to begrudge her a little rest? And it wasn't even restful—there'd been times that first week she thought she could've clawed her skin off. "I wasn't exactly sitting around watching soap operas. I've been doing a ton of stuff from my computer. Just because I'm not at the tavern pouring iced teas—"

"I know, I know." Sorrow put up a hand to mollify her. "I get it. But until Hope comes up to speed, having an extra employee is more work than not."

"Speaking of which, where is Hope?" Laura had put their new employee to work immediately, especially when she found out the woman had spent the past few years working in the state capitol. "She said she'd make some calls for me."

Hope was still learning the ropes, but she was smart and a quick study. Besides, she'd practically grown up under their roof, having been Sorrow's bosom buddy through childhood. Laura had been away at college, so she'd never gotten to know her, though she did remember the two girls griping about the other kids' teasing. But seriously, a pair of pimple-faced besties with the names *Hope* and *Sorrow*? In ninth grade, it'd just been asking for it.

"She's at the tavern," Sorrow said, "which is where I'd hoped you'd join us."

"I need to take a pass. Can't you manage without me? Those History Network people are coming"—she slid her cell from her purse to check the time—"and between that and this ranch thing, there's a ton that needs to get done."

"We need to go over menus."

"Cook whatever you want." She passed her on the way to the front door. "You rock, sis. Thanks."

She swept out and just about crashed into Hope on the porch. "There you are!"

The woman had become Laura's favorite person the moment she'd let on what she used to do for a living.

"I work for CalEPA," Hope had said quietly. "In the governor's office. On the Air Resources Board." She'd been a soft-spoken thing in high school, too. Good at her studies, not super popular, though not unpretty, either. "I oversaw the Fine Particulate Matter Monitoring Program."

Laura had tried not to gape. So that was what bookish girls did when they grew up. "Fascinating." *Not.* "Why'd you leave? To work *here*?" She'd looked at her sister, fighting a growing panic. "She knows she'll be making beds and stuff like that, right?"

But Hope had laughed it off, apparently eager to do

exactly stuff like take reservations and make beds if it meant she could get her environmental journalism blog up and running.

From there, it hadn't taken Laura long to put two and two together: people who once worked in the governor's office were people with connections.

Laura gave a tug to her jeans skirt. She'd been in a rush but was anxious to hear what their new employee had found out. "Did you call Sacramento? Can they do anything about the permit?" She turned to her sister, explaining, "Stupid Eddie is now going to build a stupid pool. Apparently, Fairview is adding kickboards and waterslides to their death blow."

"They can't do that," Hope said.

"Yeah! Right?" Laura nodded in vehement agreement.

"No," Hope said, "I mean it's possible they really can't do that."

Sorrow frowned. "As in, they're not allowed to do it?"

"I couldn't make headway on the permit issue, but I did find out that El Dorado County just approved a ten-million-dollar bond for watershed protection purposes."

"What the heck does that mean?" asked Sorrow.

Laura grinned. "It means Eddie is doing something illegal."

Hope backpedaled, looking panicked. "I didn't say *that*. I only spoke with a friend who worked on the legislation. I don't how it's enforced or what it means."

Laura headed to her car, ready to storm his job site, and the women followed her into the lot. "What *are* you saying?"

"I'm saying, that creek might be protected. *Might*. I don't know for sure. You could ask Eddie. Does he know anything about it?"

"Believe me. I'm about to find out."

Sixteen

⁓

Eddie sat on a boulder on the bank of the creek and checked his watch. Eleven thirty was early for a lunch break—he knew by late afternoon he'd regret having scarfed down his ham and cheese so soon—but he couldn't focus.

Something about this project still didn't smell right, and he'd been dragging his feet. But he'd looked and looked and couldn't find anything to back up his suspicions. He'd analyzed the property, and while the creek was on conservancy land, the ranch wasn't, and rules about preexisting structures protected him anyhow.

He'd also double-checked the historic register and that adaptive reuse paperwork, too, but it all seemed to add up.

"Eddie." It was Laura, and by the sound of her voice, she'd come with guns blazing. "We have something to discuss."

He grinned. The day was looking up.

Turning, he sized her up, and his grin turned dark. She wore an outfit that should've been on a deadly weapons list.

"Well, if it isn't my favorite ray of sunshine." He didn't know where to look, and his eyes eagerly grazed up a sleek pair of legs, to a tight little skirt, up to her flimsy yellow top. Her shirt didn't have sleeves, and he wondered if her bra straps might be peeking out—hell, maybe she wasn't even wearing a bra. A man could hope. "You look all healed. You here for some afternoon delight?"

"What do you think?" She was a little spitfire, and man how he loved to goad her. "Come closer and I'll tell you why I'm here."

"You're just in time for lunch." He smiled wide as he held up his sandwich. "Join me. If you're good, I'll give you half."

"Just come here." Scowling, she scanned the field between her and the creek bank. "You know I'm not step-ping one foot closer to you."

He held a hand to his ear. "Can't hear you."

"Liar. You can hear every word I'm saying, so listen up. Guess who's doing construction on watershed protected land? You need to stop what you're doing." She waved a bunch of papers in the air. "I have signatures from members of the community who agree. This isn't just about your stu-pid hotel—it's the whole ecology of the Sacramento River Basin we're talking about. This is something we need to look into."

We . . . we. He liked the sound of that.

"I can't hear a word you're saying," he lied. What color bra strap would be peeking out from under that little tank top? He patted the rock beside him. "You've gotta come closer, darlin'."

She scanned the distance between them, and suddenly she looked so lost and forlorn. He knew a pang of pity fol-lowed by a great stab of affection for the pain-in-the-butt city girl. He made a show of putting down his sandwich. "Best hope the bugs don't eat this by the time I come fetch you."

She took a step back, on the defensive. "Bring your sand-wich, I don't care. We can talk by the house."

"Nah, it's too pretty out here," he said, making his way back to her. "Plus there's door-to-door service." He scooped her up, and she slammed her hand—hard—into his chest. He laughed, rubbing where she'd hit him. "You're strong."

"What are you doing?"

"Carrying you to the creek."

"Put me down."

He gave her a look like he might drop her if she dared him.

"No. Wait." She had a firm grip on his shoulders now, and he could feel how she didn't want him to carry her, but she didn't want to fall, either. "What about the poison oak?"

"I cleaned it up." He gave a little hoist to his arms, readjusting her. Damn, but she felt good.

"Seriously?"

"Of course." He shook his head—what did she take him for? "I tore out every last bit."

"Thank you," she said reluctantly.

"I have an interest in the health and well-being of those legs of yours." He gave her his broadest smile, cutting her off before she could protest. "Besides, I can't have you getting a rash every time you visit me."

She rolled her eyes. "Trust me. This is the last visit, if I can help it."

"Promises, promises."

She swatted him, and as she did, some girly scent wafted up to him. "Well?" she demanded.

"Well, what?" He nestled her closer, stealing a look at her shoulder. The bra strap was lacy and light pink.

"Are you going to put me down?"

"Sure thing, sugar." He reached his goal and put her down. "Just be sure to mind the rattlesnakes."

She grabbed his arm with a squeal, and he laughed, fighting the urge to slide his arm around her and give that tanned shoulder a nip. He'd just bet Laura tasted as good as she smelled.

She shoved him. "You're a jerk."

"I do my best." He sat down, plucking his sandwich from the rock. "I'll trade you," he said, offering her half.

"I'm not hungry."

"Come on. You give me a kiss, I'll give you a bite."

She scowled at him. "I can't believe you're already hacking apart the roof."

"Though I can't decide which I'd rather take. A kiss, or a bite . . . ?"

"Be serious, Neanderthal."

"Ah, I was waiting for that one. You sure you're okay sitting with Stone Age Man here? I mean, I might chew with my mouth open or something."

"Whatever you need to do, Jessup."

He took a jaw-crackingly big bite of his sandwich and assessed her as he chewed. The scrutiny made her look uncomfortable, which made him chew slower. Finally he swallowed and asked, "To what do I owe this honor?"

"I told you." She brandished those papers she'd been clutching since her arrival. "I have signatures."

"The petition." He'd seen it posted on the bulletin board at the grocery store. "You're convincing people in Sierra Falls that I'm the bad guy."

She only shrugged, letting him fill in the blanks.

"Nice," he said, nodding. "You do realize I'll be employing a good number of local men on this project."

"It doesn't make it right."

"Whatever you say, gorgeous. Tell everyone to hate me. You can't stop the work."

"That's where you're wrong. You need to call Jack right now and tell him he'd better stop hacking off that roof, because I know something that will stop you once and for all."

"Do you now?" He cracked open his water bottle and chugged, taking a moment to figure how he was going to play it: angry or easy.

She sure hadn't wasted any time laying into him. But she

wore a little denim skirt that'd ridden up as she sat, and as he stole a glance at those long legs, he decided he'd opt for cool. It was the skirt's fault—it robbed a man's strength.

He wiped his mouth, calmly telling her, "We're not *hacking off* the roof. Those crossbeams are ancient. We've got our engineer out today, checking it out. Hotel or not, it's something that needs to be done. Can't have the walls caving in before we even start."

That silenced her for a moment, but he saw by the machinations on her face that she was working up to something else.

"El Dorado County voted in a watershed protection bond," she blurted. "What you're doing might be illegal. Or, at least, digging for a stupid pool might be."

It took him a moment to register the topic change. "How do you figure?"

"The bond was for ten million dollars," she continued, gaining steam. "All to protect the watershed. There must be implications for the land surrounding the creek."

He sighed deeply. This job was turning out to be a nightmare, in more ways than one.

"You sure you don't want any food?" He dug into his backpack and pulled out a bag of chips. "Sea salt and vinegar?" He let his eyes linger over her body—she was a workout fanatic with a tight little body, but it seemed like she'd gotten a little too thin since taking over managing the lodge. "Do you ever eat?"

She just glared, but he'd caught how her cheeks had flushed at his perusal.

"No? Your loss." He popped a chip in his mouth, giving her a wink.

"Ten million." She pressed on, undaunted. She turned away, looking back at the ranch house, and the movement tugged that flimsy yellow top tightly along her curves. "That's something."

"It *is* something." He gave an approving nod—he sure

was enjoying this argument. "Something else." He looked back up at her pretty face before she caught him staring.

He really needed to get this under control. He was a professional, dammit.

"Maybe not for Fairview," she added, "but it's enough to catch their attention." She pointed toward the mountains lining the horizon—veins of white still capped the highest elevations, the snowmelt providing water for much of Northern California. "You know as well as I do how that snow melts and fills this creek and trickles down until it eventually becomes the drinking water for all of Sacramento. If people felt strongly enough to vote in favor of a ten-million-dollar bond measure—"

"So you've said," he interjected, wondering just how many times the woman could say *ten million* in a conversation. He wanted to end this chat and get onto more interesting things . . . like dessert.

"Then they'll probably have something to say about all that's going on in this valley," she finished sternly.

He brushed the chip crumbs off his hands and shoved the trash back into his pack. "Okay, I'll look into it."

"I . . . you, what?"

The wind had mussed her hair, and a strand had stuck to her mouth, all glossy and girly and pale pink. It took everything he had not to reach out and sweep the hair from her face. He'd bet his new truck that her panties matched the bra and lip gloss.

"What do you know about bonds?" she asked again.

He cleared his throat, forcing his eyes back up to meet hers. "I don't know jack about bonds. But there was one construction project a while back—remember when they had to change the gas station site because of flood potential?—there was talk of watershed back then, too."

"You'll look into it?"

"If I say I will, I will." Of course he'd look into it—he

wanted to do the right thing. He hated being the bad guy in her eyes.

If he could ditch this whole damned job just to make her happy, he would, but it wasn't just his business at stake—it was Jack's, and he owed Jack everything.

He wanted to get the woman's mind on other things. Like on himself, for example. She was single-minded, and he had to wonder what it'd be like to have that kind of intense focus aimed at him. Would she ever see him for who he really was?

"I might be a Neanderthal, but I'm an honorable one. Despite what you might think." He polished off the rest of his sandwich and, standing, put his hand out. "But first you need to do something for me."

She was instantly on her guard. "What?"

"C'mon, I won't bite. Yet." He grinned, and her responding blush gave him the guts to lean down and simply snatch her hand. It was so small in his, he had to force himself not to look at it, to press it to his mouth and kiss it. When she didn't pull away, he dared give it a little squeeze. "There's something I need to show you."

"I just told you, you have to stop work. Until we investigate." She stood, looking like a wary animal.

"Fine."

"That's it? Just . . . fine?"

"Yeah, I told you." He gave her a tug, and she fell into step with him. He dared to sweep his thumb in a quick stroke along the side of her hand—how was it possible to have skin so soft? "But first I've been wanting to show you something." He grimaced to himself, hearing how ragged his voice had sounded. She was like a skittish colt, and he was going to scare her off.

Sure enough, she stopped in her tracks, pulling her hand free. "Edwin Jessup, you better not be up to no good."

"I'm all about the good, darlin'." But then what she'd said

registered, and it was his turn to stop short. "Hold on, how'd you know my name is Edwin?"

"You *are* called Eddie, right? Duh."

"Yeah, but most people think it's Edward."

A wicked gleam lit her eyes. "Ed-win doesn't like his na-ame . . ." She'd said it like it was a grade school taunt.

Suddenly he was ten again. He looked back toward the ranch house, as though he might find Jack watching. "Did my brothers—?"

Laura actually smiled at him. "You forget, dummy."

"Dummy?" He grinned back. "You mean I've been upgraded from Neanderthal?"

She gave his shoulder a nudge. "I've known you since kindergarten, so I think I know your name by now. Besides, *Edward* is the name of a vampire, and sorry, but you are so not vampiric."

"Hey, that's *my* line." He nudged her back. Who knew letting Laura tease him would be the way to break through her shell? "All right, Laura *Edith* Bailey."

"Ugh." She rolled her eyes. "That makes me feel like my mom." But then she stopped short, the laugh frozen in her throat. Her hand seized into a death grip in his. "What's that?" she asked, staring at some greenery along the trail.

He laughed. "That's a fern."

"Are you sure?"

"Of course I'm sure." He pulled her closer, tucking her arm in his, and she actually allowed it. "How'd you ever survive?" As they'd grown up in a small mountain town, the need for a basic understanding of the outdoors was a given. From a young age, they'd been taught how to build a snow fort, what to do if lost in the woods, all that. "How did you grow up in Sierra Falls not knowing this stuff? I mean, that was *you* I knew as a kid, right?"

"Yes." She gave him a snide look. "But don't forget, that was also me who, pretty much from fifth grade on, was counting down the days till I could flee for the city."

He spotted a cluster of mushrooms at the foot of a particularly big pine. "Wait, see those? Don't ever eat those." Suddenly everything seemed potentially perilous for the city girl.

"Jeez, I get poison oak once, and now I'm an idiot. Of course I know not to eat random mushrooms in the woods."

"Just gotta make sure." He spotted a jagged ridge of poison oak growing along the creek, and he pointed that out, too. "There, there's some more. Do you see it? Three leaves—"

"You can stop pointing it out to me," she said after he'd drawn attention to it for the fifth time. "I promise you, I'll never forget it again."

"Hey"—he took her shoulders and aimed her toward his favorite spot—"here we are." He could've just told her where to look, but he couldn't resist touching her. "Look up and tell me what you see."

She glanced back at him over her shoulder to shoot him an impatient glare. "I see a dead tree."

It was skeletal, an old beech he guessed, leafless even in the heat of summer. But it wasn't *completely* dead. "Look closer."

She fidgeted under his touch. "*This* is your favorite spot?"

Rather than reply, he simply hugged in closer from behind her and pointed his finger slowly up the trunk, stopping when he reached an old, rotted hole. A tiny patch of brown and white was barely visible through the cracking bark—it was feathers, from which a black beady eye watched them.

He felt the moment she saw it.

She blurted, "An owl!"

The creature flinched and its head swiveled, and that black beady eye twitched and disappeared. "Shh," he told her, even though he was chuckling himself. "It's a whole nest of them. A mama with her hatchlings."

"Not bad, Jessup." She looked impressed, if a bit startled.

"A forest-ranger brother is good for something." He shrugged, watching the spot for more movement. "He's the one who taught me how to look. They nest in these old trees—they like the cracks and crevices."

"They? Are there more?" She relaxed into him—it was just the slightest bit, but he felt the impact like a Mack truck.

"Look." He leaned closer again, and this time she didn't stiffen at his touch. "There and there." He pointed and pointed again. "I've counted three nests total, but there are probably more up high."

"There are three mama owls in this tree?"

"Nah, those other nests must be old. They were probably abandoned a while ago."

As she gazed up at that owl, leaning into his chest, Eddie wondered what she would do if he simply stroked down those bare arms, taking her hands in his. He risked hugging her a tiny bit closer.

As he held Laura like that, a great peace swept through him. It was an amazing life he led here in the mountains— such simplicity, but such majesty, too. Someday he'd find a woman to share it with. He knew a terrific pang of loss that it likely wouldn't be *this* woman.

"You know," he said quietly, "they're monogamous."

"Huh?" Her voice was quiet, muzzy. She was as transfixed by this magical moment as he was.

Why *couldn't* it be Laura? Maybe she was the woman for him. Hell, he'd been crushing on her since puberty— maybe he'd been right all along.

"Owls," he said, hugging her just a little tighter. And then he dared even further. He did what he'd been longing to do. He swept his hands down her smooth arms, cupping her hands gently in his. "Scott told me they take only one partner for life."

She pulled away, looking annoyed. "Unlike some people I know."

Inside, he cursed. He'd gone too far. But he was sick of

her ridiculous assumptions about him. "You think you know me."

"No, Eddie. I *know* I know you."

"Do tell." He tried to be nonchalant, but his voice was tight.

"You're like every other guy." She shouldered past him, headed out of the trees.

He'd been having fun, letting Laura think what she liked about him, but now something had changed. Maybe it was those little lacy pink straps that'd done it, but he figured it was time to show her who he really was. "Why? Because I like a pretty girl?"

"Because you'd make a move on anything in a skirt. And on your own job site, no less."

He caught up to her, keeping pace as she strode back across the field to the house. She was so tense, so quick to jump to conclusions. It struck him that he'd never seen her easy with any man. It was as if the situation had tilted, and suddenly he saw her in a new light. "Look, Laura. I don't know who the jackass is who hurt you—"

She spun on him. "Nobody hurt me." But the pain that flashed in her eyes put the lie to her words.

"But I'm not out to," he finished.

"You will if you finish this stupid hotel."

"I don't think we're talking about the hotel."

She sputtered, but when no words came, she turned and made for her car. "Just look into the water thing," she shot at him, going at a brisk trot now. "And I will, too."

"We'll figure it out." Emphasis on *we*. He slowed and let her go. There was no winning this particular battle—but he wasn't about to cede the war. "Good-bye, Laura."

For now.

Seventeen

Rob had a theory. Seven Stud was so named because seven was roughly the number of hours that could go by without his needing a break. Ever since his last big loss with the game, it's been Texas Hold 'Em for him, but he decided tonight was the night to get back up on that Seven Stud pony.

And tonight he'd gone upscale, hitting the tables at Aura, a fancy resort casino on the Reno strip. Some day, after he hit it big, he'd bring Helen here. Maybe have a second honeymoon. She could sun herself by the pool. He'd rent them one of those cabanas, and people would serve her frosty drinks with frilly umbrellas.

Aura was a classy joint. When you were on the casino floor, it was all you could drink free on the house, though he knew not to drink too much at the tables. When he did, he stayed away from beer and wine—too potent. But they watered down the liquor at these places, so his habit was to nurse a Jack and Coke, one per hour. He never got buzzed, and with those lowball glasses and all that ice, he always made it about seven hours before he needed to get up.

Helen had looked so sad when he left tonight. He wished he could tell her he did this for them. For *her*. But she wouldn't understand. All she could think about was the kids and the chores, while he had bigger concerns. Someday she'd understand. When he hired her a regular sitter and she got to cut her hours at the tavern, his plan would become clear, he had no doubt about that.

He'd known the moment he first saw her that she was the one for him. Even as a teenager, she'd been something else, with her sexy red hair and those curves—good Lord, those curves—any Hollywood starlet would envy them. He'd seen how other men looked at her. He knew he had to step up his game if he was going to be good enough for curves like that.

Which meant he had another mistress to consider, and at the moment, she wasn't anything like the queen of hearts. What he longed for was the three of clubs, the card that would complete a straight flush, prettier than any queen.

The dealer doled out the last cards. "Down and dirty."

A master at the poker face, he schooled his features. Three, three, come on three. He hadn't seen any yet, which was unusual for Seven Stud. So many cards showing, and none of them threes.

His hole card was placed before him with a crisp flick. Rob rubbed his buffalo nickel for good luck. Rubbed the card. Peeked up at the corner. An eight.

His poker face shattered. "Shit." Nada. And with a measly deuce, jack, six showing, he couldn't even make a reasonable bluff, not when the young cowboy across from him was showing a pair of aces and his Colgate smile. "Fold."

He'd been up for a while, but that last pot brought him back down to a hundred, and one lone Benjamin was definitely not going to do it. He needed more cash to get his mojo going, and that was exactly why he'd come to Aura tonight—their generous credit program.

He headed to the cashier and flashed his platinum Aura Player's Rewards card. "I need a marker."

The woman was a tiny thing, with chipped purple nails and a tag that read:

Aura Resort Casino
~ A Fairview Property ~
Hello my name is
THUY

He gave Thuy a killer smile, willing her to recognize him. She must have because there was a quick *buzz-buzz*, the gate clicked open, and a suited thug appeared to escort him to the back office.

It wasn't his first time back there, not by a long shot. He stole a surreptitious glance at the secretary's name tag. Sheryl, it looked like.

She swiped his card. "Good evening, Mister Haskell. What can I do for you?"

"I need a marker."

She glanced down at her computer screen. "I'm sorry, sir. You've reached your limit."

"What?"

"You've hit your limit for the month."

His vision wavered for a moment, anger a sudden boil in his veins. But he kept his most charming smile plastered on his face. "It's Sheryl, right?"

"Sharon."

"My bad. *Sharon.* I guess I was too distracted by your pretty brown eyes to remember right." He turned up that megawatt smile—he knew he wasn't a bad-looking guy, and it'd served him well before. "Sharon, I get paid next week." He heard an office door open, but ignored it, focused only on sweet-talking this Sharon who was the only thing standing between him and winning the pot of his dreams. "I just need a marker till then. I'm a lucky guy."

"How can we help you, sir?" It was one of the pit bosses, and Rob finally registered that two men had entered the room, the blue-blazered boss and some other guy who was so fancy, he didn't even have a name tag.

Rob shared his broad grin with them. "I was hoping to get a marker."

"Shouldn't be a problem," the pit boss said, but then he went to stand at her desk, looking over her shoulder at her screen, and he grew thoughtful. "I can see you've hit a bad run, Mister Haskell."

The fancy man joined him, looking at the screen. "A local, are you?" With a clap on the pit boss's back, he added, "I think Mister Haskell here looks lucky. Another five hundred shouldn't be a problem." He caught Rob's eye and gave him a chummy wink. "You're good for it, aren't you, Haskell?"

Rob nodded like crazy. "Yes, sir."

"I'll let you nice folks get back to business then." Rob's rainmaker shook the pit boss's hand. "I'm over a barrel here. You're confident you can stay on top of that project we talked about?"

A look of fear and respect stilled the man's features. "I sent my boys out to the ranch, Mister Fox. It's just, they were worried . . ." He pitched his voice lower. "They're worried it might be, you know, illegal."

The man in the fancy suit nodded grimly. "It's good of them to be concerned. But you tell them what we're doing will eventually be *good* for the land. Hell, think of all those rich dot-commers, anxious to spend their stock options on organic mud baths, hemp robes, hundred-dollar salads with local greens, heirloom this and that, and whatever the hell else we're pushing these days. Now *that's* eco-friendly. It's just business, and business means making the tough decisions. The smart decisions. You can't let this little glitch stop progress. We can't stop building, which means you need to make this disappear for me. Because I can find someone else who will . . . do you hear what I'm saying?"

"I understand, sir." The pit boss added nervously, "The eagle has landed."

Then the two men laughed like he'd made some great joke.

Meanwhile, Rob was growing impatient. These dudes were jawing while he needed to get his five bills and get back to the tables. It was right back to Texas Hold 'Em for him. Screw Seven Stud.

Finally the mysterious suit left. The pit boss unlocked the safe and counted out Rob's chips. "We don't usually raise the credit limit like this. Not without running it through corporate."

"I'm good for it." Once he saw those stacks of blue and red, only then did his shoulders begin to loosen. He could feel the weight of them in his hand already.

"You've got some timing, hitting us up when one of the Fairview suits was in." He handed off a pretty little tray of chips. "Mister Fox is here all the way from New York."

Rob took his money and grinned. "I told you I was lucky."

Eighteen

~

"Is everything all set?" Laura cornered her sister as she emerged from the kitchen into the main tavern. "You've got enough food? Dan texted me about an hour ago." She checked her watch. "They stopped in Fresh Pond for gas, which would put them here by four o'clock."

"What? You meant they were coming *today*?" Sorrow waited a beat, then grinned evilly. "Of course, everything's all set. For the thousandth time, we're rea—"

A shadow crossed the window—a large white van, pulling into the lot. "Oh my God, they're here." The day had finally arrived—the History Network people had come to start filming—and if that weren't good enough, an old colleague of hers was acting as producer. She ran out to the lot to greet them.

People were spilling from the van door, and it was like she was back in the city, seeing the array of tattoos, wildly dyed hair, and a showcase of tattered clothing that'd probably cost a fortune. She glimpsed an impressive amount of gear stowed in the back—mikes, boom poles, cameras, lenses. It was a total thrill.

"Hey, guys," she called, and cursed herself for sounding like such an eager goofball. She tempered her voice and expression to play it cool. "Come on in. Have a beer on the house before you get settled."

Sorrow appeared on the porch to shoo them inside, but Laura had her eye on the driver, still in the van, fiddling with his phone. It'd been years since she'd seen him, but that profile was instantly recognizable—her old pal, Dan Harper. Finally a door slammed, and he walked around the van to her, beaming. "Hey, stranger."

She felt the grin pop back onto her face, bigger than ever. "Danny, I can't believe it." They'd once moved in the same San Francisco circles but had lost touch after he moved to Los Angeles.

He took her hand, letting his eyes rove blatantly up and down her body. "Laura Bailey. As I live and breathe."

She tugged her hand away. "Easy, sailor. I'm not that cheap."

He barked a laugh. "You haven't changed one bit." He leaned in to buss her on the cheek. "Seriously, it's awesome to see you. I'm so happy we could make this work out."

"*You're* happy? I couldn't believe when I saw your name." After planning had begun in earnest, she'd been shocked when, cc'ed on an e-mail message, one of the names had popped from the rest. "How's life in Smell-Ay?"

"You Northern California types are such snobs." He shook his head in mock dismay. "Watch it, or I won't share any of my celebrity gossip."

"You've got gossip?" She motioned zipping her lips. "I will not be denied."

Bear appeared, walking from the lodge to the tavern. "You going to make the man sleep out here?"

She and Dan shared an amused look. "Meet my dear father."

Her dad simply grunted and continued his way into the tavern.

Sweeping an arm toward the porch, she added in a mockingly formal tone, "Mister Daniel Harper, would you like to come in?"

"As long as I don't have to sit down." He rubbed his lower back. "The drive was fine till I hit the mountains. Thirty miles an hour of this." His hand snaked through the air, gesturing the twists and turns. "Good thing I don't get carsick." When a woman emerged from the passenger van, looking rumpled and slightly green, he added, "Unlike Kat, here."

She gave the woman a sympathetic look. "The drive is pretty, but it can be winding."

"Can be?" Kat raked a hand through her spiky black hair and croaked, "Is there a place I can lie down?"

Sorrow had been watching from the porch and, seeing she was needed, jogged down the stairs. "I'll show her a room."

"Can't Hope show her?" Laura did a quick scan through the tavern windows for their new employee. "I thought she was going to be waiting tables for you. Isn't that why tonight's special is lasagna—anyone can serve it up?"

Hope might've proved knowledgeable about environmental issues, but when it came to actual helpfulness, so far she was pulling a goose egg.

Sorrow hedged. "Well . . . I told her . . ."

"And you were headed out tonight. You can't take two hours off?" Laura gave her a stare down. *She* couldn't take time off, but at least her sister could. Sorrow had been working so hard, as if she'd sensed just how important this all was to Laura, and she wanted to reward her sister with some downtime. "I thought you had plans with Billy."

"We did. We *do*. But Hope was nervous about going it alone, especially with all the new guests. Speaking of which . . ." They both glanced at Kat, looking green and wobbly.

"You go," Laura said. "Get the woman a bed and some ginger ale."

Dan put a casual arm around her shoulders. "I'm hoping you have something a little stronger for the rest of us."

"Right this way."

"Wait a sec." He stopped and, with a concerned glance back at the locked van, asked, "Will our gear be okay out here?"

"What?" It took her a moment to get what he was saying. "Ohh. Danny, this is *Sierra Falls.* The only thing that'll break into your van is a raccoon, or a bear maybe."

Worry flashed across his face, and Laura had to laugh. She'd always thought he was cute—they'd even had a couple of dates back in the day—but in his funky black-framed glasses and pretend-vintage concert T-shirt, he was more metrosexual than manly-sexual. She'd become so accustomed to the brawny mountain men that the cool LA club vibe just looked helpless. Almost comically out of place. Dan had a sharp wit, but she doubted he'd know what to do if faced with anything baring sharp teeth.

Oddly, it gave her a stab of affection for him . . . for all of them. It made her realize that she'd made the right decision coming home, but also just how much she'd missed her city friends. She leaned in for another hug. "It's *so* great to see you."

Gravel crunched as another vehicle pulled into the drive—a red pickup. Even through the windshield, she could discern the grim set to the driver's jaw.

Eddie and his impeccable timing.

Just like his timing with that stupid tree. He'd thought he could seduce her by showing her a couple of stupid birds' nests. And damn the man, he almost had. He'd taken her hand, and she'd felt his touch like a pulse of electricity. She'd been too shocked to pull away, too curious to see if the feeling faded, if it'd just been surprise—not attraction—that'd surged through her. But that warmth had intensified. The sweep of his hands down her arms had left her weak, hot and shivery both. No, it'd definitely, unfortunately, been attraction she'd felt.

And now he was showing up, here. Just when she was hitting her stride. He pulled in right next to where they were standing. Total Neanderthal move.

He got out, and his eyes flicked ever so briefly—and disdainfully—over Dan. "Evening," he said in a tight voice.

She bared her teeth in a smile. "Miller time again?"

He only shrugged, and she told herself it wasn't hurt that'd furrowed his brow.

The contrast between him and Dan was pronounced. Her old friend looked like he belonged in some grungy, ultrahip LA nightclub, while there went Eddie, seeming like something out of a Levi's ad. As he walked into the tavern, she had to look away.

But that brought her attention to the back of his pickup instead. Yet again, he had ten tons of gear in the back. Did he ever clean the thing out?

A small slash of color caught her eye. Stepping closer, she registered what she was looking at and felt it like a punch in the gut. It was a small red sneaker.

A child's sneaker.

Did he have a kid? She glared at the door he'd just walked through, as if that might offer some clue. Did this explain where he was always off to? Was he paying regular visits to his mistress and secret love child?

She smothered her extreme response. Why should *she* care?

The film crew was here. She knew the producer. Her world was taking off. She wouldn't let Eddie ruin her moment—she'd been looking forward to this for weeks. More than that, she'd worked her butt off to make it happen.

"Come on." She tucked Dan's arm firmly in hers and led him inside, headed toward his friends who were settling noisily into a booth.

"I've had my fill of the crew for the moment," he said,

steering her away. "I've spent the past two hours forced to
listen to their arguing."

"Here, then." She pointed him to a seat by the window
and dashed behind the bar for two bottles of beer. She wasn't
normally a drinker, but right then, she was in the mood for
a change. "Arguing, huh?" she asked as she returned to the
table.

"Oh, yeah." He cracked open both bottles, then handed
Laura hers. "The only time they shut up was to tweet."

She laughed. "Were they arguing about the shoot?"

"Nah, not that." He shook his head as he took a healthy
swig.

"Then what?"

He put the beer on the table with a contented sigh. "You
name it. Why vegetarians should be allowed to eat bacon.
Why the valley isn't really LA. Why *Battlestar Galactica*
is superior to *Star Trek*."

"Duh," she said distractedly. She forced herself to focus
on Dan instead of watching Eddie stand and lean against
the bar. The guy really did have a great ass. Did he do regular squats or was that all from skiing and hiking? Too bad
it was attached to *him*—total waste.

Focus. She'd been saying something. Gathering her wits,
she took a long pull of that beer, not really tasting it.
"Though I have to agree about the other thing. Who doesn't
want to be a baconatarian?" She laughed at her own comment, but it came out too brightly, even to her own ears.

Then Eddie's laugh rose above the tavern din. His energy
seemed to pull at the entire room, till her chest felt tight
from it. She rubbed her arms, wiping away the memory of
his touch.

She felt him make his way to the end of the bar, chat with
Bear, grab his own beer. Generally making himself at
home—in *her* workplace. Why did she feel him like this?
Feel him move through the room as though they were tied
together by an invisible string?

It made her want to flirt—with *Dan*. She reached across the table and tugged at his sleeve. "Tell me what you've been up to."

Dan met her eyes and held them a second longer than average. "Me? What about you? Is this temporary?" He glanced around the bar, lingering on the deer head over the fireplace. "Some sort of punishment, maybe?"

She gave him a playful shove. "Shut up."

"She tells you to shut up, too, huh?" Eddie had come over, practically casting a shadow over the entire table.

Dan grinned and asked her, "You've had this habit since childhood?"

Eddie pulled up a chair. "Since kindergarten, to be exact. Mind if I join you?" He'd directed the question to Dan, not her.

She glowered up at him. "Sorry, we're busy—"

"Not at all," Dan said eagerly. He introduced himself and scooted over to make room at the table. "Sorry, Laura, but I've got to hear the dirt." He turned his full attention to Eddie. "So she was a little hellion even as a five-year-old?"

Eddie's laugh was rolling. "Never heard it put that way, but yeah." He took a swig of his beer, and when he spoke again, Laura detected the slightest tightness in his voice. "She was a hellion all right. Still is." There'd been something off in how he'd said it, and an odd pause followed, but then he spoke again, his tone so easy, she wondered if she'd imagined the rest. "So, how do you guys know each other?"

Eddie had inserted himself into their conversation. She didn't want him there, but a part of her didn't want him to go, either. It was almost like she wanted to see him, but she wanted him to see *her*, too, with Dan. It was a jumble of adolescent impulses, and it gave her the inexplicable urge to be cruel—to make it clear that they were from two different worlds, and he was currently intruding on hers.

"Dan directed a webisode for us," she said blithely. "Ages ago."

"Back when they called that crap *webisodes*," Dan said, and she shared a knowing laugh with him.

"Webisode?" Eddie asked.

"I worked for an Internet company that did online reviews," she said in an impatient voice. "Each episode was called a webisode." She turned to Dan, effectively shutting Eddie out and ending that conversation. "What's the plan for the shoot?"

"I thought we'd start out by getting some B-roll," he said, switching into producer mode. "Scout some locations, that sort of thing."

"How can I help?" She couldn't wait to get to it. It'd been so long since she'd been engaged in any sort of professional endeavor that didn't involve clean linens or electric bills.

"We need a place we can set up a small studio. Something soundproof."

She nodded. "I know exactly the spot. There's a room upstairs—too small to be a guest room—you can do pickups there."

"Pickups?" Eddie grinned, trying to insert himself again. "Can *I* come around for a pickup?"

She glared at him—he *would* have to turn it sexual. "Is everything an innuendo with you?"

"Only where you're concerned." He winked.

"I meant audio pickups." How was it he always managed to throw her off stride? Terrified that she was blushing, she had to look away as she added in a tight voice, "We're talking about recording *audio*."

"Dude, *I* thought it was a good one." Dan clinked his bottle with Eddie's. "And anyway, I don't want to talk shop yet." He twisted in his seat, studying the array of pictures on the far wall—vintage signs with sayings about bounty and friendship, and old print ads for things like Kiltie Brand Lemons. They were all bordered with matching blue gingham mats that'd already been faded by the sun back when she was a kid. She'd been meaning to renovate them . . . right into the Dumpster.

Dan's voice brought her back into the present, saying, "I want to hear about this place. Why are you here?"

She bristled at his tone. "You make it sound like I've moved to Mars."

"You kind of have." He saw the pained expression on her face and dialed it back. "Maybe not Mars. Maybe just . . . the moon. But seriously, your man can't like this new development very much."

Eddie exclaimed, "Your man?"

She realized with annoyance how aware of him she'd been, how much she'd felt him sitting there in judgment. She'd refused to meet his eye, so she didn't know what expression he wore, but she did hear something in his voice. It was disbelief.

"Don't sound so shocked," she snapped, then gathered her wits with a quick sip of her beer. It was still mostly full, well on its way to becoming tepid, and she put it down and pushed it away. "He's not *my* man. Patrick and I have been over for a while."

Dan's eyes goggled. "Oh really?" He jokingly spread his arms like he was yawning, and when he brought down his hands they rested on hers.

Eddie's gaze flicked to their hands and away again. "Who's Patrick?" He kept his face a careful blank, and she found herself wishing to see something else there. Jealousy, anger . . . something.

Dan ignored him and kept his avid attention on her. "Don't tell me the queen bee is without a drone."

"Patrick wasn't a drone," she said. There wasn't any aspect of this that she was enjoying.

"Babe, you're made of honey." Dan grinned. "Gotta be some drones hiding out somewhere."

"Who's Patrick?" Eddie asked again, sharply this time.

Dan finally emerged from his entrancement to answer, "Her fiancé. The lucky dog."

"You have a fiancé?" Eddie's expression remained unreadable.

"Had," she said sharply, feeling peeved that Eddie had chosen this moment to become so mysterious.

Dan chuckled. "But I can't imagine a little filly like Lola here flying solo for long."

"Lola?" Eddie asked wide-eyed, and this time his eyes didn't budge from hers. What *was* that look on his face?

Forget Eddie. Who cared what he thought, anyway?

She turned to Dan instead, giving him a withering look. "I hate when you call me that."

"It's a nickname from her wilder days," Dan explained.

"It's not a nickname if you were the only one who used it."

"Laura was wild?" Eddie gave her a slow appreciative assessment—his expression had suddenly become readable, and she didn't like it one bit. "I'd have liked to see that."

She was one second away from leaving these two to themselves. She slid her hands out from under Dan's and braced herself on the table like she might spring up. "Well, this has been fun," she said in a voice thick with sarcasm.

"Okay, okay. I'll stop teasing." Dan patted her arm. He probably felt how stiffly she held herself because he snatched her fist in his hands, prying it open to give her an affection-ate jiggle and squeeze. "I'm just psyched to see you, and I guess it's bringing out my inner twelve-year-old. I've thought about this day, Laura."

"You have?" She was dying to sneak a glimpse at Eddie.

"Oh, once or twice," Dan said, playfully playing it down. "I've missed you."

That was it. She had to peek at Eddie. His eyes were waiting for her, staring, smoldering, a vivid, crystalline blue. His jaw was clenched. She glanced away quickly, unable to hold that look.

"I always wondered where you ended up," Dan continued, "what you were up to, what it'd be like to run into you again. Although," he added with a laugh, "I must say, I imagined reuniting in LA, or New York. Chicago maybe. But here we are . . . in the middle of nowhere." He looked up at the boar head looming high over the table and barked out a laugh. "It's awesome."

"Totally awesome," Eddie said flatly.

Shut up, she mouthed at him.

"Seriously," Dan continued, unaware of the exchange. "I bet you don't exactly get a lot of film crews out here."

Eddie nodded in mock amazement. "How will us country folk handle the excitement?"

"Shut up." And this time she'd said it aloud, scooting her chair back as she did, springing up. "I need some water." Mostly she needed to get away from both of these men.

Dan's eyes lit. "Please tell me your water comes from a well. Or is pumped from a mountain spring or something."

"Daniel, this isn't *Little House on the Prairie*. We have hot and cold running water." She stood over the table, her arms wrapped tightly around her chest. She'd been so happy to see him, but he was acting so oblivious. Couldn't he hear how disdainful he sounded? This was her new life he was joking about. Her new priorities. She was reminded with a brilliant flash of clarity why she'd given up men.

Eddie chose that moment to get back in on the conversation. "I'll bet in LA, you only drink organic bottled vitamin water shipped in from a Peruvian hot spring."

That was it. She stormed to the bar. She felt one of the men follow her, and somehow she knew it wouldn't be Dan she saw when she turned around. She'd felt Eddie's judgment from the moment he came in—as if *he* were one to judge.

She rounded on him. "What is your problem?"

Eddie assessed her quietly. "Just feeling a little protective, country girl." He paused a moment, his eyes focused on her, looking like he wanted to say something more.

She couldn't look away. His eyes were a bright, unusual blue, and she'd never noticed how long his lashes were.

When he spoke again, he sounded sincere. "I'm sorry. I didn't mean to be an ass . . ." But then he spoke again in a voice like he was testing her, adding, "*Lola.*"

He was baiting her, and she refused to bite. Instead, she kept her voice dead serious when she asked him, "Why are you even hanging around if you've got such a low opinion of everyone?"

"I came because . . ." A look of wariness crept over his face. "I have news, Laura."

"What news?" She curled her fingers into her arms, because now she read wariness *and* regret.

"I looked into the watershed thing for you."

"You did?" The words were out before she had a chance to temper the shock from her voice. Though, thinking about it, she didn't know why she was so surprised. He'd remeasured the property lines when she'd asked him to do that, too.

"Yes," he said, looking oddly insulted. "I told you I'd look into it, and I'm a man of my word. I'm sorry, Laura, the bond goes to identifying and protecting flood zones. Timber Creek has never flooded. There are no restrictions to building on that land."

"Of course there aren't." Sudden emotion clutched at her throat, and she spun away to gather herself, acting as if she needed to get herself a drink. She forced her voice to steady as she said, "Next time, just shoot me an e-mail, okay?"

He was already walking back to the booth, and the wave of his hand was all that told her he'd heard. So why had he come to deliver the news? She stole a look at him as she filled a glass with ice. Was he there to rub it in?

And then there was the Dan thing. Dan was clueless, but *she* could tell how much Eddie was mocking him. It was like he was mocking her old life, and that mocked *her*. How could she take it any other way? So why was he even there if he judged her so much?

Why did she care?

Filling a glass with club soda, she stole another glance. Eddie was leaning back, jawing easily with Dan. That was how he acted—easy with everyone. Flirty with everyone. It wasn't just with her. Those blue-eyed winks weren't because she was special.

She'd need to shore up her defenses.

By the time she returned to the table, she'd schooled all emotion from her face. She gave Eddie a flat look. "I didn't realize you were still here."

Something flashed in his eyes, and she waited for him to make a crack, but he only sighed and stood. "I'll leave you to it," he said politely. "And Laura, I really am sorry."

She let her eyes linger on his back as he left. Giving Eddie the cold shoulder didn't feel as good as she'd hoped it would.

But she had no choice. She'd failed once before, because of a man. Patrick had become her fiancé, but he'd begun as her co-worker. Eventually she'd lost her job because of him, and hearing his name only reminded her of one crystal-clear fact: she couldn't lose again.

Never again.

Nineteen

❧

Damn. Eddie's tires spun in gravel as he sped into the ranch's lot and slammed his truck into park.

Damn that woman.

He hadn't been able to get her out of his mind all weekend. Not even spending a couple of nights at Camp Richardson with a bunch of rowdy kids had tired him out.

But dammit, he wasn't a bad guy. He was a good guy. *The* good guy, who was doing what he could to rein in this construction project.

Fairview could easily have given the contract to some other outfit, and they'd probably have razed the whole thing by now, erecting some postmodern glass-and-steel thing, with fake stone fountains and a giant Buddha in the foyer.

But they'd given the job to him and Jack instead, and *he* was the one running around, double-checking paperwork, resurveying the land, investigating *watershed bonds*, God help him.

He scowled at his reflection in the driver's-side mirror.

"Rough," he muttered, and reached for the glove box to grab his electric razor. A couple of nights of no sleep would leave any man looking rough, but camping with a van full of kids from the Reno community center had to be the killing blow.

It was how he spent many of his weekends, leading at-risk youth on guided hiking and camping trips. Not many people knew about it—it wasn't something he advertised. On the contrary, it was something that felt very private to him.

He'd been a screw-up, just like so many of these kids.

There hadn't been a lot to do, growing up in a small town. His home life hadn't been bad, but still, his parents had spent years tiptoeing on the brink of divorce. They'd focused mostly on their own needs, which had made it easy for a teenage boy in a big family to get away with some bad behavior.

As he'd gotten older, it'd only gotten worse. Temptations became more within reach. It'd only gotten easier to find someone to buy him booze before he'd been legal. And, most exciting for him, the girls eventually got older and filled out, and he had, too.

But it wasn't just the partying. The youngest of four boys, he'd had big shoes to fill, following in the shadow of Mark, who'd become some fancy doctor in Silver City, and then there was Scott, who'd known practically from infancy that his vocation was to be a park ranger. Meanwhile, the only thing that'd called to Eddie had been the Gas-n-Go the next town over, where the attendant was always happy to overlook the fake ID and sell him a case of beer.

Only the strong hand of his oldest brother, Jack, had saved him. All Eddie had ever been good at was football, flirting, and fast driving, but when Jack realized the road his little brother was headed down, he'd made extra time for him.

Growing up in Sierra Falls, Eddie had always appreciated a blue-sky day or waking to a fresh blanket of snow, but it was Jack who really showed him what nature was all about.

Fishing trips, hiking, camping, living off the land for days with nobody else for miles around . . . those things had shown him how deep was the connection he felt with the land.

It was the mountains that'd shown him what it was to be a man.

The first time a bear walked through his camp was when it all really clicked. He saw how insignificant he was. How meaningless all the partying and girl chasing.

Jack had turned Eddie's world around. At the time, his brother had been building his business, and when Eddie graduated from high school, Jack gave him a job. A reason to get out of bed and comb his hair in the morning.

People credited both of them for their success—and sure, Eddie worked hard—but it'd been Jack's vision that'd made it happen.

He thought of his latest trip. Those kids might've been born in the shadow of the Sierras, but many of them had never been out of the Reno city limits, and this latest batch, like Eddie so many years ago, had just experienced their first bear encounter.

They'd hiked out to Mount Tallac, not an easy day, and were taking a break before turning back around when a black bear ambled by. The guy didn't pose a threat, but as Eddie could attest, there was nothing like the sight of one's first bear to forget your troubles. Meth-cooking moms, dads doing hard time—it all tended to fade to the background.

One would've thought that, after a weekend like that, he'd have been dead to the world when he finally hit his own mattress last night. But he couldn't get Laura out of his mind. She pissed him off. She was cold and prickly and uptight, capable of thinking only of her own ambitions.

But she also riled him up in a way that made him want to pull that hot body close to his. She was sexy and sassy and smart, but she was vulnerable, too, and that right there was the crux of it. In her eyes, he'd seen flickers of the emotion—the sadness even—that she kept bottled up, under tight control. He guessed something or someone had hurt her badly, and though her vulnerability was something she kept hidden, he knew she had her demons, secreted way down deep.

He longed to touch her . . . to finally, really touch her. To shoulder her burdens for a little while. To watch her let go and forget herself, with one of those knockout smiles lighting up her face, her greatest ambition only to melt into him.

He often caught her eyes on him. He longed to see the spark in those eyes transform, for the switch to flick from cold wariness into something white-hot. Something that forgot about arguments and bottom lines . . . something that didn't think at all. He'd seen it once, by the creek.

Maybe that was the trick—to get her away from the world she knew so well. Get her away from things she thought she could control. He wanted to show her how to lose control. That losing control could be *good*.

The way she responded to his touch, he knew she had it in her. She'd relaxed into him, warmed to him. But then it was like she remembered she wasn't supposed to show her tender side, like she was afraid of it.

And he knew it wasn't just *him*. She kept herself strung tight, looking ready to shatter before she'd let *anyone* in.

It was good to see that she and Sorrow had reconciled. He was glad Laura had someone to turn to. But still, he sensed she was lonely. If she weren't, she wouldn't have that thing in her eyes he spotted sometimes—that look of fear, that flicker of sadness.

He longed to hold her and kiss her till she forgot about the things that didn't matter. Kiss her till she shut the hell up about ten-million-dollar watershed bonds. Till she kissed him back, caving to the desire he'd seen glimmer in her eyes on that day by the creek.

Would she ever let it happen? He rapped his razor against the dash to clean it out, thinking probably not.

It was sad, really. If she wouldn't look twice at him, he wished she'd at least let go with *somebody*.

And it sounded like she'd been with someone for a while. When that annoying History Network guy mentioned her fiancé, Eddie wasn't sure what'd been more of a shock—that she'd been engaged or the jealousy that clenched his gut to hear it.

But she was back home in Sierra Falls and still alone. It seemed to him like she was afraid to let anyone in. She was terrified to fail. Terrified that someone might see she couldn't do it alone.

There was more to that girl than she let on, he knew it. Even as a teenager, there'd been something in her eyes that had reminded him of a cat, cornered and hissing, not because she posed any sort of threat, but because she was over-whelmed by her own feelings of fear and uncertainty.

Why a smart, gorgeous woman like her would ever feel uncertain was beyond him. Eddie had never made it to college—with bills to pay and a business to run, he didn't see how it'd ever happen. But Laura, she was A-list. The full package. She'd put herself through school, a real self-made woman. Hot, successful, whip smart.

So why no boyfriend? Clearly it was her own choice. If she put herself on the market, she'd be snapped up in a second.

He couldn't figure out what was between her and that hipster film guy. Was that what Laura was attracted to? Guys with tight jeans and hair gel? Hair gel, for God's sake. Eddie wouldn't be caught dead slicking a ton of crap into his hair. And then there were those bracelets—the guy had a wrist full of them. He hoped his brothers would just shoot him if he ever bought himself bracelets.

Laura had made it clear that when she looked at him, all she saw was country boy. They'd known each other for years, yet she clung to her judgments of him, refusing to see who he really was. He might not have a college degree, but he read, and he worked hard, and he had his Reno kids, but did she notice any of that? No, all Laura saw was a big pickup truck. But hell, he worked construction, took his campers off-roading, drove in the snow—he didn't know what she'd have him drive instead. Sometimes he just wanted to pin her up against the side of that truck and kiss her till she saw him for the man he really was.

He slammed the glove box shut, decided. Maybe she'd never let go of whatever it was that had her strung tight, but he could at least do what he could to prove he wasn't a bad guy.

He needed this gig. *Jessup Brothers* needed this gig. As much as he hated being public enemy number one in her eyes, he couldn't back out. He owed it to his brother.

For Eddie, with no family to support, it wasn't so much about the money. He'd built his cabin himself and owned it outright. Hell, lately all his spare cash went to the Reno kids, for gear like kid-sized sleeping bags and hiking boots for feet that seemed to grow overnight. But Jack had a family and needed the income. What's more, with his only son just off to boot camp, his brother needed the *work*, too—the preoccupation that came with such a big job.

They may have needed the gig, but still, it didn't mean he couldn't do it right.

He snatched his cell from atop the seat. He owed his brother, but he owed something to himself, too: to listen to his gut. And right now, doing the job as it was spec'd in the plans didn't feel right. Something was fishy. He'd run the job and get the paycheck, but he'd be responsible about it. Laura had been right—he owed it to Sierra Falls to do no less than that.

"Hunter, hey," he said in a sure voice. There'd be no more *Yes, sir, Mister Fox* for him. He checked the clock on the dash, suddenly worried he'd called too early, but there was no need for concern. The Fairview exec sounded as crisp and clear as if he were already on his second pot of coffee.

"There have been some developments you need to know about," Eddie told him. Once he assured the man that all was well with the construction, he dove in. "Sierra Falls was one of the original gold rush towns."

He detailed the story of the letters, of Buck Larsen, but Fox soon interrupted. "It's eight A.M. on a Monday morning," the man said. "I appreciate your town spirit, son, but I'm busy. You need to wrap it up and tell me what the hell this has to do with me."

"The History Network is here, filming a story focused on how *historic* Sierra Falls is." He sat tall, staring blindly at the ranch house through the windshield, weighing his words carefully. He wasn't a shark in a suit like Fox was, but he would get this right. "Our draw is history. Tourists have been coming for a glimpse into the past, to see where Buck Larsen slept, where he drank. If you fundamentally change the look of the old Timber Creek ranch, you'll be changing its history. If you lose the essence—"

But Fox cut him off. "TV people, you say? Are you sure?"

"I'm sure," Eddie replied, a bit thrown by the man's tone. He'd have thought these corporate types would jump at the sort of publicity that television would bring. "I met them myself."

"You met them," Fox repeated in a flat voice, then grew silent. When he spoke again, his manner was exaggeratedly chummy. "You're absolutely right, you know."

"I . . . oh." Eddie had been about to deploy his planned rebuttal and was thrown by Fox's sudden agreement. "Good, then."

"I'm thrilled you've brought this to my attention," Fox said. "If they're filming about how historic the town is, well, we can't have their story become how we're changing history. Besides, I sure don't want a bunch of TV folks going out to your job site and bothering you while you work."

"I guess that's another good point." Eddie thought fast. He wasn't done yet and wasn't about to let some slick

company man get the upper hand. "So you agree we need
to go back to our original plans. Refurbish the ranch, pretty
it up, you can get your solarium, spa, pool, all that. But we
keep it to a single story."

A few minutes later, he clicked off his cell, amazed that
Fox *had* agreed.

He couldn't wait to break the news to Laura. He could
just picture her, building up steam, getting worked up, and
that was when he'd tell her.

Laura, all worked up.

Now there was a thing to consider. She was a passionate
woman, that was for sure. All that fire, it was hard for him
not to fantasize about working out their disagreements in
the bedroom instead.

In fact, it was *all* he thought about lately.

His groin tightened as though on cue.

"What the hell . . ." He raked his hands through his hair
and blew out a breath. He needed to focus. Get to work.
Hammering something would take his mind off things, he
thought. Hammer. Drill. Screw . . . And like that, his mind
went to the dirtiest of places. He scrubbed his freshly shaved
cheeks. "Get a grip."

Suddenly, he felt hot.

There'd been an early-morning chill in the Sierra air, and
he'd thrown on a sweatshirt, but he pulled it off now and
dug through his duffel for a clean T-shirt.

A knock on his window startled him. The glass had
fogged, so he simply opened the door, expecting to see Jack
or one of his crew.

But instead, there was Laura.

Her hair was loose at her shoulders, and she wore jeans
and an old concert tee that hugged in just the right places.
She was always so sophisticated and put together, but casual
like this was when she was at her sexiest.

He couldn't help the genuine smile that popped onto his
face. "Morning, sunshine. I was just thinking about you."

Twenty

~

"You . . . why . . ." The sight of Eddie half-dressed robbed the words from her brain. She couldn't help her eyes from dipping to his chest, then back up again. He was cut with muscle in the mark of a man who took full advantage of his body, using it to work and to play, hefting lumber and operating tools and throwing balls. "Where's your shirt?" she blurted, then felt her cheeks redden at the gaffe.

"Warm morning. And looks like it's getting warmer." He smiled his trademark cocky-guy smile, but before she managed to get in a barb, he asked, "What brings you out so early, sugar?" He spoke in a husky morning voice.

Though he still sat in his truck, suddenly he felt too close, and she took a step back.

Why *had* she come? Why was she seeking him out this early? She should've known he'd be alone. Most of all, why was he half-naked?

"I have things to discuss," she managed.

"Of course you do." He got out of the truck. It was high

off the ground, and yet as his taut body unfolded from the cab and he stood, he still loomed so close and so tall over her. It was unsettling.

"I have things, too," he added with a smile. "But you first."

There was that arrogant grin again—she was sure it portended gloom. He was about to stick it to her in some way, she just knew it.

"Me first?" She cinched her arms at her chest. "Don't tell me . . . age before beauty?"

"Oh, darlin', no." He gave a playful pinch to her chin. "Pearls before swine." He winked and let go, but the ghost of his touch left her skin hot. "So what brings you here looking like you might like to eat me for breakfast?" He raised a brow, implying so much more than her current temper.

She took another step backward. She was painfully aware of his proximity, like she'd all of a sudden become claustrophobic.

Her reaction to him annoyed her. His ease annoyed her. It sharpened her words. "I found precedent."

"Precedent, huh? Sounds important." He paused. "Precedent for what?"

"For stopping this construction," she said, trying to keep her temper. "What else? There have been similar cases. In each, a federal lawsuit was filed, citing a violation of the National Historic Preservation Act."

He nodded, thinking, then asked, "That all?"

"You are maddening. No, that's not—"

"Because if it's my turn, I wanted to tell you *my* news. I got Fairview to back out of their phase two plans."

"You . . . what?" She felt herself gape. Surely she didn't just hear what she thought she heard.

"There's no stopping the resort," Eddie quickly amended, "but Fairview has agreed to scale back."

She searched his words for some hidden trick. "What does *scale back* mean?"

"We're keeping the building to just one story after all."

He smiled, looking proud of himself. "I told you I'm not a bad guy."

"You said *there's no stopping the resort*." She still suspected he was, in fact, a bad guy. "I still want to *stop the resort*, Eddie."

"Come on, Laura, you know there's no stopping a company like Fairview."

"In fact"—she ignored him and tapped a finger on her chin—"I think I'd like to *kill* the resort."

"Hey, I just put my ass on the line to scale back plans for a whole damned international hotel. Which, by the way, will mean less money for Jessup Brothers."

Baby steps, she told herself. Of course he wouldn't do something that would hurt his own business.

He saw her waffling and held out his hand. "Peace? Please? Let's shake on it."

He wouldn't stop the construction completely, but she still could. She'd think of a way. In the meantime, she let her hand slip into his, and there it was again, that warm rush at feeling his large, worn hand envelop hers.

"I guess." She let him shake her hand. Scaling back was something, she told herself. Scaling back was good.

He squeezed, doing a little rub with his thumb, and all sorts of alarms sounded in her head. When she pulled her hand free, he laughed again. "The least I could get is a smile. Maybe a *Thank you, Eddie, for being so awesome*."

"Forgive me if I don't trust you," she said. "Why'd you do it, anyway?"

"I did it for you, dummy."

She stiffened. "Why?"

"Because I respect you, Laura."

Respect. Wasn't that what she'd wanted? She'd lost it at work, had been scrambling to reclaim it at home. Why did it feel so strange getting it now, so freely, from *Eddie*?

How was this guy she'd known all her life—who'd bugged her all her life—how was he the one to be giving her what she'd so longed for? And not just that, but he was sacrificing some of his own money in the process.

Suddenly, it wasn't Edwin Jessup from Mrs. Patmore's kindergarten class standing there. It was a man she saw with fresh eyes. A currently *shirtless* man.

And he looked good.

She fought it.

She edged sideways—had Eddie always been this big?— but as she did, she caught a glimpse of a large duffel on the passenger's side.

She *knew* it. Same old Eddie. "Doing the drive of shame?"

"I don't get your meaning." He pulled on his T-shirt— finally—and as he did, she heard him murmur, "Sure is chilly with you."

She hated the stab of jealousy she felt . . . at him frolicking around all over town, at her always being the chilly one. It riled her even more and she stabbed a finger at the junk littering the inside of his pickup. "Just getting in from an all-nighter? Real classy, Eddie."

"All-nighter?"

Razor, dirty shirts and socks, an extra pair of shoes . . . he'd clearly been based out of his truck for a couple of days. Was it with someone she knew? Or maybe he'd crashed with whatever hottie it was in Reno he was always dashing off to see. The mother of his child. Her stomach lurched for reasons she didn't want to contemplate.

"Actually"—she put up her hand—"I don't want to hear it."

"What are you talking about?" He glanced into the cab at his stuff, and as her meaning registered, his face fell. He gave her a flat look to match his flat tone. "Yeah, Laura, I was out all night with my many mistresses, having hot times in my pickup." He shouldered by her, slamming the door behind him. "Why do you insist on seeing the worst in me?"

What right did *he* have to look so hurt? He was the one sleeping around, not her.

"I was just asking," she muttered.

He stopped, turning slowly to look at her. "I can't figure you out." The way he shook his head said he was about to give up trying.

But she didn't want him to give up, and that was what *she* couldn't figure out. She fell into step behind him as he went to the back of his truck. "That's because I'm complicated. Unlike you."

"Oh, I'm easy as pie."

"*Easy.* I'll just bet you are." She scowled at his head—his hair stuck up every which way, like a man who hadn't showered that morning.

Why on earth was she feeling her heart crack? Why did it seem like everyone had their secret lives except for her?

He caught her staring and gave a beleaguered sigh. "Hat head, Laura. Because I went to bed with wet hair. Not because I was out all night partying."

He reached into the truck bed for his hat, a black Giants cap he settled onto his thick, brown waves. And did he have to be so damned *cute*?

He kicked back, half sitting, half leaning against the bumper, arms crossed at his chest. "But enough about me. How about you? How's your *fiancé*? Or did you throw him over for that TV douchebag? Gotta hand it to the guy—all that jewelry and hair gel, he sure is pretty."

"At least *he* works an honest job."

Eddie popped to standing. "Don't talk to me about a good day's work. Nobody works harder than me and Jack."

She felt a stab of regret at her hurtful words, but there he was, looming over her again. Her defenses kicked in and she sidled out of his way. "It's *Jack and me.* 'Me first is the worst.' "

He stepped closer, angling his body to face hers. "You think I'm some sort of redneck idiot, don't you?"

She forced herself not to retreat. "No."

He took another step closer. "So, is that the kind of guy you like? Pretty?"

This time she stepped out of the way, a move that put her up against the side of his truck. "Of course not."

"Then what do you like?" His voice was a mesmerizingly low rasp. He placed the gentlest finger beneath her chin, tilting her face up to his.

She should've said, *Not you.*

She could've said an urban professional.

A well-groomed man, someone who wore Burberry for work and James Perse for weekends.

She should've said, *Anyone but you.*

But for some reason, her tongue stuck in her mouth as her eyes locked with his. They were a vibrant blue, glittering with desire that'd become unchecked. He looked like he was going to kiss her.

And it was looking like she might let him.

Twenty-one

❧

Eddie couldn't help it. His years of wanting her, his frustration and anger. The way she lashed out, intentionally misunderstanding him. He couldn't hold back anymore. She'd always gotten to him, even when they were kids. Except back then, when she riled him, all he'd had to do was tug her ponytail. Now he wanted more.

To touch her, just once. He needed to bring this thing—whatever it was—to a head.

He placed the gentlest finger beneath her chin. "You didn't answer me."

He'd expected her to flinch, but instead her breath caught. Those gorgeous, sparkling eyes were wide, staring at him. The barest suggestion of tears appeared, shimmering, making them even bluer.

He pulled his hand away, fisting it at his side. Was she scared of him? She ate men like him for breakfast. What was going on in her head?

She could've taken up her concerns with Jack, but instead

she'd dogged *him*. She could've been colder, but the anger she hurled at him was fueled by a deep-seated passion. Passion that ran hot.

"Who are you really, Laura Bailey? What are you doing here?"

"I came to stop you."

He sighed, so tired of this backing and forthing. "No, I mean *here*. In Sierra Falls. Why are you alone? What happened?" The need to touch her again was unbearable, but he fought it. He'd never touch what wasn't his to take.

"Nothing happened."

"Why are you alone?"

"I just am," she said, looking ready to snap.

"But you're so goddamned beautiful. I know you know it. I see you running along the side of the road in those little short shorts. What are you running from?"

"Nothing."

Why wouldn't she trust him? "You're running from me."

A strand of hair blew into her lashes. The whites of her eyes had turned pink in the corners, like she was holding back some fierce and secret emotion. He ached to smooth the hair from her face. To cup her cheeks and kiss her once on each eye, to make them shine bright again.

"I don't run from anyone." Her voice wavered, like she didn't really believe it.

"Then why no boyfriend?" She was so near, he could feel the heat of her, smell her feminine scent, like flowery soap. He was dying to close the gap, but he'd never touch a woman against her will.

"I don't need a boyfriend. I'm not interested in you or anyone." She looked away, and he watched as she bristled, her gaze sharpening, focusing inside the truck bed.

He followed her eyes to a gray hoodie. One of the kids had left it behind in the van.

She added primly, "I'm especially not interested in a man who won't take responsibility for his own kid. Or is it kids?"

He was stunned speechless. He'd come to expect her crazy accusations, but this was ridiculous.

"Well?" she demanded. "Do you have a kid?"

"I have a lot of kids." He did an exaggerated silent count on his fingers. "Seven. I spent the weekend with my *seven* kids."

"Don't joke like that. I'm being serious." She looked so brittle, like she was barely keeping herself in one piece.

Why would Laura care so much about whether he had a kid? It made him want to goad her even more. What would it take for her to break through to the other side? For her to tell him what was really going on in that pretty head of hers? "I'm always serious, darlin'."

"Why can't you own up to your obligations? Are you saying you're not someone's father? Just cop to it already." Her cheeks were flushed. Would she be taking this so seriously if she didn't have some sort of feelings for him?

There was chemistry between them, no doubt about it. There always had been. What would it take for her to accept it? Accept him? It was time to clear the air. "Laura, slow down and listen for a minute."

"I am—"

"I don't have a kid," he said, cutting her off before she could reel back and hurl more his way. "I take care of kids."

She stilled, frowning. "What do you mean? Like . . . you babysit?"

He barked out a laugh. "No." His laugh faded as he considered it. "God, no. Though sometimes it feels like it. I take at-risk kids camping. That's all. I promise."

"Camping?" She was staring at him like he'd begun to speak Greek. "That's why you're always going to Reno? To pick up at-risk kids?"

He nodded. "I work with the community center there, downtown."

"Oh," she said quietly. She stared at him, dumbfounded.

"See?" He smiled nervously. What was that look on her

face? What was she seeing when she looked at him? "I'm not such a monster."

She sighed, lifting her face to the sky. "No, *I* am."

The statement shocked another laugh from him. "Hardly."

She shook her head, clearly needing a moment to wrap her mind around it. "To jump to conclusions like that when all the while you're taking poor kids *camping*? I'm horrible."

"Okay, maybe a little horrible." He grinned. "In the prettiest of ways."

She shoved him. "Why didn't you say something?" Then, studying his truck, she said, "Is that why you got such a ridiculously big vehicle? So you can drive kids around?"

"Nah, they wouldn't even fit in this old girl. I borrow a van from the center instead." He patted the shiny red paint job. "You're coming around to her, aren't you?"

"Nope. Not one little bit." She glanced at the gear in the back. "So who pays for all this?"

He shrugged. "I do."

"*You* do?"

"It's no big deal. I don't have any bills to pay, not really. There aren't a lot of good local programs for these kids, so I figure, how hard is it for me to buy stuff like food? They barely eat anything. And then the gear I use over and over again. Other people kick in a little extra here and there. Doctor Mark is always good for some supplies."

"Other people know about this?"

"Not many, no. I don't advertise or anything. There's just too much explaining to do." He added with a smile, "Kind of like I'm having to do now." Seeing her crestfallen expression, he chucked her chin. "Kidding."

"Jeez, what must you think of me?"

"I think you're a businesswoman looking out for your own."

"You must've thought I was insane." She sagged against the side of the truck. "I've been such a shrew. I've just felt so . . . alone in all this. It's overwhelming. I feel like it's up to me to carry the family."

He wanted nothing more than to give the poor woman a hug, but he knew to keep his hands to himself. "Seems like you and Sorrow are getting along now."

"I can't bug her with everything—she's got her own thing going on, plus with Sully gone, she's the one managing all the cooking. And then there's Dad. Since his stroke, our medical bills have been nuts. You wouldn't believe the paperwork I have to sift through just when he gets a simple checkup. I did the books recently, and it's getting harder and harder to balance the damned things. When I ran the numbers, the loss I projected with your, your . . . Slumbertimes Spa"—their eyes met as they shared an amused look—"I just don't see how we can pull through."

Her folks always had seen her as the professional, business-savvy kid in the family, so it was no surprise she'd felt she had to be the one to shoulder all the financial concerns. Still, he couldn't believe she'd been holding all this in.

He was just glad he'd made that phone call to Fox. It'd been some lucky damned timing on his part, that was for sure. "Will it help that we're scaling back the project?"

"I guess." Her eyes went to his, and for once there was warmth there. "I mean, yes. Yes, of course. Every little bit helps."

"I'd do more if I could, but Fairview is big."

"I still want to stop them," she said, her voice suddenly fierce.

"You know there's no stopping them completely."

"I'll figure out a way."

"Jack and I need the business. It'd be a blot on our record if we biffed this now."

"I get that. I get it, I do." Her gaze drifted back to the camping equipment in his truck bed. "Though I guess it's not just that. If you lost the job, I'd be taking food and gear away from at-risk inner-city youth? Nice . . ."

He drew the back of his finger down her cheek. "You had no way of knowing."

His touch brought her eyes back to him. There was something else there now, something that was seeing him for the first time. Something that smoldered.

"Did you come out here for anything else?" he asked, hoping.

She wet her lips. "I just . . . I want this to stop."

It was the flick of her tongue that did it. He didn't need more than that. She'd licked her lower lip. Darted her eyes to his mouth then quickly back up again. He could read signals.

He knew women, but it was Laura he wanted.

He stepped closer.

"Stop the construction, or stop *this*?" He cupped her cheek. Stepped closer, till he felt the heat of her body along his. He moved slowly, giving her every opportunity to stop him.

She didn't stop him. She only stared up at him, looking as disbelieving as he felt.

"I want you, Laura." His desire for her was intense, blinding him to everything but that luscious mouth. How many times had he stolen glimpses of it, fantasizing about the dirtiest of things. She'd been his teenage fantasy. His high school crush. And now here she was before him, lips parted slightly, his for the taking. "You know I want you."

"I know," she said, and he had to smile at that, such a Laura thing to say. But he knew she was just nervous. He saw now how vulnerable *the* Laura Bailey could be.

He leaned down to her, and for a moment, he hovered just a breath away. He didn't believe this was actually happening. He'd wanted her for so long. As long as he could remember.

And then she shocked him.

"Dammit, Eddie." She snagged his T-shirt in her fists and pulled him the final inch to her. Her mouth slammed into his, devouring him instantly.

His whole body stiffened, hardened, lust swamping him until his head rang with it.

He kissed her back. Kissed her like he'd wanted to kiss her since they were kids. Only they weren't kids now, and his hunger was a man's hunger, ravenous, wanting to take her, have her.

He wrapped his hands around her hips and braced her against the side of his truck. And—oh, God—he'd fantasized that, too. Taking her against the side of the truck. In the truck. In the woods. On the tavern bar. Beneath their high school bleachers. So many times, so many ways, and God help him, he wanted them all.

He kissed her deeply, and she kissed him back, just as deeply, just as hungrily.

But then she pushed him away, keeping his shirt clenched in her fingers. Breathlessly, she said, "This doesn't change anything."

"Not a thing." He leaned down, nipping at her ear. He'd consider it later. For now, he just wanted to get back to kissing.

"You're not listening, Eddie. I'm going to make Fairview regret the day they found us on the map." She was so damned sexy. So hot and so passionate.

His eyes found hers. "Bring it, gorgeous."

She shifted. Damn, was she pulling away? But, oh . . . *oh*, she was only adjusting, repositioning herself to drag him down to her. She nuzzled into him. He felt her mouth on his jaw, tasting his neck, tugging his shirt lower to lick and suck at his throat.

He growled with pleasure and pressed his body into hers, his groin so hard he was sure she couldn't help but feel it. Would it scare her off? But then she writhed into him, adjusting her body, nestling him against her.

He couldn't catch his breath. He couldn't believe it. Laura Bailey.

He wanted to feel her. He had to feel her, but he was

afraid. If he'd fantasized about kissing her, how much had
he dreamed of running his hands along that taut body? Of
cupping those hot little breasts?

He couldn't stop himself. He had to. Slowly he inched
his hand up. The fabric of her shirt tugged beneath his palm.
He rested his hand on her rib cage. Her chest rose and fell
as though she were panting to catch her breath. Her heart
hammered through her bones, through her skin. He felt it
beating against his hand, pounding through his body.

"Yes," she whispered, and brought her mouth back to his,
kissing him harder, more frantically.

He didn't need more urging than that and slid his hand
the last few inches to her breast. So firm, her nipple was a
hard peak under his thumb.

She moaned, and he did, too. He pulled from her, so
starved for her, he had to speak through his clenched jaw.
"I've wanted you so bad."

"You, too." She stole small kisses along his jaw. "God,
Eddie, you, too."

He pulled from her in disbelief. His heart was punching
against his chest, but he had to ask, "You have?"

"I did. I have." She looked as frustrated as he felt. "But
you were so damned stupid in high school. I wanted you,
but you never asked me out."

He couldn't believe his ears. "I was totally in love with
you in high school."

"You were a jerk."

He pressed his body against hers and gently raked his
hands through her hair, cradling her head close against his
chest. "Not anymore, Laura. I swear. If you still want me,
I'm all yours."

Twenty-two

❧

"Finally," Helen murmured, seeing Laura walk in the front door. And what was with the dopey smile?

Laura's eyes found her instantly. "There you are, Helen."

There *she* was? She'd been trying to call the girl all morning. When Laura finally got around to answering, she was the one who'd acted put out. She'd been out at the old Timber Creek ranch . . . of course. She seemed to make a hobby out of pestering poor Eddie. She'd invited these television people and then proceeded to take off, running around, waving her petitions, hounding Eddie, flittering around, doing whatever it was she did. Laura got to be free and easy, *so* busy keeping herself fit and pretty, while most days all *Helen* felt was used up.

"I've been here all—"

"Hey, Dad," Laura greeted her father at the end of the bar. "I take it that's the window?" She stormed to the shattered window and torn screen, and Helen heard her mutter, "Of course *he* couldn't deal with this."

Helen followed her. "Your film people broke it with their microphone pole."

"It's called a boom," Laura said distractedly.

Fine. "Your film people broke it with their *boom.*"

"They're not *my* film people." Laura rounded on her. "They're here for the whole town."

Helen could only shrug at that. She didn't care who they'd come for; all she knew was they were about to be the straw that broke her back. They disappeared during the day, but mornings and evenings they crawled all over the place, making themselves at home, ordering her around, asking for things way outside her normal responsibilities . . . would she order pizzas, find them duct tape, buy the woman a box of tampons, for goodness' sake.

She studied the window—didn't seem like such an emergency, really. "Can't we just tape it up till it gets fixed?"

"No, we can't just *tape it up.*" Laura looked at her like she'd grown a second head. "We have people *filming* here."

"Can Hope help?" Their new girl had yet to prove her worth. She was book smart, sure, but she seemed pretty helpless when it came to simple day-to-day chores.

"Where *is* Hope?"

"I haven't seen her." She already had three kids to keep track of—babysitting new employees definitely was not in her job description.

The Bailey girl exploded into action, calling back to the kitchen, "Hey, Sorrow. We've lost Hope."

The Kidd sisters sat at a nearby booth. Pearl turned and said, "You can't lose hope, dear."

Laura looked like she was strung tight enough to snap. "But she hasn't—"

"Not that kind of hope." Helen patted the woman on the shoulder, feeling glad to have Laura's laser eyes shifting off *her* back for the moment.

Understanding registered in Laura's eyes. "Oh. Hope is

the name of the new girl," she told Pearl, using a louder, slower, talking-to-senior-citizens voice.

"We're old," Ruby told her. "We're not deaf, dear."

Helen would bet money that the younger of the two Kidd sisters was, in fact, quite deaf. She hid her smile as she went to grab the pitcher to refill their waters. A few decades ago, those women could've given someone like the Bailey girl a run for her money.

Pearl smiled blandly. "I've always thought Hope was a lovely name."

"Is that the plump girl?" Ruby asked.

"She is not plump," Helen chimed in, feeling a bit put out. Just because those women were skin and bones in their orthopedic sandals gave them no right.

"And Faith," Pearl said, still in her own thoughts. "That's another pretty name."

"You talking about that Hope girl?" Bear swiveled around in his seat. "Sure seems plump to me."

The man next to him at the bar elbowed him. "Gotta have something to hold on to."

"Prudence is pretty, too," Pearl continued, "though you never hear that anymore."

Ruby leaned in. "Do you remember Prudence Jacobson?"

Pearl gasped. "Scarlet fever took her."

"Such a tragedy." Ruby clucked.

A man at the end of the bar chimed in, "Are you kidding? Hope is hot."

Pearl nodded. "If you mean the plump girl, she's lovely."

Ruby pitched her voice loud for her sister. "She's not plump, dear."

Laura gave a funny little aggravated cry. "Would you all just—" There was a buzzing, and she slid her phone from her jeans pocket to check it. She made a weird face, then tucked it back away. "Dammit."

It was the third time since walking in the door that Laura

had screened a call, checking the ID, then letting it go to voice mail.

It didn't bode well for Helen. Were the Baileys hiring her replacement, and Laura didn't want to field the call in front of her? Or, had Laura met someone? Was that where she'd disappeared to this morning? A man would take the girl's mind off things for a while . . . until it went south and she took it out on *them*.

She couldn't resist probing. "New boyfriend?"

Laura's head shot up, and her deer-in-the-headlights expression made Helen think for a moment she'd hit the nail on the head, but then the girl waved it off. "No, it's a work thing."

"A tavern thing?" she asked, doing her best to keep her voice even, while inside she cursed because, *dammit*, Laura *was* looking to replace her.

She should've known. Lately, the woman had watched her every move, acting like she was just waiting for an excuse to chuck her out the door. And with Rob more remote than ever, she was in a panic about it.

If her husband was sleeping around . . . Her stomach churned at the thought. If he left her the way she feared he might, she'd need some way to support her family.

Jobs like this didn't exactly abound in a town the size of Sierra Falls, and what else was she qualified for besides waitressing and tending bar? It was all she'd ever done. She supposed she could drive all the way to Silver City for work, but then who'd help with the kids?

"No," Laura said distractedly, "it's my old CEO from San Francisco."

It took her a moment to register the reply, and then she exclaimed, "Oh!" It *hadn't* been tavern business. Her job was safe. For now. "You mean your boss from your old company?"

"Yeah, he's called . . ." But then Laura seemed to tune

in to just who she was talking to. "Never mind. We've got
to deal with this window."

She was busy, not stupid. "I went ahead and put a call in
to Eddie," she said, but then paled to see the girl's strange
reaction.

Stupidly, she hadn't considered Laura's hatred of the guy.
At the time, all she'd thought was how she didn't want to be
phoning Jack, a married man, so she'd just called the other
Jessup instead.

Helen cringed. She'd messed up now. She wanted to rail
at Laura to grow up, but she needed to play nicey-nice if she
wanted to keep her job. "Sorry, I guess I should've called
his brother."

"No. Eddie's . . ." And then the woman went and blushed.
"Eddie's good."

Holy cow. There was no explosion. No bitching. The girl
actually *blushed*.

Helen was treading dangerous personal territory, but
curiosity got the better of her. "I thought you hated Eddie."

"I don't hate Eddie," Laura snapped. "I've never hated
Eddie."

What was the saying about protesting too much? She just
shrugged. "Whatever you say."

Laura sharpened her eyes and crossed her arms at her
chest. The bitch was back. "So, table four? You *are* on the
clock, right?"

"Sure thing, boss." She forced a smile on her face.
Nicey-nice.

She'd been avoiding table four. June Harlan lunching with
Jack Jessup's wife, Tina. But Laura was right, it looked like
their iced teas needed freshening.

She shuddered to think what they might be talking about,
heads leaned close together like that. Every time she
approached, their voices got louder and their faces brighter,
like they'd only been chatting instead of doing the gossiping
she suspected they were doing.

June's husband ran the hardware store and was Rob's boss, so they probably had plenty to jaw about where she was concerned. Had Rob's mistress ever been in to see him at work? Maybe that was where he'd met her.

Maybe she was here even now. Frowning, she scanned the room as she went to the bar to grab the pitcher.

Billy had come in, headed straight for Sorrow in the kitchen, and she overheard them back there. Sorrow was teasing, something about being bad and needing a patdown.

It was the last thing she needed to hear. Her morning coffee sloshed in her belly, sour and burning. If only she had a reliable man, it would all be so much easier. The Baileys thought they had trouble—one broken window, for God's sake—but she could school them on trouble. Trouble was her middle name.

She refilled the tea pitcher, wiped her hands on a rag, grabbed a fresh bowl of cut lemons, and headed back to serve June and Tina.

If Rob was getting it on the side, it was only a matter of time before he kicked her to the curb. And if her husband left, there'd be no meeting anyone for *her*. No nice sheriff would ride into *her* life. She could always try that Internet dating stuff, but what man out there wanted a woman with three young kids?

The ladies were leaned closer than ever, and she braced herself to face them. Would that she had a friend to gossip with, but she could only dream of having that kind of time. It made her feel more the outsider than ever. Slowing, she overheard snippets as she approached.

". . . never in."

"Three kids. What would she do?"

It was like she'd been punched. She forced a cheery smile, though she was gutted. Dying inside. "Can I get you anything else?"

Their heads sprang apart. "Thanks, Helen."

"We were just talking about Craig," June said, referring

to Tina's son, just off to boot camp. "He says Lake Michigan is pretty in the summer."

"Mm-hm." She topped off their teas. Sure they were.

She lived in a town full of judgmental biddies. All she needed was for Marlene Jessup to drive back into town, and then it'd be a party.

"Three kids." There was no doubt—that had to be her.

So that was how it was. Rob was probably fixing to leave her. Maybe he'd already made the plans. Did everyone at the hardware store know it? Did everyone in town know except for her? She made herself smile, though she feared she probably just looked like she had a screw loose.

That was it, then. Fine. She handed the ladies their check, grinning like a wild woman.

More than ever she needed to keep that grin pasted on her face. Maybe one day it'd turn real. Maybe one day she'd really feel like smiling.

But for now she needed a plan.

Twenty-three

Eddie was getting out of his truck, and as Laura watched him from a distance like this, everyone else faded away. He'd always been one of the best-looking guys in school, but now that he was older . . . *Good Lord*, but the man was hot. White T-shirt, faded jeans, tan work boots.

Memories of their kiss had been so unreal in her head, but here he was, in the flesh. She'd known a flicker of such relief in his arms, like she could let go for a second. It was probably just hearing news of Fairview's scaled-back construction, but still, that fleeting comfort, the momentary feeling of finding something, had haunted her all day.

She'd spent the morning racking her brain for excuses to go see him again or have him out to the lodge. Lucky for her, the History Network guys—hungover, no doubt—had given her the opportunity in the form of a shattered window. She hoped finally to shake this feeling of unreality.

She needed to focus. Regroup. She didn't want to hurt Eddie and Jack's business or—God forbid—to take money away from impoverished kids, but surely there was a way to stop Fairview in a way that worked for everyone.

And now, to complicate matters, the president of her old company had been calling, leaving messages saying how he'd fired the wrong person. Hired the wrong vice president. She was the one who'd been right for the job, but he'd been blinded by her no-good ex, Patrick. His apologies were effusive, and he had an offer, too. If she'd come back, he'd double her pay. Healthy stock bonus package. Top-of-the-line insurance, and her whole family could be covered. He was a smart man. He'd caught that her dad had had a stroke, and it didn't take a genius to deduce what their premiums must've been.

Talk about vindication. She still hadn't taken any of his calls, but the attention only made her more confident she'd be able to solve these problems at home.

A whole other possible future opened itself to her, and it'd given her pause.

In the same way Eddie was giving her pause.

For so long, she'd had it in her head that she was giving up men, and it was a shock to find one preoccupying her thoughts. Surely Eddie didn't count, though. They'd known each other all their lives.

It wasn't like she was going to marry the guy or anything. No way. She was accustomed to certain things—nice car, nice restaurants—things that Eddie couldn't provide.

But they could mess around. Especially now that he'd proven he wasn't that bad a guy. He'd challenged Fairview on her behalf, and that was something.

He walked through the tavern door, strode to the bar like he owned the place, and slung his tools by a stool on the floor. He scanned the room till he found her, then gave her a smile that was darker and more meaningful than his usual carefree grins. "Hey, darlin'."

She felt her face turn red to the roots. "Hi, Eddie." He'd been calling her *darlin'* since they were teens, but now it was different. Now she knew what it felt like to have him whisper the endearment hot in her ear as she offered her body to him for the taking. She took a steadying breath. "Thanks for coming. I know you're . . . busy."

And that was when she remembered just one of the many reasons why his hotness had been so far from her mind lately. He'd been busy . . . at the ranch. The threat to her family's business.

"You know I'll always come for you." He got a naughty look on his face.

She cleared her throat. "Helen, would you please get Eddie a beer?" She knew *she* could use a cold one.

"Make it a Coke. Thanks." He gave the waitress a genuine smile. "I never drink and work."

He went to the window to assess the damage. Opening the sash all the way, he jiggled the screen free and pulled it through to the inside. "Hey, Bear," he called to her father, sitting in his spot by at bar. "You're not having the best luck with these screens, are you?"

Bear only grunted.

"You could use this as an opportunity, you know. Finally upgrade to better-insulated windows. They have really good energy-efficient ones now. You get a tax break and everything."

Bear grunted again.

"I take that as a no." Eddie tilted the screen this way and that. "Well, I'm afraid this is beyond patching. But"—he leaned down, studying the window, knocking at the sash, scraping his thumbnail against the old wood—"the mullion is old, but it'll be easy enough to pop out the glass and replace it."

"Hey, pretty lady." Dan appeared at her shoulder, and she had to bite her cheek, seeing his gelled hair and thumb ring through new eyes. "Sorry again."

She watched Eddie's shoulders stiffen and had a brief internal debate, feeling oddly tempted to flirt with Dan just to see how Eddie would respond.

He said he'd called Fairview for her. That he respected her. Part of her couldn't believe that Eddie might actually, truly like her for her. She believed he *wanted* her, but his being fond of her was a different story all together.

"Don't sweat it," she told the producer. "You can stop apologizing. Stuff happens."

Actually, more than the usual stuff was happening. If the lodge hadn't needed the publicity so much, she'd have kicked Dan's crew out by now. They stayed up till all hours every night, and the front parking lot had become the guys' communal ashtray.

He slung an easy arm around her shoulders. "Let me make it up to you."

She became acutely aware of Eddie, watching how his movements slowed. Was he listening? He'd made fun of the city guys—was he jealous? Protective? Possessive?

Dan gave her a nudge. "You checking out the hired help?"

"What?" She realized she'd been staring at Eddie's backside, and man, was it one fine specimen. "No."

"Hey, Lola." Kat, their camerawoman, came over to see what was going on. "Sorry again about the window." Her eyes roved from the broken glass to Eddie, then simply snagged and hung there. She mouthed, *Is he single?*

Her chest tightened. *Was* he single?

No. Yes. Maybe. Not for girls with spiked hair, she bet.

What was wrong with her? Why was she fuming? Why didn't she answer Kat?

Eddie took that moment to turn around. Seeing the tableau, he got a funny look on his face. "Can I have your help here for a sec, Laura?"

She jumped into action, realizing she'd hoped for just this sort of excuse to talk to him, even if it was about windows. She'd always been such a pro with men, but something about this situation made her feel shy.

"I need something to put the broken glass in. Like a trash bin. Or even a large bowl." He'd put on his work gloves, and she was momentarily mesmerized by the masculine sight. The worn leather framed his forearms, highlighting ropes of muscle that flexed with each movement. There was a sun-faded dusting of hair along his weathered skin. "Laura?"

Her eyes flew to his, and a knowing smile was waiting for her. He pitched his voice low. "How about I finish this up and buy you dinner?"

Dan ambled up, too close. "What's the damage?"

She fled behind the bar to grab the small plastic trash can they kept for rags. It gave her a second to gather her wits. Dinner with Eddie? She hadn't really thought past that first kiss.

Meanwhile, the producer was peering at the window like he was studying something of great importance. "Can you fix it?"

Eddie gave him a funny look. "This thing? Sure, I can fix it. A child could fix it."

Dan's posture went stiff, making him look like he'd challenge the other man to arm-wrestle if only Eddie wouldn't have whupped his butt at it.

All the male posturing was making her uneasy. She put the trash can on the floor and occupied herself by starting to pick up the shards. "I can help you get the glass."

"You won't dare," Eddie said instantly. "I got this." He stepped in to take over. "Since the window was broken from the inside, most of the glass went out, anyway. I'll clean up those bits when I'm done here." He began to scoop up the shards. "Can't let you cut those pretty hands."

Dan snorted. "Cheeky."

Eddie stood and tossed the pieces in the plastic bin. With a nod to the window, he asked, "What idiot did this, anyway?"

Laura had to bite back a smirk. She was pretty sure Helen had mentioned precisely which idiot it'd been, but she said evenly, "It was an accident."

Dan came to stand beside her again, whispering in her ear, "He doesn't like me much."

She flinched away, wondering how much *she* was liking Dan at the moment. "Doesn't appear so."

"Our boom smashed it," Dan said more loudly in answer. "Accident, dude."

"Dude," Eddie mumbled.

They watched as he deftly popped out shards of the broken pane, then used a tool to scrape out the remaining dirt, paint, and glass.

"Cool," Dan said. "What is that you're using?"

Eddie didn't look up from his work. "Five-in-one tool."

"Gotta get me one of those."

"Seriously, Danny?" She raised a brow. "For your toolbox?"

"Hey, I'm handy." He inched closer, studying Eddie's work. "Not as handy as this guy. But I guess when you do it for a living . . ." He clapped a chummy hand on Eddie's shoulder.

At the unexpected contact, Eddie's arm slipped, and his hand flew through the opening, his forearm grazing along the mullion still jagged with glass.

"What the—" Eddie hopped back, shaking out his hand, looking like he'd rather be using it to punch Dan. "A little space, please."

Laura gasped, seeing the blood gush along his skin. "Oh my God, Eddie, you're hurt."

"Dude, so sorry." Dan looked panicked.

"No big thing." Eddie scowled at the cut, fisting and unfisting his hand. "This part of the arm bleeds a lot."

"I'll say." She ran to get a clean rag from behind the bar. "Here, wrap it up."

He wound it around his arm, cinching it tight. "It's fine. Really."

Dan backed away. "Hey, I should be going, anyway. The guys want to check out that bar cross town."

The look she gave him said that was probably a good idea.

The dinnertime rush was starting in earnest. The hum of diners swirled around her, and Helen and Sorrow could've probably used help, but she was worried about Eddie, already back at it.

She let herself take a moment to sit down. She needed to think. Her phone buzzed and buzzed again as the calls from her old boss had been replaced by a text assault, and they were all so flattering.

Come back. We need you. Stock + incentives.
I'm sorry.
Patrick's gone. Fired his ass.
There's nobody better than you.
You're an ace. Come back.

She'd longed for respect. Had felt so stung when the job that should've been hers was taken away.

And now she wished she could've told someone about this new job offer, but she was too wary. Nobody would understand. She didn't have the best track record in Sierra Falls, and in some ways it'd become more important to prove herself at home. If her family heard she'd been offered her old job back—check that, offered an even better job—even if she swore she was home to stay, they'd just be waiting for her to leave.

But she didn't want to leave Sierra Falls. Against all odds and despite what she would've guessed, she was actually contented. Challenged, even. Never in her wildest dreams would she have imagined she'd want to stay, but there she was, watching Eddie Jessup patch her window, and she was *happy* about it.

And what an engrossing sight it was. The windows were a standard size, and he'd cut a replacement pane before coming. She tried not to stare too unabashedly as he made quick work of it, but it was hard when right in front of her was a white T-shirt tugged tight over a broad set of shoulders, muscles flexing as he chipped and sanded and pried, doing all manner of capable man things.

He was such a guy's guy, hanging in there till he finished the job, despite the gash on his arm that must've been killing him. He was acting immune to the pain.

She'd known guys like this—she'd grown up around mountain men, and heck, she had an overly macho brother. But her dating life had mostly been in San Francisco, and she'd never *been* with a guy like this. The most dangerous thing her dates had ever faced was weaving in and out of rush-hour traffic. The most painful thing her fiancé had ever encountered was the hangover after his best friend's bachelor party.

"All done." He dropped his tools back in his box and recinched the rag around his arm.

She slid to her feet, feeling a little bummed the show was over. "That was fast."

"I told you. A kid could've done it."

She gestured to his arm. "May I?" She didn't know what she was doing—she needed to get back to work—but she kept prolonging their time together. "Maybe someone should take a look at it for you."

"Like a doctor?" he asked incredulously.

"Yes, like a doctor."

He stuck it out for her perusal. "You're cute."

"Cute?" She gingerly peeled the rag away, and a fresh line of blood appeared along his cut.

"Yeah. Cute." He stretched and tilted his arm. "It's not that big a deal."

"Maybe I'm just worried you'll turn around and sue us," she joked as she wound it back up. She'd known men like this, which meant she also knew they could be tough-guy idiots who'd rather bleed to death than actually ask for help. "Come on, let me at least clean it. I'll fix you right up . . ."

And then you can get out of here, she'd meant to say, but

he stepped closer, and suddenly the room felt ten degrees hotter.

"Can't say no to that, Doctor Laura."

"We have to go back to the lodge," she said, her face hot. "That's where the good first-aid kit is."

"Even better."

She was painfully aware—of her stride, of the patrons' glances, of Helen's stare—as they made what felt like an endless trek across the dining room and back to the main lodge.

She led him upstairs, but he paused by her bedroom door. "Hey, this your room?"

"Yes," she said warily. "How did you know?" She leaned in to peek, searching for the clue that'd given it away.

"It's obvious." He strolled in, and she had no choice but to follow.

"It is?"

He pointed. "Purple bedspread and lamp. I went to school with you, remember?"

"Yeah, so?"

"Everything was purple with you. Purple backpack. Purple winter coat. Purple jeans." He grinned. "I especially liked those purple jeans."

She'd forgotten the purple. "The color is plum."

"Purple, plum, whatever. It's clear it hasn't been changed since you were a kid." He pulled out her desk chair and plopped down, leaning on an elbow to avidly study all her memorabilia.

She felt herself blush. "My parents didn't see the need to change it, and it didn't seem to matter. I guess I always assumed Mom would eventually get rid of everything and turn it into a sewing room."

"Nah, not your folks. You could be an old woman, and they'll still have your room done up like it was yesterday."

The comment gave her pause. Was that really true? Was she really so valued?

He peered at the photos pinned on her bulletin board. "I'd have thought you'd be the one to have redone it by now. Some modern Ikea look, or maybe Japanese antiques."

"Are you making fun of me?"

"Sugar, I wouldn't dream of it."

"Mm-hm," she mumbled doubtfully. She went to the bathroom to grab the first-aid stuff, and when she returned, Eddie was standing, eyeing every last item on that bulletin board.

It was the same junk she'd had in high school. A Hello Kitty postcard. A 13.1 sticker from when she'd run a half marathon in Sonoma. A picture of her in her cheerleading uniform. She'd been meaning to go through it with a big trash bag, but there was never any time.

"I didn't know you *climbed*."

She came up behind him to study the picture of her on an indoor rock wall. "Oh, that. That's from a couple years ago. I sent it to Mom, and for some reason she hung it up." She did a little self-effacing shrug—parents could be embarrassing, even if you *were* twenty-eight. "It was from a team-building thing at my old company."

"Let me see." He shocked her by taking one of her hands in his. Goose bumps shivered up her arms at the feel of those warm, large hands enveloping hers. "They don't look like they belong to a climber."

She tugged away. "I'm not a *real* climber," she said, though it was kind of a lie. It'd been one of her favorite workouts. It was indoors and perfectly safe, but she found such joy in it nonetheless. She was always so regimented in her life, and dangling high above the ground was the one time she felt free. Felt dangerous. "I used to go to a climbing gym in the city. No big deal."

"Seems like a big deal to me." He turned his attention to an old shot from her high school cheerleading days. "Not as big a deal as *this*, though." He leaned closer, grinning. "God, I had such fantasies about you in that little skirt."

She plucked the picture from the wall and put it face-down.

He turned back to her and suddenly he was *right there.* "You always were a hottie, Laura Bailey."

The compliment overwhelmed her. There was a depth to his gaze that suggested he spoke to so much more than her looks—that she was a hottie because of those photos and trinkets and purple bedspread.

It felt like she'd inadvertently spilled a secret she hadn't meant to tell. She felt vulnerable, and vulnerability made her nervous.

Instead of responding, she opened the bottle of hydrogen peroxide and soaked a cotton ball with it. "Give me your arm." She dabbed the peroxide with abandon.

"Still are," he said in that voice . . . that voice he got. "Hotter than ever."

She ignored him and dabbed harder. "This doesn't look so bad." Now that he'd stopped bleeding, she could tell the cut wasn't nearly as horrific as all that blood had implied.

"Hey, that stuff stinks. Whoa"—he flinched—"and stings."

He tried to pull away, but she held on. "It's good for you. Now stand still."

She finished with the cotton ball and felt his eyes on her as she put on the antibiotic ointment. "Maybe you should have your brother check it out," she said. "It might scar."

She was liking him too much. Liking *this* too much.

"I thought women went for men with scars." The moment she sealed the last Band-Aid on his skin, he brought his hand to her face, tucking her hair behind her ear. "How about you, Laura? You always liked the bad boys."

She ignored the comment and instead backed away from his touch. "Be sure to keep it covered."

She hadn't wanted this. She didn't want a boyfriend, least of all Eddie. They'd known each other just too long for this not to end with either a ring or a breakup. In her mind, in this small town, both options were completely unpalatable.

"If it got infected, you'd have a big problem," she said tersely.

"Laura, babe. Look at me." He cupped her cheek.

She held her breath. Looking at him was a bad idea. It was all too easy to lose her way in those blue eyes.

"I've got only one problem at the moment," he said.

"What?"

"I *really* need you to kiss me again."

Twenty-four

≈

Laura knew she desired Eddie—what hot-blooded American woman wouldn't? But how badly did she *want* him? "I need to think."

He quirked a smile. "What's there to think about?"

"Well, for one, consider what you're getting into."

"What I'm getting into?" A medley of expressions crossed his face, all of them some variation of amused and dirty. "Darlin', I can think of ten responses to that, and I don't think you'd like one of them."

She removed his hand from her face. "You know what I mean."

"No, Laura, I'm afraid I don't."

"Think about it. Sierra Falls is tiny. We'll see each other everywhere. At the gas station, tavern, grocery store . . ."

"Sounds good to me."

"And what will people think?" Did she want everyone to see her as his girlfriend—or someday ex-girlfriend? And what about her family? Or his family? She ran into Jessups *everywhere*.

He stepped closer. "I don't give a good Goddamn what people think. *I* think I'd like to kiss you."

She wanted that, too, but . . . She tried to think of another reason. "Eddie, really . . ."

"*Really*," he coaxed in a husky voice. He wrapped his hand around her waist, easing her closer, and *God*, he felt so good.

"I've got work to do," she said weakly.

"Just one kiss."

She clutched that bottle of peroxide to her like armor and pressed her other palm against his chest to hold him back. Did he have to have such a thin T-shirt and such a hard, hot body? "I've got to get back to the tavern."

She couldn't be doing this. Couldn't be doing it with Eddie. *Eddie Jessup*, for goodness' sake, the twelfth-grade screwup. The guy who'd toilet-papered the principal's house. Who'd shown up to prom drunk.

Who used his own money to take underprivileged kids on camping trips.

"Just one kiss." He ran a finger down her cheek. "Come on. I see you caving."

She had to get a handle on this. "We *cannot* be hooking up in my childhood bedroom."

"Why the hell not?" When she didn't reply, his face warmed into the sweetest smile, his eyes crinkling at the corners. "Fine, sugar. It's your show. No hooking up." He added innocently, "Just one kiss."

She wasn't strong enough to simply turn and walk out on him, but she knew a man like him would need mollifying. "One kiss. Fine." She stood on her tippy-toes and gave him a quick, chaste peck on the cheek. "Okay?" But as she returned to her feet, her chest brushed against his and her body began to pulse.

Their eyes met. Held.

"That all you got for me?" His voice was a deep, rich rasp. His eyes were glued on her mouth, and they were hooded, dark in a way that made her shiver. He angled his pelvis to hers and, with a wicked half smile, brushed his jeans against her ever so slightly. He was a rock.

Her breath caught. "I don't usually go this fast," she managed.

"Fast?" He gave a husky little laugh. "Laura, we've known each other since we were five. Any slower and our next kiss will be in a retirement home. Come on." He leaned close to whisper, "Just one more."

"Aw, hell." The peroxide bottle dropped to the ground as she wrapped her arms around his neck, pulling him down and kissing him hard.

He moaned, and the feel of it reverberated through her. She opened her mouth wider, grabbed his shoulders and tugged him closer. For a moment, she couldn't get him close enough. Couldn't touch him enough. She ran her hands through his hair, pressed her breasts against his chest, chafed her palms against the sandpaper stubble along his cheeks.

He was two people. He was Eddie Jessup, the bad boy. The one you didn't bring home to Mama. The Eddie who'd always tickled her imagination. Who'd made her wonder *how* and *if.* The Eddie it felt so deliciously wrong to kiss.

But then he was also Eddie the man, who'd fixed their window, and called her dad *sir,* and phoned Fairview just for her. The one who mentored at-risk kids.

Which Eddie was her body responding to? Young Eddie might've been a bad boy, but Eddie the man was far more dangerous.

When they parted, his eyes bored into hers like he might peer down to her soul.

What was happening?

She didn't want to think about it. Didn't want to think about this feeling she had when he looked at her like that. This feeling of relief. Of security. Of protection.

So she kissed him again. Told herself she was kissing Eddie the bad boy. The one she'd sneaked peeks at in homeroom. The one she'd ogled whenever he'd played any sort of ball on all kinds of fields ever since they were twelve.

She'd made the move, and his response was instant. Now he was the one to angle his mouth and take the kiss deeper. This time it was his fingers in her hair, tipping back her head. It was his hand roving her body, kneading her, and— *oh God . . .*

She pulled away with a gasp. His fingers were cupped over her breast, where he'd been doing amazing, magical things. She cradled her hand over his and felt the thumping of her own heart.

He grazed a thumb over her peak, giving her a questioning look. "You still with me?" His gaze was quiet and intense, like he might be able to read the real her.

Yes, she realized. She was. "I'm with you."

He gave her his crinkle-eyed smile, and a feeling of such tenderness warmed her, but then it was heat that followed, cascading from her chest all the way down to her toes. Had she always loved his smile? Was it just that she'd been afraid of what it meant? Afraid of how it'd made her think dirty things with this bad boy?

She promised herself she'd consider all of it . . . later. For now, she had to kiss him just one more time. She stood on her toes, running her hands up the nape of his neck. "So kiss me already."

He did, but then this time he was the one to pull away first. "I thought you said slower."

"Whatever," she muttered. Feeling a bit breathless, she tugged him back.

With a low, rumbling laugh, he brought his mouth down, trailing kisses along her jaw, down her neck. He was going lower, and every atom in her body wanted and feared it both.

She swallowed hard, trying to calm her body down a

notch. "I can't believe we're making out in my high school bedroom."

"Another of my fantasies to check off the list." He kissed below her throat, dipping even lower. Her shirt had a low scoop neck, and he was grazing dangerously close to the neckline.

She finally registered his words. "This was a fantasy?"

"Oh yeah." He roamed back up to kiss her jaw. Her cheek. Dipped in to take her mouth.

She pulled back. "What else did you fantasize about?"

His eyes sparkled. "You still got that cheerleading costume lying around?"

"Pig." She gave him a little shove, but there was laughter in her voice.

He laughed broadly, scooping her tightly to him. "You pushing me around like that . . . that might be somewhere on the list, too."

She froze. "Seriously?"

"No." His voice pitched deeper. "But this is."

He lifted her, and instinctively she wrapped her legs around his waist. She felt so exhilaratingly small in his arms. He carried her across the room until her back touched the wall.

She curved her body, grinding into him. She'd told him slower, but now all she could think was faster, faster, more.

He braced his hand on her purple-flowered wall, kissing her in bad-boy ways that would've horrified the popular girl who'd done the decorating.

There was a knock. The door creaked. Then, "Oh, jeez, sorry. Oh."

She unhooked her legs and swung her feet to the ground. "What the—?"

Eddie's firm, protective hand didn't budge from the small of her back, as Hope looked from her, to him, and back again.

"Sorry," the woman sputtered. "I was . . . So sorry, Laura. I just couldn't . . ."

"What?" Her voice sounded angry even to her own ears. She took a calming breath. "What do you need, Hope?"

"I couldn't find the hand towels."

"You couldn't find the hand towels," she repeated flatly. She stepped away, and finally Eddie let her. "They're in the linen closet, with all the other towels." She registered the stack of sheets balanced in Hope's arms. "Wait, what have you got?"

"We have a couple checking in tomorrow morning, so I thought I'd get the room ready now."

"I thought they were staying in the Gold Rush room."

"They are."

"Those sheets are for the Pioneer Suite."

"Oh. Sorry. But these are"—Hope glanced at the sheets then back at her—"they looked like they'd fit."

"Go to the room. I'll be right there." When Hope left, she looked up at Eddie, who wore an aggravatingly amused expression. "I should help her."

"It is really a disaster if the Pioneers use the Gold Rush sheets?"

"There's a system, Eddie."

"I can see." He wandered to her bureau and began to nonchalantly poke at the stuff she kept there. She knew he was probably disappointed, but was that uncertainty she read on his face? *Eddie Jessup*, uncertain? "Can I buy you dinner?" he asked.

She paused, shook her head. "There's no time."

"Then I guess I'll just have to be happy I got dessert." Before she had a chance to respond, he added, "So when's the next time we get to make out in your room?"

He picked up her pinecone, and instantly she said, "Please don't touch that."

"This?" He raised his brows, incredulous. "It's just a pinecone. There are a thousand of them on the ground outside your front door."

She nervously eyed it in his hands. "Please."

"Hey, sorry." His voice got tender, and he put it back down. "I didn't know it was special."

"I know, I'm sorry." Now it was her turn to feel uncertain. "I didn't mean to get weird on you. It's just . . . my grandfather gave it to me when I was little. I know . . . heirloom pinecone. Probably sounds stupid, huh?"

But he remained serious. "Your dad's dad?"

"No, Grandpa Jim on my mom's side."

"I remember him."

That surprised her. "You do?"

"I pay attention, Laura."

"Well, it's not *just* a pinecone." She came and shifted it to its proper place. "He used to burn them in the fireplace. Dad hated the smell." She smirked. "Sometimes I think that's why Grandpa did it. Anyway, he'd help me gather them. He had a special basket for me and everything."

"That's kind of adorable."

It was, she supposed. More than that, it had always made her feel special. "It was just something we did, just him and me. He'd bake with Sorrow and play backgammon with BJ. But with me it was walks and pinecones. He'd take me out to the falls . . . I still go sometimes, when I'm feeling low. I always take a quick detour on the road back to the city. When I'm there, I feel connected, like he's looking down on me and I'm not alone anymore." She shrugged, a little abashed. "I always bring him a pinecone."

She realized Eddie was looking at her funny. "What?"

He tucked his hand along her waist and slid it around her. "Just . . . you."

"Just me what?" Had she said too much? She had to lean away to look up at him. "Am I being silly?"

"No, on the contrary. Sometimes you act all tough. But really I think you're a lot softer than you let on. You're kind of like that pinecone there," he said, nuzzling her playfully. "Hard on the outside with the tender meat inside."

She pulled away. "Tender meat? Um, ew."

"Sure, nature girl. Didn't your grandfather tell you on your walks?" He pointed to the pinecone. "You can eat those, you know."

She thought about those petit fours she'd had with the Kidd sisters, and their talk of how the hard shell masked the sweetness inside. She'd been told the same thing twice now. Did she really act *that* tough? Might she really have a tender side? She guessed both were maybe true.

People always saw just one thing with her. Commenting on how rigid she was. How disciplined. How controlling. How thin or how fit. How this, how that. So how was it Eddie Jessup saw past all that? It was unsettling but comforting, too.

"You can really eat these?" She plucked the pinecone from her dresser, and even after all these years, the hard, sharp ridges poked her. "Wouldn't you hurt yourself?"

"No, goof. Where do you think pine *nuts* come from?" He pointed to the tips. "If you're ever stuck in the woods, find a pinecone."

"How do you get the nuts out of there?"

"You can't do it with your bare hands. I'll show you sometime." He carefully took it and put it back in its exact place. "You deny it, but I think you really are nature girl at heart."

She almost said no. She wasn't this secretly soft, nature person he was talking about, and there would be no next time besides.

But instead she heard herself say, "Yes. Show me."

Twenty-five

~

Laura sat in the chair at Claire's Cuts studying herself in the mirror. She and her sister had taken a break from the lodge for a little personal maintenance. It'd been Sorrow's idea, and Laura had acted resistant, but really, she didn't mind the idea of a little prettying up. She told herself it was just for her, that she liked looking good for herself.

It certainly had nothing to do with any Jessups.

"It'd be easy to brighten it up." Claire ran her fingers through Laura's freshly trimmed waves as they discussed adding some highlights. "Conceal the grays."

"Conceal the *whats*?" She spun in the chair.

"Some grays." Claire caught her eyes in the mirror. "Don't worry, it's just a few."

She darted her eyes to Sorrow, seated in a neighboring chair. "Can you see them?"

"Yeah. No." Her sister gave her an apologetic shrug. "Maybe."

"Damn," she whispered as she peered at herself in the mirror. "I can't believe you found gray hair."

"You should do it," Sorrow said. "Why not?" She was in a neighboring chair where she was flipping through an old *InStyle* magazine. She shut it, looked at the cover, then opened it again. "Claire, this is two years old. It's not even 'in style' anymore."

"It's the 'Best Of' issue *and* it has Carrie Underwood on the cover."

Sorrow displayed the cover. "Hey, Laura, you can learn *Ten Ways to Reduce Stress*."

She was still stuck on the gray hair sighting and shot back, "How come *you* don't have any gray?"

"There's not a lot," the stylist said reassuringly.

"I didn't even see it till she pointed it out." Sorrow traded the *InStyle* for a more recent *Us Weekly*. "This is more like it."

Claire riffled through her hair, bouncing it in her palms. "My advice? We take the highlights up a bit, but"—she put her hands on her shoulders to stress her point—"then *you* need to relax more. That's the only thing that'll stop the premature aging."

She slouched in her chair, grumbling. "Premature aging."

Sorrow held up a photo spread. "Hey, ladies, *who wore it better*?"

She only needed to give it a quick glance. "Easy. Kate Middleton. Duh. She's always going to win that one."

"That girl?" Claire tsked. "Too skinny."

She glanced over again. "What did that other woman do to her eyes?" Then leaned in for a closer look. "Who is that, anyway?"

"Who knows anymore?" Sorrow flipped to another page. "So many of these people are just famous for being famous."

The stylist steered Laura back upright. "Are we going to do this or not? I've got to pick up Abbie from swim team soon."

"You think I should?" If she still lived in the city, she wouldn't have thought twice about lightening her natural highlights. But now the prospect made her feel oddly self-conscious. "I'd feel kind of weird about strolling into the tavern with Marilyn Monroe hair."

Sorrow rolled her eyes. "It's not going to be Marilyn Monroe. You're too thin for that, anyway. I'm the one who got the curves in the family."

Laura's mind flashed back to Eddie and his skilled hands. He seemed to like her curves just fine.

"Nobody will be able to tell," Claire assured her. "You'll just look . . . brighter."

"And by that, she doesn't mean smarter." Sorrow smirked, not looking up from her magazine.

"Shut up." She rolled up the ancient *People* magazine that was in her lap, reached over, and swatted her baby sister. "You're the one sitting there reading old news about Brangelina." She sat back up, all settled. "Okay, Claire. Do it." She shot Sorrow an evil grin. "My sister will just have to wait for me."

An hour later, Claire left to pick up her ninth-grader, and Laura sat there with dozens of tiny foil strips in her hair, Sorrow at her side.

Her sister was clearly engrossed in some article, but *she* wanted to talk. "What are you reading?"

Sorrow didn't even look up. "My magazine."

"I can see that. What is it?"

"Johnny Depp interview." Sorrow held it closer, reading the fine print on the photo spread. "H-O-T hot."

"He tries not to be," Laura said, trying to make conversation. "You know, he tries to play it down. Living in France. Wearing all those hobo clothes." She paused, but her sister wasn't taking the bait. "But there's no stopping the *hawt*." Finally she just leaned over. "Can I see?"

Sorrow sighed and flopped the magazine onto her lap. "What is it?"

"What is what?" She gave Sorrow an innocent look. "I just wanted to see the Johnny Depp pictures."

"Are you all right?"

She slouched in the chair as much as she could without mussing her bleaching hair. "Eddie's ranch project is still freaking me out."

"I thought you said he was scaling back the construction."

"He is, but I ran the numbers again, estimating the size of their hotel. Even with the new smaller scale, our projected loss is still too high."

"I think you're making too big a deal out if it," Sorrow said. "Think about it for a sec."

"That's *all* I've been doing," she shot back.

Sorrow kept her patience and said gently, "I know, but the numbers will work out. Their resort will be totally different from the lodge. It'll be more like a spa. Mud baths, massages . . . it'll draw visitors to Sierra Falls we'd never get otherwise."

"I guess we do mostly get hunter-hiker types."

"Now we'll get hunter-hiker *wives*." Sorrow reached over and put a hand on her knee. Earnestly, she said, "We'll be fine. It might even be good for us. Have you thought about that?"

"I guess it would be nice to have a place to get a decent mani-pedi without having to drive all the way to Silver City."

"There you go," Sorrow said brightly as she riffled through the stack and grabbed a new magazine. "You've got to have a good attitude about it, because I don't think there's any stopping it. If Eddie tried—"

"How hard, really?"

Sorrow laughed. "Enough already. Stop fretting over Eddie. He's a good guy. He wouldn't intentionally do something that was bad—for us or for the town."

Laura sulked at that, knowing it was the absolute truth. He'd been so much safer when he wasn't a good guy. She turned her attention to her own magazine, blindly flipping through.

Good guy. That was the trouble. He *was* a good guy.

"Why do you have such a bee in your bonnet about him, anyway?" Sorrow's hands grew still. Not looking up from her *Vanity Fair*, she said, "Unless you secretly like him."

She groaned. That was the problem.

"I know," Sorrow said, misunderstanding. "You're holding out for your zillionaire."

Would she really want a zillionaire? She certainly wouldn't find one in Sierra Falls.

For half a second, she considered telling her sister about the job offer from her old CEO. She considered the offer itself. If she took her old job back, it'd solve all kinds of financial problems for the family. It'd mean better health insurance. A bigger cushion for all of them. Not to mention the fact that she'd meet all kinds of single executive types.

And she was sure very few of them spent their free weekends taking kids camping.

"This one's kind of boring." Sorrow traded *Vanity Fair* for *Vogue* and became engrossed in several pages of ads.

"Did you know he takes poor kids camping?" she blurted.

"Who, Eddie?" It took Sorrow a second to get what she was talking about. "Yeah," she said warily. "Billy helped him a couple months ago with one of the kids."

She waited a moment, letting the silence hang, then demanded, "Well?" She stared at Sorrow, who was aggravatingly engrossed in her reading. "What happened?"

Her sister shrugged. "One of the older boys got into a scrape, but Eddie vouched for him, and Billy intervened. Convinced Reno PD the kid just needed a talking-to, rather than sending him to juvie."

"Why didn't you tell me?"

Sorrow looked at her like she was nuts. "I didn't think you'd care."

"Hmph." She went back to her magazine, more flustered than ever, and flipped angrily through the pages.

So, he was a good guy. A nice guy. A good egg.

She looked up with a huff. "Well, he could be a saint for all I care, but he needs to get his business in order."

Sorrow finally spun her salon chair, facing Laura completely. "What on earth are you talking about?"

"I can't finalize our fourth-quarter budget until I have a full picture of what our expenses will be." She turned her attention back to a spread on fall dresses. "If he's such a good guy, you can tell him he needs to bill us."

"Bill us for what?" Sorrow asked, sounding perplexed.

"For all the stuff he's done around the lodge. Who knows what that's all going to come to."

"I do," Sorrow said. "Nothing."

"What do you mean, nothing? It'll add up to *something*, believe me. These contractors charge a fortune."

"Eddie never charges Dad. They've got something worked out. I mean, we pay for materials, but his labor is always free."

"What?"

"You'll note he never has a bar tab," Sorrow said with a smirk.

"This is serious. Our expenses are out of control. Somebody needs to keep track of everything, and that somebody is *me*."

"Jeez, Laura. It's fine. It all works out in the end."

"That's a horrible way to do business," she shot back.

"Well it's how *we* do business." Her sister uncrossed her legs and gave her a pointed look. "Eddie's like family. They're just little jobs, anyway. I'm sure Dad would insist on paying him if he did something big. Like when he patched the roof. We paid him then." Sorrow turned her attention back to her magazine, flipping through like it was no big deal. "I know you have a thing against the guy, which is why I don't really talk about him. But I promise, he's got no secret plans to destroy us. He doesn't want to take us down. He's not going to stick us with some crazy unexpected bill. He's a good guy."

"So you keep saying," she mumbled.

"He's such a cutie-pie, too. It'll be interesting to see if he ever settles down. It's gotta happen eventually."

"Does it?"

"Sure." Her sister continued to flip through her magazine, blithely prattling on about things that were turning knots in Laura's belly. "He's so great with those kids—I'm sure he must want some of his own someday. If any woman could catch him, he'd be awesome husband material."

"Eddie?"

"No, old Stanley down at the recycling center. Yes, dummy. *Eddie.* I've seen so many girls throw themselves at him. He's got to be holding out for something. I wonder what it'd take to get a guy like that to settle on just one woman." Sorrow got a swoony little look on her face. "For him to tell her, hey babe, that's it, *I'm yours.*"

But Laura knew. He already had.

"I'm all yours," he'd said.

And he'd said it to *her.*

Twenty-six

~

"No, I said we're going with the PEX pipe, not the PVC."
Eddie leaned his elbows on the counter, breathing slowly to
keep his temper.

"I heard you," Rob said, then surreptitiously checked his
watch.

"Don't let me keep you." He was only half joking. "Shift
over soon?"

"Yeah." Rob gave him a guilty smile. "I've been here
since seven."

He wondered where the guy would be running off to at
one in the afternoon, because Eddie sure as hell never saw
him with his wife or kids. He felt sorry for poor Helen—her
husband surely had something going on the side, though
concealing it in a town this small was some feat. Rob
must've been dipping into action outside the town limits.

As far as he was concerned, the guy needed to man up
and deal with himself. It wasn't like Eddie didn't understand
the concept of wanting to be somewhere else. In fact, he

could think of a whole mess of other places he wanted to be. Like . . .

Instead of coming with Jack to the hardware store to pick up an order, he could be picking up Laura.

Instead of doing errands, he could be doing Laura.

She consumed his thoughts. He just wanted to lose himself in her.

He blew out a breath and checked the clock on the back wall. He'd call her later. Convince her about that dinner. Laura needed pursuing, and he was more than up for the challenge.

For now, though, he had responsibilities. He wanted to be all kinds of elsewhere, but he kept his word. Which meant he was standing at this counter, waiting for this guy to do his job.

"All set," Rob said, and Eddie zoned back in.

"Cool, thank—Wait." He pointed to the ancient screen. "You typed PVC again. I said we don't need PVC."

He loved Up Country Hardware, but wasn't it time they upgraded? Got a new system . . . maybe a new employee even.

"Oh, oh." Rob peered at the order like he was seeing it for the first time. "Got it."

Did he? Because demo on the ranch had gone fast. They were down to the studs, and work needed to happen quickly. They couldn't get stopped up now with the wrong gauge of the wrong pipe. He'd stuck out his neck enough, asking Fox to scale back the project. He couldn't be pushing back the date on top of it.

Rob pecked at the keys. "Sorry. The PEX won't be in till tomorrow."

"We all set?" Jack came up from behind and dumped some stuff onto the counter. "I'll pull my truck around. Let's load up the pipe."

He hung his head, rubbing the rim of his ball cap. "Can't."

His brother gave him a flat look. "What do you mean, *can't?*"

"Rob here ordered the PVC, not the PEX."

"It'll be in first thing tomorrow," Rob assured them.

"But we need it this afternoon." Jack caught sight of the bright yellow flyer pinned behind the register. "And what the hell is that?"

STOP THE DESTRUCTION—END THE CONSTRUCTION

He smirked, clapping Jack on the shoulder. Laura was a challenge unlike any he'd ever encountered. "That, big brother, is Laura Bailey."

"Not cool, Eddie. If Fairview gets wind—"

"Chill out." He spotted a familiar car pull into the lot and broke into a grin. "I'm all over this."

Jack saw whom he'd spotted and said, "You're in over your head with that one." Then he turned his attention back to Rob. "So tomorrow . . . *for sure*?"

Rob checked the screen one more time. "Yes, for sure that order will be in tomorrow, first thing."

"Well, today is shot." Jack checked the time on his cell. "I guess it's paperwork for me this afternoon. Come on, I'll drive you home."

"Nah, I'm cool." He watched Laura stride in, a baby-blue sundress fluttering around her gleaming, tanned legs. "Looks like my ride just got here." He gave her a big smile. "Isn't that right, sugar?"

She got that look she got, the one that said she couldn't decide whether she wanted to kiss him or kick him. "Isn't what right?"

Jack laughed and patted him on the shoulder. "Told you. Out of your league, brother."

"You're gonna give me a ride." He gave her an affectionate wink. "By the way, that's a real cute haircut."

That flummoxed her. "Thanks."

He couldn't wait to run his fingers through those soft waves. "It's lighter, too."

She touched it, looking a little self-conscious. "You're not supposed to be able to tell."

"I notice everything about you, darlin'."

Her eyes darted from him to the other men, as though remembering she and Eddie weren't the only ones in the room. She put her purse on the counter and proceeded to ignore him, exchanging pleasantries with Rob.

Jack shook his head, chuckling. "So, tomorrow . . . we'll hit the site seven sharp?"

He touched a finger to his cap. "It's a plan."

Laura cut her eyes his way. "Well . . . good-bye, Eddie."

"Don't you worry." He leaned against the counter. "I'm not going anywhere. I told you, you're my ride."

She frowned, looking unsure of her next move.

Rob was the first to fill the silence, asking Laura, "What did you say you needed?"

Eddie smiled, not taking his eyes from her. "She didn't."

Her head swung toward him. "What?"

"You didn't say what you needed. Our friend here is trying to clock out."

"Did you need something?" Rob asked again.

"I think she *does* need something. Don't you, tiger?"

Rob was clueless to the flirting, focused only on how many minutes it was till one o'clock.

Her cheeks flushed. "Well, if you must know, I thought I'd swing by to . . ."

"To?" Eddie raised his brows. He was desperately curious now why was she acting so uncharacteristically shy?

Staring exclusively at Rob, she finished in a rush, "I came by to get the petition and ask you to take down the flyers."

Eddie cracked a huge smile. Progress. "Taking down the petitions, huh? Does that mean I'm not such a bad guy after all?"

"It doesn't mean anything," she shot back.

It sounded a lot like what she'd told him during their first kiss. He rubbed his jaw. "I feel like I've heard you say those words before . . ."

She grew visibly agitated.

Rob gathered all the bright yellow flyers and handed them over. "If that's all you need . . ."

"Surely you remember." He leaned against the counter, giving her his full attention. "*Doesn't mean anything.* If you don't remember saying the words . . . well, maybe that means you didn't mean them."

"Bye then." Rob looked relieved to finally be getting out of there. "If you need anything else, Tom is in the back office."

"Later, Haskell," Eddie said automatically, but his gaze hadn't budged from Laura. "Now, let's see . . . as I recall, you told me nothing was changing. Nothing would be different."

He studied her profile, watched her chest rise with a deep breath. She turned to face him.

That was the woman he knew—never one to back off in a showdown. He loved that about her. He pitched his voice lower, wishing he could pin her up against the counter, then and there. "Were you wrong? Is it different for you now, Laura?"

"I don't know what you're talking about," she said weakly.

"How about I remind you?" He took a step closer and ran his hand down her smooth, bare arm.

She didn't flinch away; she only stared up at him raptly, her lips slightly parted. She'd been with pretty city boys, but just then he wondered if Laura had ever been with a *man*.

She didn't move away, but she didn't move forward, either. But it was all good. He was happy to be the one with the moves.

He swept his hand down one last time, twining his fingers with hers. "I need to speak with you outside."

"You do?" She was wide-eyed, resembling that cornered cat again.

There was a distant phone ringing. Tom's voice carried to them from the back office.

He nodded somberly. He was barely keeping his head, he wanted her so bad. "I think maybe we should take this to my place."

"All right," she said finally. Her hand tightened, her fingers squeezing his. "Maybe we should."

Twenty-seven

❧

Laura felt so naughty. So recklessly, wickedly bad in a way she'd previously only fantasized about.

She was blowing off work for the afternoon . . . to be with *Eddie*. He'd taken her hand. It'd felt so good, and yet she'd had to make herself not pull away. Make herself keep her cool. Keep her head.

She barely remembered the car ride to his place.

She wanted him, and she told herself it was okay to want him. For once, she'd let herself be this person who said sexy things to sexy men.

She pulled into the gravel driveway, and the moment she yanked the emergency brake into place, he was reaching over the center console, sweeping the hair from her brow, cupping her face and turning it to his. "You're sure?" he asked her.

She put her hand on his cheek, ready. Now that she'd made her decision, she was eager to make out right there. "I'm sure."

But Eddie closed the gap slowly, taking a deep and gentle kiss.

"Come on, then," he whispered as he pulled away. He was out of the car and opening the door for her before she'd even caught her breath.

He kept a hand on her lower back as they went up to the porch. He'd been so slow and deliberate in the car, but the tension between them grew with each step, his movements becoming urgent. He kept his hand on her waist as he fumbled with the keys.

The door unlocked and the keys jingled in the knob as it swung open. He swept her inside, yanked off his cap, threw it across the floor. He didn't pause to shut the door. He simply closed in, his body hot and hard along her chest and thighs.

"Eddie." She pressed into him, sliding her hands along his waist. "Is this really happening?"

"Yes, hell yes." He claimed her mouth in a kiss that exploded to life. It wasn't slow, or gradual; it was frantic and hungry. A kiss that'd been simmering for years.

"Wait." He pulled away, looking winded. "Dammit," he hissed under his breath. "Not yet."

"What?" She tried tugging him back.

"I've got to shower."

She curled her fingers, holding tight to his shirt. She wanted him, and she wanted him *now*. "No, you don't."

"Yes, I do. A few hours ago, I was hauling old drywall to the dump." He cradled her face in his hands. "Laura, I've been waiting, what, fifteen years for this moment? I'd rather my smell not turn you off before we even start."

This moment? She knew what he meant, and her skin tugged tight in anticipation. She debated offering to shower with him. There were women who would have. She could've purred something sexy about washing his back.

"You smell just fine to me," she said instead, but she let his shirt slide from her fingers, anyway. She wasn't that brave. Yet.

"I'll be two minutes." He disappeared into the bathroom and soon the sound of the shower filled the tiny cabin.

Waiting made her nervous. She fought the urge to check her cell phone, vowing she'd give herself an afternoon to be this new Laura. This carefree Laura. The one who skipped out of work for a little afternoon delight.

She knew she'd find only the usual messages, anyway. Lodge reservations, cancellations, inquiries. Maybe something from the film crew—they were supposed to be shooting in the old Town Hall today, and she got the impression the Kidd ladies weren't well acquainted with the concept of *quiet on the set*. She'd probably have a few new texts from her old boss, too.

She pushed all of it from her mind. Sorrow and Hope could handle any emergencies, the film guys could deal with themselves, and as for her old CEO, she'd turned him down twice now, and it was time he got the hint.

She realized she was still standing stiffly in the same spot and wandered in, consciously trying to relax. *Eddie's place.* How strange to be standing there, able to take it all in, unwatched. The last time she'd been over, a rash had been erupting all over her legs, and what she'd seen of the cabin hadn't extended much past what she could spy from where she'd sat on the edge of his tub.

He'd built the place himself, and it was surprisingly charming. Small and tidy, holding the fresh smell of the logs it'd been built with. It had a masculine feel, decorated with rich colors, like the chocolate of the leather couch, a hunter-green throw blanket, and a soft maroon area rug atop the dark, timber plank floor.

The cabin itself was open and airy. A bar in a roughly hewn style was the only thing separating the modest living area from the kitchen. The appliances were modern, the stainless streamlined and spotless.

She wandered over, stealing a quick look in one of the cabinets. Peeking in a couple of drawers. She'd expected some bachelor scenario like in the movies, with pizza boxes and a jar of old mayo in the refrigerator. Instead, opening it, she found a small assortment of condiments, half a bag of prewashed lettuce, a six-pack of Corona with two missing, a few oranges, half a lime, some deli meats, a pack of ground beef.

Her stomach rumbled, and with a startled giggle, she slapped a hand to her belly. "Whoa." She'd shut herself down for so long, but now all her senses seemed to be coming to life, waking after their long slumber.

Spotting the new bag of hamburger buns on the counter, she had a guess what he'd been planning to make. She'd caught him on his lunch hour—had he eaten? It was late—he was probably starving.

She decided to surprise him, maybe even impress him, and throw a little something together for lunch. How hard could it be? Cook for the man—it was the advice she'd once given Sorrow, and look how that had turned out.

Besides, slowing the afternoon's momentum a bit could be just the thing. The more she saw of Eddie, the more she liked. The bigger this thing felt. It made her nervous.

She thought of his kiss. Considering how his touch had a way of lighting her like a Christmas tree, a little food was probably advisable. She had a feeling once they started kissing again, there'd be no stopping for some time.

The shower was going, but she went to the door, hesitated there for a second. It felt so intimate to make herself at home while he was on the other side of that door, naked. She vowed that next time she *would* offer to get in the shower with him. She smiled to herself—she was taking to this Eddie thing rather more quickly than she'd thought she would.

Not giving herself a moment to chicken out, she simply cracked the door and called in, "You eaten?"

"No. You?" The smell of men's soap, like pine trees, wafted out with his voice.

It gave her a shiver. "Me neither. I've got some ideas, though."

He laughed that laugh—she'd known he would. She'd even anticipated his next line, "I look forward to that."

As a no-carb girl, she knew her way around a frying pan and ground beef. She quickly formed some patties and got them going on the stove.

She'd known Eddie her whole life, and stepping into his world like this felt oddly like settling into a cozy chair. It was new, but somehow familiar, too. Almost like coming home.

She wandered back into the living room as she waited, making herself at home in a way that felt satisfying. She studied the pictures on the wall and thought it interesting that there were no personal pictures to be found, especially considering his close-knit family.

Instead, there was a series of large, black-and-white landscape photos. An alpine lake with the sharp glare of sunlight on the water. Dark, massive granite peaks that seemed all the more majestic for the absence of color. An extreme close-up of pine needles coated with clouds of fresh snow.

"You like those?" Eddie had come in, and he stood there toweling his hair.

It took her a moment to find her tongue, he was so sexy, standing there in his bare feet, his dark hair spiking every which way. "I do," she said. She liked every single thing about this cabin, including its inhabitant.

"This one's my favorite." He came up beside her, peering at a shot of a tiny winter bird. A line of fragile bird tracks trailed behind it in the powdery snow. "I took it a few years back, in the woods by the falls."

"*You* took these?"

He laughed at her disbelief. "Yup. Mom got me a Neanderthal camera when my View-Master broke."

She nudged him with her shoulder. "Don't make fun."

He nudged her back. "You either, Laura." He'd sounded almost half-serious. It showed him in a different light.

"I won't," she promised. She supposed she had been ruthless over the years, probably judging him all the more fiercely for the fact that she'd always found him so damned attractive.

"I've learned my lesson, Eddie Jessup." She crossed her heart. "As of this moment, I will never again make any assumptions about you."

He got a funny expression on his face and looked toward the kitchen. "Hang on. What's that smell?"

She'd forgotten the burgers. "Whoops." She made a *sorry* face. "I was going to surprise you."

"By filling my cabin with the smell of burned meat?"

She followed him to the stove, staring in horror at the obliterated patties.

Eddie turned off the burner and tilted the pan, studying the mess. "Did you put anything in these, or on them?"

"No." She gave him an apologetic smile. "All I know are Atkins recipes. I'm sorry. I ruined it."

He got a funny look on his face. "Not at all, actually. Grab a bottle of red," he said, nodding to a small countertop wine rack. "I've got an idea."

An hour later, he'd added a can of Ragu, some chopped tomatoes, and a few additional spices, and they'd settled at a weathered picnic table behind his house, eating pasta with Bolognese sauce.

"Refined flour," she muttered as she twirled spaghetti onto her fork. It ended up being a giant bite. "What the hell?" She shoveled it in. If she was going to be hooking up with Eddie Jessup, she might as well enjoy some carbs, too.

When the flavors hit her tongue, her eyes widened. She put a hand over her mouth and said, "Oh my God." Swallowing, she repeated, "Oh my God." She shut her eyes, washing it down with a sip of wine. "I never eat pasta, and this is so good."

"See? You're learning all kinds of things. Pasta's not half-bad. Maybe Jessups aren't half-bad, either . . ." He gave her a teasing smile. The late-afternoon sun made his skin glow, and a light breeze tousled his hair.

Not half-bad at all.

Sudden butterflies made her stomach flutter. She had to look away, shoving another bite into her mouth, and took in the view instead. A small meadow spread out before them, peppered with ragged grasses and wildflowers and ringed with pine trees. Mountain peaks loomed in the far distance.

He breathed in deeply, squinting against thc low sun. "Pretty, huh? It's why I bought the place." He pointed to the distance. "I own all the way to that fence there."

She shielded her eyes and realized that sure enough, beyond the meadow, there was a basic wire-and-post fence. "What's that for?"

"I've been meaning to get a dog. Thought a fence would come in handy."

"Why haven't you?"

"Gotten a dog?" He shrugged. "I guess I always hoped I'd meet someone, and it'd be something we could do together. You know, go to the shelter, pick out a nice mutt." He turned his attention to his plate and took a giant bite of pasta, looking a little embarrassed. It was a sight she didn't see often.

"I'll bet those kids would like it. If you brought a dog on your camping trips, I mean."

He chuffed out a laugh. "I'll just bet they would. Not a lot of dogs in Reno's low-income housing developments. Not nice ones, at any rate." He got a distant look and a faint smile, like he was remembering something. "On my very first trip, one of the little guys chased what he thought was a lost dog into the brush."

"Was it?"

"Nope." Using a heel of bread, he swabbed up the last of the sauce on his plate. He popped the bread into his mouth and shook his head as he chewed and swallowed. "At first, I didn't know what it was. And of course I had to chase after

the kid—I mean, I guess it's possible it *could've* been someone's stray dog, but I panicked, thinking of all the other stuff
it might be. Rabid raccoon. Injured fox. Wildcat. Hell, it
could've been a bear cub."

She raked up more spaghetti, realizing she'd been holding
her fork in midair, listening raptly, wondering where this
story was going. "So you chased after some boy, knowing
there might've been an angry bear waiting for you."

He looked at her like she was crazy. "Of course." He
wiped his hands on his napkin and tossed it on the table.
"When we're out there, those kids are in my care. But there
were no angry mama bears."

"Thank God." She waited a beat. "Well . . . what was it?"

He smirked, looking like he was debating telling her.
"Skunk," he said finally. He laughed then. "I dove into that
brush after the kid, and damned if that skunk didn't spray
me right in the face. I stank for a week. Whoever said tomatoes remove the smell was never tagged in the face at point-
blank range. Tomato sauce, tomato juice—I bathed in the
stuff. All it did was make me smell like an *Italian* skunk."

She was laughing, dabbing tears from her eyes, and it felt
so good. She couldn't remember the last time she'd belly-
laughed.

He made a face like he was put out of joint, but she saw
the humor in his eyes.

She patted his hand, playfully consoling him. "But you
didn't let Pepé Le Pew win, did you? You're still going out
and braving those woods."

"Don't you mean, braving those kids? But yeah, damn
right I'm still going. Only now I do all my wildlife instruc-
tion in the van on the way over." He tilted his plate, swabbed
clean of tomato sauce, muttering, "Took me months before
I could look at a tomato without gagging . . ."

She laughed and mashed the last bits of meaty sauce in
the tines of her fork. "I for one am glad you and tomatoes
have made peace. This was really good, Eddie."

"It was nothing."

"Burned patties are *nothing*. But turning them into this? That's MacGyver caliber." She sipped her wine, thinking how for every question Eddie answered, she found five more popping up in its place. "Do you cook a lot?"

He shrugged it off. "I'm all right. I can grill a steak. Feed myself."

"That's more than I do," she muttered. It occurred to her that he'd have to cook for a lot more than just two on his trips. "What do you feed the kids when you camp?"

"I make easy stuff. I've got a Sterno, and food keeps pretty well in ice chests. It's not so hard. My monkey bread is always a hit."

The light in his eyes as he'd said it made her believe he truly got something from the trips.

"Monkey bread." She grinned. "I haven't had that since I was little and Dad took us to Big Basin to see the redwoods. Look at you . . . I think you enjoy the camping. It's not just for the kids, is it?"

"Sure, it's for me. Watching them in the woods for the first time, it kills me. These kids have had it hard. Some of them have been busted for big-deal stuff, too—especially the older ones. Concealed weapons charges. Drug stuff. But then they get out there"—he waved to the mountains along the horizon—"and they're blown away that you can live off the land. That a man can actually walk into the woods with no cell phone and no gun, not even a cigarette lighter, just walk in there and then walk back out, a week later if he wanted, alive and well."

He swirled the wine in his glass, shrugging like it was no big deal. "It's all about self-sufficiency. Personal responsibility. Keeping calm and informed. The *man* stuff that every boy needs to learn. That's what I try to teach them at least. It's what Jack taught me."

"That's how you got into it?"

"It's what got me thinking about it, yeah. When I was

sixteen, seventeen, I was shaping up to be a bad seed. I'm
sure you remember."

She considered his teenage antics. "Wild child, maybe.
But egging the teacher's car seems far from *bad seed*
material."

"Either way, it doesn't make for a very good man,
does it?"

"What about your parents?" She didn't know his dad
well, but Marlene was such a lovely woman. "Surely they
rode you about stuff."

"I was the last one out of the house, and by the time I
was a junior, senior, they were pretty involved in their own
worlds. I'm sure Dad was probably having his affair by then,
which on some level I'm sure my mom knew about. And it's
not like I got arrested or anything. I got decent grades, didn't
do drugs. Still, I thought I was a real son of a bitch. But then
my brother showed me what a man really is, and that it's not
some bad-ass with a fast car and a bottle of Southern
Comfort."

"So you really were as naughty as all the girls said."

"In all the right ways, darlin'," he told her with a wink.
His grin had lightened the mood, but after a moment's
silence, he turned serious again. "I guess the bottom line is,
it's important to me these kids learn what I did the hard way.
That feeling good about themselves comes from inside. Not
from a bottle or a fistfight. That strength, courage, self-
worth . . . they've got to find it inside."

His words hit her hard. Was she any wiser than these
kids? Her self-worth had always been so wrapped up in the
trappings of her success. In the car, the fancy gym member-
ship, the clothes. Of course, that stuff didn't fulfill her. It
was just *stuff.*

"I want to meet them," she said suddenly.

He looked stunned by that. "The kids?"

She gave him a shy smile. "Hopefully not the skunks."

The sun had dipped below the mountains. She wore only

her flimsy blue sundress, and her bare arms prickled into goose bumps. She hunched into herself with a little shiver.

"Hey"—he scooted closer, chafing warmth into her arms—"let's go in."

She looked off to the meadow. A cool breeze had picked up, but it'd set the wildflowers dancing. "I don't want to go in yet."

"There's always my hot tub," he said playfully, his laugh sexy and teasing. But then he stood, giving her shoulder a gentle squeeze. "Seriously, I'll run grab you a fleece."

"Actually"—she snagged his hand, stopping him—"I kinda like the sound of that hot tub."

Twenty-eight

Eddie looked at her like he didn't understand. "I've got a fleece I can lend you," he said slowly, "but there's no bathing suit. At least not one that'd fit." The line was funny, but he'd knit his brows into a serious expression, watching her, waiting to hear her reply.

She stood. Made herself hold his gaze. "I know."

She knew what she wanted. To have needs didn't make a woman weak, she knew that now. She could be vulnerable with a man like Eddie and still be safe. Losing control was sometimes a good thing.

"Where is this hot tub?" she asked, while inside she complimented herself on how brave she sounded.

And there was no reason to be afraid anyhow. She thought of all the reasons why it'd be okay. The beige bra and panties she'd worn under her sundress were probably more sensible than her actual bikini. She didn't need to manage every situation. Not everything needed to be perfect and planned.

"It's around the side," he said.

"Can we use it?"

He gave her a smile, looking eager and wary both. "You're not kidding?"

She pretended outrage. "Can we get in your hot tub or not?"

"Sugar, you don't have to ask *me* twice." He snatched her hand and led her around to the side of the house.

It was a whole other world there, with an outdoor shower, a hammock, and a shining red barbecue. "Red truck, red barbecue . . . you like the color red, don't you?"

He came up close and traced her shoulder, tugging aside the cap sleeve to reveal her thin bra strap. "Right now, I'm liking pink."

"That color's called nude," she said weakly.

He smiled. "I like that even more."

She began to debate the whole hot-tub thing in favor of simply tearing Eddie's clothes off then and there. But then he stepped away to deal with the tub, pulling off the cover, releasing a cloud of steam. When he leaned over the side to turn on the bubbles, she let her eyes linger—that man sure did have the best backside she'd ever seen.

He stood and caught the look on her face, and instead of giving her one of his trademark grins, his expression grew dark. "I'll go grab towels," he said, his voice hoarse.

When he returned, he strode toward her with such intent in his eyes. Suddenly shy, she merely hiked up her dress and sat on the edge. The sun had yet to set, but it'd dipped below the mountains, casting the scene in a gray light. Her shoulders were chilled, but the water was hot, bubbling over her feet, and her body gave a shiver of relief as she began to warm.

He studied her, sitting there with her dress tucked tightly around her thighs. "We can still turn back."

"I know." She knew he meant more than the hot tub. And she also knew, whatever happened that night, he wouldn't hold her decision against her. But turning back was the last thing she wanted. She wanted to be fearless. She could let herself lose control.

"We could just sit and talk," Eddie said, then added playfully, "I could be a gentleman and let you keep that dress on after all." He sat next to her on the edge, putting his back to the water and resting his feet on the tub steps. "Seriously, Laura, the stars will be out soon. I could bring you a blanket."

"Are you so surprised that I'd want to get in?" Just how cautious did people think she was?

"I suppose I didn't take you for the skinny-dipping type."

"I'd have my bra and panties on," she countered.

"We'd have to see about that." He sneaked a finger under her sleeve, hunting for her bra strap. "Where'd it go?"

"Eddie!" She flicked water at him but was secretly pleased.

He stood, a challenge in his eyes. "Well, if you're not getting in, I am."

She watched avidly as he pulled off his shirt, but when he began to unzip his jeans, she said, "Hey, don't *you* have a suit?"

"Not if you don't." His hands froze on his zipper. "Why, you complaining?"

"Never."

He grinned at that, but still, he kept on his boxers, and she suspected it was to make her more comfortable. He hopped into the tub, and water whooshed over the sides, drenching the hem of her dress. "Come on in"—he playfully patted the surface, splashing her some more—"the water's fine."

She hesitated. It was tempting. *He* was tempting. Adorably so.

He'd always been such an easy charmer, and it was a delight to finally embrace his flirtations. To let herself bask in them.

But still . . . to undress in front of him? Just like that,

outside, in the daylight? She wondered if maybe she should wait for the sun to dip lower. She'd always been a little self-conscious when it came to her body—she knew in her head that it was a good one, but knowing and feeling were two different things.

His voice pulled her from her thoughts. "Still worried about what other people think, aren't you?"

"No," she said defensively. Though really, he'd hit the nail on the head.

"I promise, there's nobody but you and me in these woods."

"I'm different now. I don't care what people think."

"Is that so?" He grew quiet, studying her, and she read affectionate understanding on his face. "Look, let's go inside, Laura. All I want is to be with you." He quickly added, "I don't mean *with you* with you, though I'd love that, too . . . *God*, how I'd love that . . ." He gave her a flustered smile. "What I'm saying is, we can just hang out and watch a movie. Do the crossword. Whatever makes you happy."

She shot him a look. "You do the crossword?"

"No." He made himself look innocent. "But you strike me as someone who appreciates men who do."

She stared at him. It was finally hitting her that, yes, Eddie Jessup was the sort of guy who really would choose the crossword over a naked hot tub party, if he thought that was what she wanted.

"I appreciate you just fine, Eddie, with or without the stupid crossword. And I *am* getting in this hot tub."

She stood, and in one smooth movement, pulled the dress over her head. She squealed as the cold air hit her bare skin and she immediately plopped into the tub. She sank down to her shoulders, her grand moment of bravery spent. "That wasn't very graceful, was it?"

"The judges give you a nine-point-nine."

"Not a ten?"

"I didn't say *you* weren't a ten." He sidled close, but not too close. "You're beautiful, Laura. Don't you get that?"

"Thanks."

"Hey, I'm not so sure you do get it." He gently turned her face to his, studying her intently. "I blame that bastard fiancé of yours."

"*Ex*-fiancé." She looked away, avoiding that intense gaze, and instead placed her hand on the surface of the water, focusing on the feel of bubbles between her fingers. "It's not what you think. It wasn't like I was so in love with him. Patrick didn't break my heart. He just showed me . . . how I need to be more careful. Keep myself safe. Protect myself, you know?"

"I'll find him and kill him."

She shot her head up with a laugh. "Okay. But you've got to let me help."

"Naturally." He leaned back, spreading his arm behind her, along the back of the tub. "We'll be a duo. Only now, *I'll* be the one to keep you safe."

She felt her smile fade. "Sure."

"Hey, come here." He pulled her onto his lap, settling her sideways, and the position exposed more of her body to the cold evening air. He smoothed her wet hair from her shoulders. "You've got to let yourself be vulnerable with somebody, sometime. Vulnerable isn't weak. Sometimes vulnerable is good. Like . . . vulnerable can get you this." He kissed her neck, and the feel of his hot mouth on her cooling skin sent a delicious shiver rippling across her body. She became exquisitely aware of her breasts tightening under the thin, wet fabric of her bra.

"Or this," he said, his voice gone husky. He stroked down her arm, until his hand disappeared below the bubbles. His fingers splayed over the side of her hip, gripping her, tugging her panties against her flesh just enough to set her body on fire.

She had to open her mouth to inhale. "All right," she managed. "You're convincing me."

He nibbled her earlobe. "Only *partly* convinced?" His breath tickled her skin, and her pulse became a drumbeat. "What else do I need to do?" One hand smoothed down her thigh, finding her knee, and the other swept down her back, lower then lower still, until the very tips of his fingers dared plunge under the top of her panties.

"Oh." She'd begun to speak, but her word became a moan. Nodding, she said, "You win. Vulnerable is good. I see that now."

He stroked his other hand back up her thigh, higher and closer, until his thumb was sweeping just below the V of her thighs.

Her body was throbbing now, begging for more, and instinctively she circled her hips in his lap. "Mmm. I could maybe get used to vulnerable."

"Show me." He nipped at her shoulder, kissing along her collarbone, waiting for her to make the first move.

She tucked her knee, and in a single motion she swung her leg between them, spinning in his lap to face him.

He barked out a pleased laugh. "Hot damn, Laura."

She felt like she must've been beaming, she felt so free, so gratified, so joyous. "I used to be a cheerleader, re-member?"

"How could I forget? You were the Holy Grail of my teen years." He grasped both her hips and ground her closer. His arousal was undeniable, and it was a spark, inflaming her.

"We're not kids anymore," she said softly as she twined her hands behind his neck. She hitched her hips to nestle him in place and kissed him deeply.

When she pulled away, he looked drugged, dazed. "You are one sexy thing, darlin'."

He parted his lips, leaning closer to taste her again, but she ducked away, instead kissing along his jaw, his neck. She'd dreamed of seeing that bare chest, of touching him, and let herself explore every inch with palms and fingers and mouth.

It was perfect. Just then, in the dreamy twilight, *this* was perfect.

She roved back up and let herself sag into him, savoring the feel of his hands stroking along her back. "This is good, Eddie."

"Better than good," he said, in a voice gone fierce. He guided her mouth back to his, taking another kiss. It was passion and urgency, but mastery, too, his hands knowing just where to go, his kiss just right. *Good Lord*, but the man knew his stuff.

Her desire hitched higher, until she felt fevered with it. She stretched into him, until the chafe of her bra against her sensitive skin became an exquisite agony.

She broke the kiss, catching her breath. She wanted him. Needed him skin-to-skin. Desired him with an intensity that made the heat of the water nearly unbearable. "Too hot."

"It *is* hot," he growled, taking her mouth again.

After a minute, she broke away again. "No, the water."

Holding her in his lap, he swept them to a bench that sat higher in the tub, exposing more of her upper body to the cold air. It was instant relief. "Better?"

With a moan of pleasure, she kissed him hard in answer. She wrapped her arms more tightly around his neck and tilted her hips, craving him closer, deeper.

He reached around and unclasped her bra. Pulling away, his eyes met hers. He still held her straps in place, as if asking permission to let the scrap of fabric fall from her shoulders.

"Yes," she whispered.

He brought his hands down, drawing the bra slowly along her skin. Sensations overwhelmed her—the shiver of cold air on naked skin, coarse lace dragging over her body—it drove her desire to the edge. But it was Eddie's eyes on her, hooded, devouring her with a look of such wanting, that gaze was what pushed her over the edge. She gripped his shoulders, needing him to take her, to quench this fire.

Her breasts pebbled in the cool air. She arched her back, wanting him to taste her, take her, something. "I want you."

Instead, he slowly, reverently, brought his hand up, cupping her. "You're like an angel." She leaned into him, using her body to beg for more, and he answered with a firmer touch, squeezing her, palming her. "Magnificent," he whispered. "Perfect."

She grabbed his head and pulled his mouth to hers for a kiss. But still, it wasn't enough. She pulled away, unable to stand it any longer. "Now, Eddie. I need you."

He leaned down to steal a taste of her breast, and she pleaded, "Please."

Finally, he parted from her. "Wait . . ." Keeping her legs wrapped around his waist, he held her as he half stood, reaching for the towel, and then when he settled them back in the water, he flashed a condom pinched between his fingers.

She grinned. "Smooth."

"I'm a man with a plan," he said, grinning back.

He stretched, tossing the towel well away from the water, and the move showcased his torso and flexing muscles. It was a beautiful sight.

She swept her palm lightly along his chest, teasing him to goose bumps. "You need to go shirtless more often."

He sucked a breath in through his teeth. "Are you *trying* to kill me?"

"You bet."

With a smile, he cupped her face for a quick kiss, but it soon grew heated, deeper. The next time they parted, when they settled back again, the rest of their clothes had disappeared.

She took Eddie inside her, and he filled her, hot and perfect. The bad boy and the good man, all at once, in a single package. It was almost too much.

Afterward, he held her close, and she felt raw, overflowing with sensation, with emotion. With a sense of completion that frightened her.

"You know I'm in love with you," he said, his voice so quiet. So serious.

She held her breath. Darkness had fallen, and with it, silence had descended like a blanket, shrouding the woods from all sound but for settling leaves and the occasional distant cries of coyotes. A vast canopy of stars spread overhead.

She was overwhelmed by the night. Overwhelmed by him.

She couldn't answer his extraordinary declaration. She only clung tighter, squeezing him closer.

He seemed to understand, though, and began to caress her in long strokes, from her head, along her hair, and down her back. "I'm glad you're here," he told her gently. "Glad you're home."

"Me, too." She felt it in her heart. She wanted to be there, to be with him. She'd meant the words, but she was too afraid to consider beyond that.

It'd been a risk to come home. A risk to stay. And yet it was Eddie who felt like the greatest risk of all.

Twenty-nine

❧

Rob stowed his blue-and-yellow Up Country Hardware apron in the back and headed out—finally. He must've checked his damned watch five hundred times, but the seconds had ticked by like he was trapped in some screwed-up science fiction movie.

He had another hunch, but this time it was a good one.

When he first checked his watch that morning, it'd been eight o'clock on the nose. No big deal. But then he'd checked again, and damned if the time didn't read nine o'clock, exactly. He'd just about pissed himself. Double zeroes, then double zeroes again, right in a row, flashing like a red beacon.

Omens didn't get any more solid.

Screw the card tables, he was done with them. He wasn't going to mess around—he'd head straight to the Reno strip. It was time for roulette.

"Rob," Tom called from the back of the store. "Didn't you hear me calling?"

He stopped. Dammit, but he'd already clocked out and gotten halfway out the door. Automatically, he checked his watch, half hoping he'd hit one o'clock. But it was already seven past. "I thought I was off at one." He tried to seem calm, but really he just wanted to hop into his car and floor it. His hand was in his pocket, jiggling that buffalo nickel.

"Yeah, yeah, your shift's done," Tom said. "But you've got a phone call."

Screw Reno. Really, he just needed to cross the state line. The Indian Rock Casino had a sweet setup with a bunch of five-dollar roulette tables. Or maybe he'd head right to their ten-dollar table, if he was feeling it. It had to feel right, and he made it a rule to stay away from empty tables.

"Did you hear me?" His boss hitched a thumb in the direction of the back office. "Helen's on the line."

"Helen? She's at work." Indian Rock it was. If he went five miles over the limit, he'd be there by two, two-fifteen latest.

"I know she's at work," Tom shot back. "That's where she's calling from. Right now, on the phone."

Rob stood there for a moment, registering the information. "What about?"

"How the hell should I know?" Tom turned and disappeared into the storeroom.

Dammit. He hated interrupting his mojo like this. He told himself it didn't matter. He'd seen the double zeroes.

He strode back to the office and grabbed the phone. "Hey, Helen."

"I called your cell," she said in greeting.

"Didn't hear it." Really, he hadn't answered it. Whenever she called, it was usually just for stuff like milk or sugar, anyway. He was going to check her message later. Groceries could wait. Double zeroes didn't.

Anyway, he was doing this for *them*.

"Ellie's camp called," Helen said. "You need to go get her."

He glued his eyes to the old wall clock, watching the

second hand *tick-tick*ing along the face. "Wait, *I* need to get her? Why can't *you* get her?"

"I am working a double shift."

"She sick or something?" He calculated. He could get her, get back in the car, and be at Indian Rock by two-forty-five. But—damn damn damn—he'd need to get going. "I'll go grab her, drop her at home for you. I should run—"

"Wait," she snapped. "Don't you hang up on me. I need you to stay with her, not just drop her."

"Luke's around." Their oldest was in high school. By the time *he* was in high school, he was working fifteen hours a week at the Gas-n-Go. "He's a capable kid. Can't he watch her?"

"No, Luke can't watch her. He's down at the Kidd house on Tuesdays, running errands, remember?"

No, he didn't remember, but he only said, "Yeah, okay. Well, can't she just sit at home in front of the TV? I'll grab some ginger ales for her. Should be fine like that."

"Where do you need to be running off to that you can't take care of our sick child?"

"I got errands, Helen. And if she's so sick, won't she want you? I don't know what to do with sick kids."

"You know I can't leave here. As it is, every time I turn around, Laura's eyes are burning a hole in the back of my head. I won't get out of here till nine."

Nine-zero-zero. It mocked him.

He'd had his omens. He had to seize them.

"What's wrong with her, anyway?" Maybe a car ride might be soothing. Put her to sleep like when she was a baby.

"Croup."

"How bad can it be? You dropped her at camp in the first place."

"Yeah, and it killed me to do it," she said slowly, her resentment crackling over the phone line. "But croup's like that. Kids seem fine, until they *can't breathe*. So just go get her already."

"What do I do if she has trouble?" He checked his watch. Helen wouldn't resent him when he brought home enough to cover next month's mortgage . . . double zero paid thirty-five to one.

"Sit her in the bathroom and run the shower. Moist heat is good. Helps her breathe."

"You sure you can't do it?" He thought he'd try one last time.

"Someone needs to earn money in this family."

"Oh, and I don't earn any money?" He'd show her just how great his earning potential was.

"I'm not going there now, Rob." The wind had left her sails, and suddenly his wife just sounded tired.

There was one thing a gambler was good at, and it was a poker face. "Sure thing," he told her. "I'll go get her." It wasn't like he was lying—he was doing this for her.

"You sure?" Helen sounded so relieved that, for a moment, he believed himself the hero.

He *wanted* to be the hero. "If I said I got it, I got it, babe."

Not thirty minutes later, he was with Ellie in her room. She flopped dramatically onto her pink rug. "Can't I just watch TV?"

As he'd predicted, she didn't look so bad. She didn't even have a fever, just a voice that made her sound like a seal.

"Come on, angel girl." He leaned down and scruffed her hair. "A little field trip will fix you right up. The best thing for that throat is ice cream, and the best ice cream is in Indian Rock."

"My throat doesn't hurt. I just want to watch TV."

"They have TVs there. A whole wall of them." He pictured the screens with keno and horse races flashing by. "And they have a buffet, with soft serve and sprinkles."

"Bear's place has yummy ice cream," she argued. But she'd sat up, and that was progress.

He studied her stuffed animal shelf. Why were there so many, and who'd paid for all this crap, anyway? But he wasn't about to mess with the fragile mood of a second-grader, so instead he asked, "Which one of these is your favorite?"

"Mister Bear."

There must've been two dozen bears on that damned shelf. "Which one is Mister Bear?"

"The brown one."

That narrowed it to *one* dozen. He grabbed the biggest one, and she hopped to her feet. "That's Missus Bear."

"Shouldn't Mister Bear be bigger than Missus Bear?"

"No." She shouldered by him and pointed up. "That's him."

He plucked down the bear and then froze, trying not to grin. "Wait. Did you hear that?" He gaped at the toy. "Did you say something?" Holding the bear to his ear, he said, "Mm-hm. Yeah. Oh, sure, they've got plenty. In vanilla and chocolate."

"Is there strawberry?" Ellie asked, wide-eyed.

"Oh sure, they've got all the flavors." He handed her the stuffie. "Mister Bear says he wants to take a trip for ice cream."

Finally, a smile dawned on her face. She opened her arms to the bear, but instead Rob just scooped her up. He wasn't such a bad dad. Not such a bad one at all.

He settled her by the pool, with a big dish of strawberry ice cream with gummy bears on top—a special request from Mister Bear himself. He was in a grand mood. It'd been three-zero-zero on the dot when he'd pulled in. Granted, he'd been watching the clock like a hawk, but an omen was an omen.

Helen had said Ellie needed warm, wet air, and it didn't get much warmer than out by the pool. The air was dry, sure, but surely the pool water added some humidity to the place. It was a pretty clever solution, actually.

"Daddy will be right back, angel girl." Just an hour was all he'd need. Maybe not even that long. Maybe even twenty minutes. He leaned down to lay a kiss on her head. "Mister Bear here is in charge till I get back."

He left his daughter, smiling poolside. His double zeroes were waiting.

Thirty

Eddie traced his finger down Laura's naked back. Every inch of her was perfection, and she was in *his* bed, lying on her stomach, her blond hair a wild tangle. God, she was gorgeous—and what a sight when she finally let loose and let go.

She squirmed from his touch. "You're tickling."

"I'll do more than that." He swept aside her hair to lay kisses along her shoulders but felt the tension there at once. "What's with all the knots?" Leaning on his elbow, he began to rub her back. "Sweetheart, you're wound so tight you're gonna snap."

She shifted to get a better look at him. "Then maybe you should unwind me."

Her eyes were all crackle and fire, and in them he saw the passion he'd always admired, only now she wasn't fighting him. Now she was loving him.

It would've felled him, if he hadn't already been lying down.

"Unwind you, or wind you up? Which is it?" He eased
onto her back, wanting her again. He doubted he'd ever stop
wanting her. Just touching her like that, he'd begun to stiffen
already. He smoothed his hands along her arms, spreading
them over her head. Nuzzling at her neck, he said, "Shall
we go for three?"

"You're a machine."

"It's the mountain air, darlin'. And you."

She arched her back, wriggling her hips, teasing
him. "Me?"

"All you," he said, suddenly serious. He rolled to the
other side of her, turning her to face him. Strands of her hair
had tangled in her lashes, and he carefully brushed them
aside. "You're amazing, Laura."

"A girl tries." She gave him a light smile, clearly not
getting his exact meaning.

"Hey"—he chucked her chin—"I don't just mean your
looks. Which, by the way, are stellar. It's who you are. *You*
amaze me."

He wasn't the biggest wordsmith, so he thought carefully
about how to express it. It amazed him how alive he felt with
her. Amazing how she'd gotten under his skin. She'd thought
she was afraid to be vulnerable, but he'd never felt so
exposed before, and it scared him. But it felt great, too.
Intense. He was ready for it. For her. Ready to let it all
hang out.

He took a deep breath. "I won't make you say or feel
anything you're not ready to say or feel, but hear this. I think
you are the greatest goddamn woman I have ever met. You're
so smart. So sharp. Look at you—you plucked yourself up
by your bootstraps and got out of here. Paid your way
through school. Then when your family needed you, you
came back again. You're tough when you have to be, but
you know what you want. You protect your own—your
town, your family. You love fiercely, Laura. I've seen it.
That's what's amazing."

"Really?" she asked, a little abashed. "I didn't know any-one noticed that stuff."

They lay belly-to-belly on the bed, and when she looked up at him, he saw this strong woman's eyes cloud with emotion. For once, she was letting herself be vulnerable, and it was for *him*. A tidal wave of affection swept him. Swamped him.

He cupped her head, pulling her close to kiss her fore-head. "I noticed. I noticed you from the get-go—all the way back on that first day in kindergarten."

She laughed, wiping the corner of her eye. "No, you didn't."

"All right. Maybe it took me till first grade. But you get my gist." He rained kisses along her face. "Plus you're beauti-ful. You're so beautiful, like an angel. Like a painting." He had too much to say . . . he didn't know what to express first.

She giggled and poked him in the ribs. "Like a painting of an angel?"

"Hey, I'm new at this."

"Eddie Jessup, new at women? I don't think so."

"All right, yeah, I know how to pay a compliment. I can appreciate a pretty face. But I've never been floored by one, and Laura, you floor me."

She grew serious. "You floor me, too, Eddie. I . . . You've blown me away. I had no idea, you, this . . ."

She ran out of words, but it was okay. It was enough. He was a patient man.

The ringing phone startled them.

He frowned. "Who the hell is that?"

"Can you let it go?" she asked, but the look they shared said they knew he couldn't. Late-night phone calls were too unusual—and too alarming—to send to voice mail.

He scampered naked to the living room, where he'd dropped his cell on the table with his keys and wallet. He checked, and the Caller ID was a weird one. It couldn't be a telemarketer at ten P.M., could it? "Hello?"

"Is this Jessup Brothers Construction?"

"Yeah," he said warily, peering at the clock on the microwave. "It's way after hours, though."

He strolled back into the bedroom and gave Laura a look that said they were far from done.

"Apologies for the late hour, but I'm calling from Indian Rock, from the urgent care clinic here?"

She'd said it like a question, so he said, "Yeah," even though he wasn't entirely sure of the place. He'd been to Indian Rock a few times through the years, but those late-night clinics all looked the same. Single story, lights on late, sign with a red cross out front.

Laura gave him a questioning look, mouthing, *Who is it?* and he could only shrug.

"We weren't sure who to call," the woman said, and by the time she finished telling him her reasons, he'd dashed outside, grabbed their clothes from beside the hot tub, and begun tugging on his jeans.

"So who was it?" The question burst from Laura the moment he clicked off. She was sitting up in bed, holding the sheet to her chest, where she'd been avidly watching his every move.

"Some clinic in Indian Rock. They've got an anonymous girl there, unconscious." He pulled on a clean shirt. "I'm heading over."

"Right now?"

"She's just a little thing. They think she's from Sierra Falls."

She hopped out of bed, dressing quickly. "Why'd they call *you*?"

"They think I might know her. She's wearing a shirt with a Jessup Brothers logo. A soccer shirt," he recalled. They'd donated money for the peewee jerseys last year.

It wasn't even a question that she go with him, and he loved the feel of that. Like they were a team. "I told you we'd be a duo," he said as they hit the road.

"You were right." She'd put her hand on his thigh the moment they'd gotten in his truck, and she gave it a squeeze. "Do you think they called Billy, too?"

"I assume the sheriff was the first person they called. I didn't think to ask."

"We'll see when we get there, I guess."

He filled her in on the remaining details. A girl, approximately six to eight years old, was sitting poolside at the Indian Rock Casino when she began to have trouble breathing. "The hotel called 911," he finished, "and you know the rest."

"Who could it be?"

"I don't know. I can't think of anyone who'd vacation there."

"Not from *here*," she said, and he had to agree. Indian Rock was kind of threadbare. And where were her parents?

Laura used the GPS on her phone to navigate, and with the late hour, they made good time. They ran inside, though the scene was far from urgent when they arrived.

A tired-looking nurse greeted them when they arrived. She'd minimized her computer window, but not before Eddie spotted a solitaire game. She asked, "You're here for Ellie?"

Laura blurted, "Ellie . . . *Haskell*?"

At the nurse's nod, she didn't wait for an invitation, she simply stormed through the waiting room door into the back, and Eddie followed.

The clinic was a small one, with just a tiny kitchenette, two patient rooms, and a bathroom in the back. The doctor didn't even have his own office, just a niche in the hallway bearing an ancient-looking PC with a stack of files beside it.

They saw Ellie right away, and Laura went to her, sweeping the sleeping girl into her arms. "What the heck is *she* doing here?" she demanded in a whisper.

"She said her father brought her for ice cream," the nurse said, standing in the doorway to join them. She was shaking her head like it was something she saw everyday, and after spending time with his Reno kids, Eddie imagined it was possible she did.

Laura mouthed over the girl's head, *I'll kill him.*

Though he'd never seen this side to Laura, he didn't doubt she would.

As Ellie snuggled into her, she asked, "Did you call Helen? Her mom?"

"The mother reported the girl missing to the sheriff's office not two minutes ago—about the same time Ellie woke up enough to tell us who she is."

At the mention of Helen, Ellie roused. "Is Mommy here?"

"We'll take you home, honey." Laura rocked her. "Your mom is waiting for you there. She'll be so happy to see you." She turned to the nurse. "Helen is my employee at the lodge and tavern in Sierra Falls."

"*Can* we take her?" he asked. "We're close with the family."

"We'll have to contact Mrs. Haskell," the nurse said. "But you've got such a big head start on her, I can't imagine she'd mind."

The doctor appeared at the door. "Denise will finish up the paperwork. If it's okay with the girl's mother, it shouldn't be a problem to discharge her into your care."

Eddie put one hand on Laura's shoulder and the other on Ellie's forehead. "Is she okay to leave? You don't need to do any tests or anything?" The kid actually didn't look that bad. Her breathing was loud and her cheeks a bit flushed, but otherwise she seemed fine.

"She's all set," the doctor told them. "I imagine she'll sleep well the rest of the night. It's how croup is. The child appears normal, with just a minor cold, until the laryngeal muscles spasm. Does Ellie have asthma?" He signed off on the paperwork, then handed the clipboard to the nurse. "When she's better, she should be tested. To be on the safe side, we put her on the nebulizer—some extra oxygen and a little Albuterol fixed her right up."

Laura gathered her more tightly in her arms. "We'll get you home, honey."

They settled back in the car, and by the time Laura phoned what seemed like pretty much everybody in Sierra Falls, Ellie was fast asleep in the backseat of the truck.

"Poor Helen," Laura whispered. She turned in her seat, craning to check on the sleeping girl one more time. "I'm going to kill Rob. I *knew* something was up with him, but bringing his kid so he can meet his mistress? I can't . . . it's just beyond the pale."

"His mistress?" Eddie had other suspicions. "I have a feeling his mistress just might be a stack of chips."

Thirty-one

❧

Helen was beat. She was on for the lunch shift, but all she wanted to do was curl onto the couch with Ellie and zone out in front of as many stupid kid movies as her girl wanted to watch. She'd gather her boys on the couch, too. They'd have themselves what she called one of their desert-island days, when they spent the day in their jammies, eating whatever was in the cupboards.

She sighed. She might've been beat, but it was nothing compared to the whupping last night's bill gave her. Late-night visits to urgent care clinics didn't run cheap, and even with insurance, emergency co-pays were nuts.

Her damned husband.

He'd acted all penitent that morning and offered to watch Ellie—had seemed desperate to watch her—but she wasn't about to let her girl leave her side. Her baby currently sat in one of the tavern's corner booths, listlessly coloring the back of a children's menu.

Helen watched as Laura brought Ellie a ginger ale. She braced herself for some lecture on how she shouldn't be bringing a sick child to work, or maybe about how she'd had to drive to Indian Rock in the middle of the night, interrupting whatever it was she'd been doing with Eddie Jessup, and didn't Helen just wonder about *that* development.

She spoke before her boss had a chance to lay into her. "Sorry about Ellie. I can't leave her alone."

But Laura surprised her with a vehement and instant reply. "Of course you can't." The significant nod that followed was a knife in the gut—her sympathetic expression said it'd be a given that she couldn't leave Rob at home with the girl. And then Laura shocked her even more when she said, "That's why you should go home. Hope's in the kitchen doing lunch prep. We're all set to cover your shift."

"I . . . oh . . . thank you." She fantasized about it for a second, then tied on her apron, knotting it with a sharp tug. "But I can't. Emergency clinics aren't exactly cheap."

"I'm sorry. Believe me, I remember how it was with Dad." Laura frowned and reached out to her, putting a hand on her arm. "You let us know if there's anything we can do."

Helen made herself not flinch away from the unexpected contact. The woman's sympathy seemed genuine, and it wasn't what she would've expected.

She gave her a sad smile. "You could rob a bank for me."

"I'm afraid this won't be the first of your bills, either. Make sure they itemize it all for you. They'll get you for every Band-Aid and cotton swab. I'd be happy to help you review it all as it comes in. Unfortunately, I've gotten good at parsing medical invoices."

The offer floored her, and Helen was thanking her when Edith bustled in. "Where's our little patient?" Mrs. Bailey went straight to the booth, wrapping an arm around the girl, tucking her close and stroking her hair. "Ellie Lynn Haskell, I am taking you up to the house right now. You're going to spend the day with me. I'll even let you sit in Bear's chair."

Laura smiled. "Just like Goldilocks."

Ellie went wide-eyed. "Can I?"

Edith looked to Helen. "Please say I can take her."

She felt something unclench in her chest. "Really? You sure you don't mind?"

"Are you kidding? It'll be nice to have a little one under-foot again." Edith plucked Ellie's glass from the table and bustled behind the bar. "How about a refill? Do you want to try Sprite? That was always my girls' favorite."

Laura laughed. "Mom's a big believer in the clear fluids. Hopefully you won't mind your daughter drinking a gallon of soda today."

"No, I appreciate it," she said, meaning every word. "I wanted to thank you again for driving her home last night. And also . . ." She gave Laura a probing look. "Thank Eddie for me."

The girl blushed, and it was a sight Helen never thought she'd see. "The cat's out of the bag, huh?"

So, her and Eddie . . . would wonders never cease? But the Bailey girl seemed to live a charmed life, so in some ways it was no surprise. She told her genuinely, "He's a good one, Laura."

"I'm getting that." She got a faraway look on her face. "He really dealt last night, didn't he?"

What she wouldn't give for a man who dealt. A man who could be a source of comfort and strength instead of trouble. "You're lucky."

Laura opened her mouth to speak, but she just stood there for a moment, at a loss for words. Their eyes met for a strange, prolonged moment. So, they really were a couple now, though it appeared maybe Laura was still getting used to the idea. Helen had to wonder if she truly understood what a good man she'd found.

The bell jingled as a different Jessup walked in.

Laura brightened, appearing a bit relieved that their moment of bonding was over. "Hey, Scott." He was in his ranger uniform, so he was clearly on duty. "Grabbing an early lunch?"

He went straight to Ellie. "Nah, just came to check on this girl here." He fished in his pocket and brought out a pack of cards. "I brought a little get-well present."

Helen felt herself choke up. It stunned her how the town was rallying around her. For years, she'd kept herself at arm's length, assuming everyone was so judgmental, but that wasn't it at all. Everyone cared; they'd just been looking for a reason to cross the divide.

Touched, she turned her back, swallowing hard, busying herself with refilling ketchup bottles. "Whatcha got?"

"A pack of Junior Ranger cards." He settled next to Ellie in the booth.

Edith joined them. Using her dramatic mother voice, she said, "Oh, look, Ellie. How nice is that?" The woman was going to make a wonderful grandmother someday.

"Each one pictures some bit of California wildlife," Scott said, peeling off a sticker and putting it on Ellie's shirt. "You've got to study up, if you're going to be an honorary forest ranger."

With her daughter so happily occupied, she set about doing the lunch prep, and Laura joined her. They got into a rhythm, where one unscrewed and wiped down ketchup bottles while the other filled them back up.

Laura shot a look at Scott, then muttered, "Studly job, good looking, *and* he likes animals? That man must get laid right and left."

Helen snickered at the unexpected comment, and boy, how she appreciated a topic other than medical bills and wayward husbands. She stole a peek, too, and had to agree— Scott sure did fill out his uniform nicely. "Can't argue there."

They shared a laugh, and it felt so good to have a nice, normal, easy exchange with another woman for once. "I guess Eddie must've called him and told him what happened."

"Eddie called *everyone*," Laura said. "Doctor Mark was first on the list, though. He prescribed clear fluids, fresh air, and lots of Nickelodeon."

"Too bad Rob's cure isn't so easy." Helen bit her tongue, unsure she should've divulged so much.

Laura hesitated, then asked, "Did Mark talk to you about it? He said he called you, but wouldn't elaborate. Patient confidentiality and all that."

It felt good to be confiding in someone, even if that person was Laura Bailey. "Yeah," she admitted, "we talked."

"And?"

Helen let herself have a moment of gallows humor. "I asked if he could prescribe my husband a pill that'd make him less of a jackass."

Laura smirked. "No luck, I take it?"

She shook her head. "He said compulsive gambling is an addiction like any other. Sorry to say, there are no magic pills for my husband."

"I looked around on the Web late last night," Laura said, and with a rueful smile, added, "You can imagine I was pretty amped when we got home. Anyway, I read that the biggest challenge is getting the person to admit he has a problem. But if he recognizes it and takes it day by day . . ." She tapered off. "Does Rob get that his gambling is a problem?"

"If he doesn't, he will when I'm through with him." She sighed heavily. The line would've sounded funnier and felt better if it weren't just so damned sad. "He says he's sorry. I don't know . . . maybe the scare was big enough to shock some sense into him." She shrugged. "He said he thought he was helping us. As if he might've actually hit some jackpot." She forced a smirk, because if she didn't, she'd cry.

"I say make him grovel." Laura had noted Helen's attempts at levity and was trying to play along.

But she felt her smile fall from her face. "I don't know if I can ever forgive him."

There was nothing to say to that, and the women grew silent. Gradually, she tuned back into the sound of Scott, flipping through his ranger cards.

"Here's a black bear," he was saying, explaining each animal to Ellie. "We've got lots of those around here, and that's why we lock up our trash. We all have to live together, though, don't we? Hey, here's a chipmunk. And a gray fox. Ooh, you've got a mountain lion, too—don't run into many of those, thankfully. Oh, and these guys are special. A spotted owl. You don't see many of them anymore."

"One sec," Laura muttered, and left her with the ketchup bottles. "Can I see?"

"He has polka-dots," Ellie said.

"Oh, I've seen owls like that," Laura said. "Near Timber Creek."

"You sure?" Scott asked. "They're pretty rare."

"Is it endangered?"

Helen wiped her hands and joined them, wondering at the woman's sudden nature curiosity.

"Technically, it's just a threatened species," Scott said, "but a lot of people are fighting to get it on the endangered list. I'd be surprised if they had a nesting ground near the creek. Usually stuff like logging and construction is limited around critical habitat areas."

There was a clattering in the kitchen, and Hope burst through the door, a plate in hand. "I made Ellie . . ." Her eyes snagged on Scott, and her cheeks flamed bright red. "I made cinnamon toast. For Ellie. I thought she'd like toast. With cinnamon." She glanced again at Scott. "Hi," she said awkwardly.

Scott's eyes widened. "Hi."

Laura and Helen shared a quick, loaded look, and the

Bailey girl said, "You two don't know each other? Scott Jessup, Hope Fitzpatrick, our new employee."

"Hi," he repeated lamely.

The look she and Laura shared was longer this time, and they didn't have to say anything, because the meaning was clear: a speechless Jessup was rarer than any owl.

Thirty-two

～

Laura stood behind the bar, going through the motions . . .
wiping down the counter, checking stock, cutting limes,
refilling the glass tray. But mostly she was thinking.

She had what she needed. She'd done some research. The
northern spotted owl was federally protected as a threatened
species. She'd seen the job site—the construction wouldn't
go near the nesting ground, and Eddie's project wasn't nearly
big enough to be a threat, anyhow. But still, she knew it'd
be enough to put a hold on their work for a good, long while.
She could stop the construction.

But would she?

She could make a stink about it. Notify environmental
groups. Call television stations in Reno, get it on the evening
news. Just one hint of bad press, and she had no doubt Fairview would pull out. They'd spent years, not to mention a
bundle of marketing dollars, pitching smaller, boutique
resorts just like this one as eco-friendly destinations. Tourists came from all over to meditate and get back to nature,

all the while dishing out beaucoup bucks for things like mud facials and seaweed wraps.

She could make a stink, and Fairview would pull out, removing all competition for the lodge. The Bailey family business could continue to thrive.

But at what cost to Eddie?

"Heya, Lola."

She sighed. Dan. The last person she felt like seeing just then, and she forced tired cheer into her voice. "Done filming for the day?"

She tore into a big bag of Chex Mix and considered her conundrum as she filled several bowls for the evening tavern crowd. She could make a fuss, but she had a new perspective now. If Fairview pulled out, it'd cut into Eddie's bottom line. It would also take food, savings, and security from Jack's family.

Worst, it would take away from the at-risk kids in Reno—kids who'd lost so much already.

"Ooh, gimme." Dan leaned on the bar, reaching for the snacks. "I'm going to miss all this middle-America awesomeness." He pulled a bowl his way and shoved a fistful into his mouth. "I'm starving. We took off a day of filming to, you know, explore. Dude, have you been to Silver Town?"

"Silver City? Of course I have." Stopping Fairview had been all she'd wanted—could she let it go now? She remembered her talk with Sorrow . . . the family business would probably survive a little competition, especially because the two properties were so different.

"I swear, we had the worst sushi ever. We went to some place . . . what was it called? The Sushi Zone," he exclaimed. Dan snagged another handful of snacks, then added in a mocking voice, "We were . . . *in the zone . . . the sushi zone.*"

"Yeah? How was it?" She wiped down the counter for the third time, mostly to appear busy to the producer. She really needed silence to think this through.

There was the whole environmental question still to consider. Of course, she *could* just discuss it with Eddie. Maybe she should. He'd make sure to give the owls a wide berth. The impact would be negligible.

But he was Mister Outdoors Guy. If he knew those owls were special, he'd stop the work until he could sort it all out. More than that, if he knew they were protected by law, he'd halt construction all together.

Did she want to be responsible for the loss to his business? Worse, might he think this was just another ruse on her part, another way to hound him?

"Did you hear me?" Dan asked, chomping away.

"Did you want a beer?"

"Oh, yeah, that, too, thanks. But I was saying there was mayo on the sashimi rice. Actual *mayonnaise*. The ahi was chewy, and you know they only had that gross crab stick stuff on the Cali roll."

"Gross," she said distractedly. No wonder they were taking so long to film if Dan was having his crew drive all over creation in search of raw fish. When would they be done, anyway? They hadn't even gotten any lodge footage, which she'd been hoping for. It'd all been shots of the town, the falls, interviews with the community. They must've had hours of B-roll by now.

"Dude, how can you live here without decent sushi?" He sounded outraged, and just then it struck her as so ridiculous.

"I find a way to carry on," she said drily.

"The last time I had food that crappy was at The Supermarket. You heard of it? It's *the* new place on Melrose. They serve only food purchased from grocery stores . . . like an ironic statement about the global economy. You get it?"

She struggled to open a jar of cocktail onions. "Sorry, get what?"

"The Supermarket."

Her cell rang, and she answered without thinking.

Dammit. She'd been too distracted and had forgotten she was screening. Now she had to deal with her old CEO—as if she didn't have enough on her plate at that moment.

"Hold on," she told him and, putting a hand over the phone, said to Dan, "Ask Sorrow. She can tell you how to get there."

"Get where?"

"The supermarket."

"What? No. No, no, dude. The Supermarket is a restaurant in LA. Anyway, I'll let you get that." He waved at her phone. "I'll wait."

Fabulous. She turned her back to him, trying to keep it down. But the dinner crowd had yet to appear, and even in a whisper, it felt like her voice echoed through the place.

She listened to the same litany. Double her salary. Hand-picked team. Stock options. Benefits for her and her family.

That last bit tripped a switch in her brain. *Benefits.*

Watching Helen wrestle with just one small urgent care clinic visit had given her flashbacks, back to the days after Dad's stroke. Forget the challenge of getting him back to health; they'd struggled for years to recover financially.

Her parents weren't getting any younger. How would she pay for their care when the day came that they needed extra help? There was Medicare, but would that be enough? What if, God forbid, something catastrophic happened? It would bankrupt them. Talk about failing the family business.

She nestled the phone closer to her mouth and found herself asking, "Full coverage? If I came back, you'd give my *parents* coverage, too?"

But Dan had overheard. He spun in his seat. "Get out. You're moving back?"

She shushed him, angling farther away. "Did you ever establish that pretax benefits plan?"

What a relief it would be, if she could feel like her parents were covered. Sorrow and Billy would be married soon, and she was sure the sheriff's department would have them covered, but if *she* could establish a bigger nest egg for Mom and Dad, then if the day ever came when her folks needed something like in-home care, she'd be able to provide it.

"Because I *so* cannot see you living here," Dan said with a smirk.

Tucking her head for more privacy, she told her old boss she'd consider it.

San Francisco wasn't so far away, not really. She *could* go back, just for a little while. Sorrow could stay and run things at the lodge, and *she'd* have her high-powered job back, pulling in an easy six figures. She could scrimp, setting aside enough money to take the stress off her parents.

"There's not even any decent sushi here," Dan said, continuing his rant at her back.

She nodded, moving farther down the bar. "I'd need a guarantee in writing," she told him in a low but stern voice. It felt good to be business Laura again—she *was* good at it. "A more ironclad contract. And no noncompete clause this time."

Maybe Eddie would even move with her. They could always come back to Sierra Falls when it was time to have kids.

They . . . she smiled at the thought.

"I knew it," Dan exclaimed the moment she hung up.

"What are you talking about?"

"I've seen you screening your calls. Checking your texts. Lola's back. The master negotiator."

Eddie walked in, and as she watched him approach, all her concerns fell away. Their eyes locked.

"I love this idea," Dan said, then added in a conspiratorial whisper, "But forget San Francisco. You belong in LA." He held up a hand, and it hung in the air until she gave him an automatic but distracted high-five, her attention pinned only on the Jessup heading straight for her.

Eddie reached them, and all she wanted was to sink into his arms—if only he were holding her, she'd be able to sort out this confusion. If she could be with Eddie, she'd be home, wherever she was.

"Hey," she told him quietly. "There you are."

"Here I am, darlin'." He gave her his Eddie smile, all ease and promise and comfort. "I came to take you to dinner."

"Just no sushi," the producer chimed in. "Am I right, Lola?"

Eddie looked askance at the guy. "No worries there."

"Lola, tell Teddie here where they have the best sushi."

"It's *Eddie*."

"San Francisco is where it's at," Dan yammered on. "They've got the best sushi, and now they'll have our Lola back, too."

"Dammit, Dan." She paled, watching Eddie's face go blank, and quickly assured him, "It's not like that."

"Not like what?" he asked her slowly.

"Didn't you hear?" Dan raised his beer in a toast. "Our girl is moving back to San Francisco."

Thirty-three

Eddie's blood turned to ice. "What did you say?"

"It's not set in stone," Laura said.

"What do you mean?" Dread spread through him like a cold, black shadow. "What's not set in stone?"

"My old boss called," she began, and she didn't need to say more than that.

"You're *leaving*. Again." It felt like he'd been punched. Her leaving was no real surprise anymore, and it gutted him. But on top of the hurt was anger. Why hadn't she told him?

"It might be a good option," she hedged. She hadn't disagreed.

Eddie watched her, waiting for this to be some misunderstanding, but he could tell by the look on her face that he'd heard correctly. "That's all it takes? A phone call from some guy who treated you like crap, and then you're back in your car, outta here?"

That idiot producer chimed in. "She's off to San Fran,

but I'm telling her, LA is the place to be. City of Angels, baby. Am I right?" And then the jackass actually gave him a chummy punch on the arm.

Eddie flinched away. He couldn't believe this. She wasn't leaving. Not again. He tried to understand—surely there was something he was missing. "So, what, this guy just called you?"

"He's been doing the hard sell," Dan answered instead. "Calling, texting."

"Dan," Laura scolded.

Eddie finally broke his gaze away from her, shooting a glare at Dan-the-douche, then back at her again. "Is that true?"

"Yes, but—"

"Dude's been calling her for a while now. But who wouldn't chase Lola?" Dan gave a knowing leer. "She's even got *you* chasing her."

Eddie cut his eyes at him. "How about you shut the hell up?"

"What's *your* problem?" the guy muttered, grabbing another fistful of bar snacks.

Laura sighed. "Take it easy, boys."

He was done being easy. He'd been easy his whole life, and look what it was getting him. No, he finally had everything he'd ever wanted, and he wasn't letting it go without a fight. "Don't you think you might have mentioned this? Remind me . . . *what* have we been doing these past weeks? Because I know what I've been doing. I've been with you. Thinking about you."

In love, *with you.*

While clearly *she'd* been back to her old ways—coming home, doing the emotional slash and burn, which meant soon she'd be hightailing it back to the city, leaving scorched earth in her wake. Right on schedule.

"I know," she said in a pleading voice. "I didn't think his calls would come to anything."

"Or, hey," he barreled on, "here's a thought. You could've mentioned it to me, maybe before you told *this* guy." He angrily hitched his thumb Dan's way.

"Chill out," Dan told him, sounding indignant. "Take it easy on her." He added under his breath, "Dude, I would lose my shit living here."

"Fine, *dude*," Eddie mocked. "Then maybe it's time for you to leave."

"You could come with me," Laura argued. "We can still be together."

Dan's eyes widened, and he swung around on his stool with a shout. "Get out!" He shook his head, repeating, "Get the hell out. You two are a thing?"

"I could take care of things for a while," she said, ignoring Dan. "Till you got on your feet. You could find a construction job in the city. I can pay for stuff."

"You think that's what I care about? Whether I have enough *stuff*? Have you not been listening to a word I've said? Haven't you gotten who I am?"

"He's right. What would a mountain dude do in the city?" Dan laughed to himself, shaking his head, muttering, "Lola sowing her oats with the locals. Classic."

Eddie spun on him. "How about you shut your mouth before I shut it for you?"

"Forget him." Laura reached for his hand. "Listen to me. You have to admit you've been struggling, but there's work in the city. Jack could run Jessup Brothers on his own."

He pulled away. "The only thing I'm struggling with right now is you, Laura."

Dan chuckled to himself. "She's a spitfire, all right."

"I'm warning you," Eddie told him through gritted teeth. He would not be held responsible for mopping the floor with this guy.

Dan smirked. *"Nice."*

"I need to think of my finances," Laura continued. "Our finances."

"What's so wrong with our finances? We've got food, family, a roof over our heads. Hell, several roofs."

"But what if I need more? People will pay me a lot to use my business sense. It's how I've survived."

"We survive because this is our home. We've got family here. *I've* got family, and I'm not leaving them." He did a quick scan of the bar. Bear was in the corner, playing cards with his buddies. Sorrow was in the back. Helen worked the floor, while Edith was at the lodge caring for her kid. "We're a community, Laura. But we're not good enough for you, are we? We never were."

"That's not fair."

"You know what's not fair? Jerking me around like this. What, you just wanted to see what it was like with a townie? Is that all I am? But how big of you, you're not done with me yet, so you'll find the country bumpkin a job in the big city."

"That's not it at all. I didn't think I'd consider leaving until just now."

"And you didn't for a moment think your leaving was something I might like to have a say in?"

She shot back, "Since when do you have a say in my professional life?"

He got quiet. "It's like you need to control every aspect of your life. You can't let it go for one minute, can you?"

"That's not true."

"I should've known. Whenever the going gets too scary, Laura Bailey cuts and runs." He felt so stupid. Stupid, and embarrassed. "And I can't believe you told this guy about it before me. You could've at least told me your old boss was calling. We have had some time together lately. I trusted you. I thought I was finally making headway with you. I told you stuff, Laura. And then you turn around and tell your news to this prick."

Dan pulled his shoulders back, trying to look tough. "Don't be getting up in my grill. Lola, I can't believe you're

letting mountain man here talk to you like that. He's out of
your system, now you should get him out of your bar."

Eddie took a step closer. He had half a mind to show this
guy the meaning of *mountain man*. "You're on thin ice,
pretty boy."

"Just come with me to the city," Laura pleaded. "I can
take care of things for a while, until we figure it out."

"Don't sweat Teddie here," Dan told her. "If he doesn't
want you, you can be *my* sugar mama, any day of the week."

That was it. Eddie grabbed a fistful of that gelled, spiked
hair, pulled the guy from his stool, and punched him in the
face.

Dan grabbed his head with a sharp yelp and skittered
backward. "What the hell?"

"Stop it," Laura shrieked. The bar had fallen silent.
"What are you doing?"

He flexed his fist, shaking it out. "Just being a country boy."

Dan grabbed his asinine black glasses from where they'd
flown to the floor and settled them back on his face. "Don't
mess with me." He blew out a breath, rolling his shoulders
like he might actually try something, but Eddie had about
five inches and forty pounds on the guy that said he wouldn't.

"Screw this," Dan said. "I'm loading up. We're out of
here. I thought we'd get some footage of your stupid hotel,
but I'm over it. Done."

As the producer stormed out, Laura turned on him.
"Thanks, Eddie. Thanks a whole hell of a lot. Your business
sense is staggering."

That was all she was thinking about? *Business?* She'd
just broken his heart.

"I thought you had a tender side," he told her. "But everyone was right. You're out for yourself."

"And *I* was right, too. You're a Neanderthal."

"Yeah, at least I'm not a robot. I'd rather know how to
feel, and get angry, than be good at . . . what are you good

at . . . spreadsheets? All you care about is the bottom line. Well, you can take your cold numbers to bed with you."

She stood rigidly, arms wrapped tight around her chest. "You say you don't want anyone to think you're a bumpkin, but look at you. You can't just go around punching people when things don't go your way. Talk about looking the part. What do you expect people to think?"

"They'll think maybe I'm in love with you."

The bar was utterly silent. Laura was silent.

He felt it in his chest, gutting him, like silence might be a physical thing.

"You think you're better than us," he told her quietly. "You always did. I tell you I love you, and not even *that's* good enough." He let his eyes lock with hers, one last time. He had to get her out of his sight. The pain was too great. "You know what, Laura? Just go. And this time, stay gone."

Thirty-four

Rob dallied under the tavern's awning, putting off the inevitable.

It'd been a sort of horror . . . watching from a distance as a man did such unfathomable things, only to realize *you* were that man. When clarity had descended, and he grasped what he'd done, it'd been like rousing from a dream into a waking nightmare.

Last night, he'd left his daughter. It was incomprehensible. His sick, tiny daughter. He'd left her alone to fend for herself. Helen would never forgive him.

He'd never forgive himself.

He reached for the doorknob, but it flew open, and out burst Laura Bailey. She froze, stopping short before they ran into each other, and then she gave him a look of such disgust it shamed him. "Men," she snarled, her lip curled, then stormed away to the lodge.

Not the greatest indication of how he'd be received. He took a deep breath and warily entered the tavern. Inside, the silence was so deafening, it made his skin crawl. Was the silence because *he'd* shown up?

"Great," he heard his wife say. "Now it's a party."

Guilt, humiliation . . . it choked him. But it was a horror of his own making, and so he made himself face it.

He found her—his Helen—his eyes went straight for her. "Can we talk?"

She put her hands on her hips. "You've got a tongue. What's stopping you?" So pretty she was, with that thick, red hair. That saucy body. There used to be such fire in her eyes, and he knew he was the one who'd dampened it.

"Someplace private?" he pleaded. By the time he'd made it home last night, she'd secured the chain on the door. She wouldn't let him in. Wouldn't take his calls. His only choice was to plead his case in public, but he hoped it wouldn't have to be *this* public.

She scanned the floor, until Bear caught her eyes and gave her a nod. She led him to a corner booth and sat. "Tell me one thing," she demanded at once. "Is there another woman? Because I can't figure how else you could leave our girl like that."

"Of course not. Just you. Only you." He leaned forward, desperate to take her hands.

She stared at his outstretched arms like he was diseased. "That's all you've got?" She bolted to standing. "I can't do this."

"No. Please." Panic made his mouth taste metallic, made his ears ring. "Just give me one minute. Sixty seconds is all I ask."

She considered it for a painful moment, then sat stiffly across from him. "Sixty seconds." She glared at her watch like she might actually be timing him.

She seemed so far away. He was losing her. Losing his family. He'd awoken from his haze into a cold, black place. But it was a place he'd made himself. Even now he felt the itch to try, just one last time. To head to the nearest casino and finally get his big payday. But he knew now, the impulse was a madness, chasing smoke. He had his payday, and it was Helen and the kids. And they'd locked him out of their lives.

He forced himself to keep his hands extended toward her, praying the day would come when she'd take them again. "I'm sorry. So sorry."

"Tell it to Ellie. I can get you wanting to leave me, but her? Chrissakes, Rob, she's only seven years old."

"I'll never forgive myself."

Her eyes were flat on him. "That and two bucks will buy you a cup of coffee."

"I have a problem," he said. "I know that now. But I promise I'll work hard. I'm going to work on getting better." It would be a lifelong struggle, but his wake-up call had been just too terrifying. The stakes were too high—he had to back away from the ledge. There was no choice in this one. He needed to turn his back on gambling forever. "Doctor Mark found me a group in Silver City."

He heard someone in the tavern say, "As long as it's far from the strip." There was a low, answering laugh.

He pretended not to hear. "I went, and it's good, Helen. It'll be a good thing. They told me how gambling is an addiction. Like heroin or something."

He heard voices discussing him. The talk came to him in snippets . . . what he should do, what Helen should do, what others have done. There were Bible quotes about forgiveness. About fortitude. Pithy, pitiful crap.

It all made him so angry. People didn't understand. Easy quotes and anecdotes meant nothing when you were facing a battle like this. But he knew that his anger and shame were the flip sides of the same coin. He had no right to be angry, and the shame was his to feel. He was the one who'd made himself an outsider.

He pushed those other voices from his head. They didn't matter. All that mattered was Helen. His kids. "Gamblers like me, we think we can hit the tables like anyone else. I thought I could go to the casino like a normal person."

"I swear to you," Helen snapped, "the day you enter another casino will be the day I take your kids from you forever."

Her voice was steel, but he'd earned that cold wrath. He made himself hear it. "I won't. I swear I won't." He'd been studying the steps to recovery. First was to admit he was powerless. Then, to turn his will. Now, it was time to make amends.

"Can you try to forgive me?" he asked quietly.

"I'm tired, Rob." She leaned her head back, looking defeated. Her pretty face had aged.

He'd done that to her. "Marrying me was a bad bargain."

"Our kids are the only reason I'm even looking at you right now."

"I vow I'll spend the rest of my life making it up to all of you."

"You've said vows before." She shook her head. "They're just words."

"Not if you mean them like I do. You said vows once, too. *In sickness and in health.* Please, just one more chance. Let me be a husband to you."

She stared at him a moment, speechless, looking like she was seeing him for the first time. "I'm done."

Panic clawed him. "Don't say that. Don't say you're done."

He'd emerged from a fog to realize his angel girl could've died, and it would've been *his* fault. He'd awoken to find his wife on the other side of a glass wall, staring at him like a pitiable thing. Like a criminal. "I love you, Helen. I'm nothing without you."

"Then it looks like you've got a problem."

He felt someone looming over them and looked up to find Eddie Jessup staring daggers.

"Hey, Helen," Eddie said. "Do you need help over here? Do you need me to ask him to leave?"

"I have to talk to my wife."

"And I have to make sure your wife wants to listen."

He stood and faced Eddie. This would be the last time she'd need another man to step up for her, even if it meant breaking his back to prove he was the only one for her. He'd face everyone, one by one, if that was what he needed to do to make it right. To make Helen *his* again. "She doesn't need protection from me."

"Your kid sure needed protecting when I dropped her at your house last night."

"What are you doing lurking around our house?" Eddie made himself at home while he'd been locked out. Jealousy and shame burned him. Fed his anger. "You hot for my wife?"

Helen got up, every inch of her five-foot-four frame standing erect. "Robert, don't you dare."

"You have got to be kidding me." Eddie laughed grimly. "This is *not* the best moment to push it with me, Haskell."

"What do you care, anyway?" He considered the guy for a moment. He knew Jessup had been there for his wife and child, and it stung. He wanted to lash out, but since he couldn't take the guy with his fists, he'd take him with words. "If I were you, I'd be worrying about minding my own damned business. Fairview's got a casino in Reno, and the place has been crawling with suits. I heard them talk, and there's something fishy with that construction project of yours. So you need to stop throwing stones when you live in your own damned glass house."

Eddie squinted at him. "What the hell are you talking about? You're so full of it, trying to make this about me, when you should be *thanking* me. I was there last night for your family, doing what you should've been doing."

"You need to stay away from my wife."

"And you need to get a grip," Eddie said. "Look at

you . . . look at all your bullshit. The gambling, the money, this big-guy attitude of yours, screw all of it. You've got a wife and kids who love you. That's the jackpot right there. And you're going to lose it all."

The statement hung, reverberating, until Helen added quietly, "It's one thing to neglect *me*, Rob, but Ellie could have died."

He broke then.

He began to weep, in front of all those people. But he didn't care. He'd strip naked and walk through Sierra Falls if it meant his wife would forgive him. "I don't want to neglect you, Helen. I love you."

Eddie scowled at him. "Then you need to man up."

"That's enough, Eddie." Helen inserted herself between the two men. "I've got this."

Rob took her hands and told her earnestly, "All I ever wanted was to take care of you. To treat you to things. Treat you right."

She flinched, and it was a knife in his belly. "You've got a funny way of showing it."

"I just wanted some extra cash," he pleaded. "For *us*. I wanted enough money to hire a sitter for you. To get you some help every once in a while."

"I love the kids," she shot back. "I love spending time with them. I wanted to spend time with *you*, too."

"But you're always flirting with other men."

"Hoping to catch *your* attention," she snapped. "I don't want them. I thought you had a mistress."

The front door jingled, and Ellie ran in, with Edith right behind. His angel girl, and she ran right into his arms. "Daddy!"

"I tried to keep her on the couch." Edith shot a glance at Helen, and it was loaded with uncertainty and apology. "She saw his truck in the lot and insisted."

His daughter forgave him, and he swore to himself he'd

do all he could to make himself worthy of it. He scrubbed his face dry. "Hey, pretty lady. How are you feeling?"

Ellie was clueless to the discomfort of the adults in the room and reported with a wide smile, "Missus Edith gave me a special wallet for my money."

"What money?" Helen was instantly suspicious, and it made him feel like a thief. She took the beaded wallet from their daughter and opened it, but when she saw what was inside, her expression crumpled.

"Daddy gave me his buffalo nickel," Ellie said proudly.

Helen gave him a pointed look. "That's your lucky coin."

"I don't need it anymore." He reached for her hand. "That's what I've been trying to tell you."

She held herself stiffly, but finally she didn't pull away. "I don't need babysitters and fancy cars," she said, sounding so tired. "I need *you*."

"Really? Do you really mean that?" He would erase that sadness from her eyes—he'd dedicate himself to it.

Finally he felt Jessup, Edith, and the others drift away, giving them some privacy, and he let it all out. "I see you . . . you're so damned sexy, Helen. And I'm such a screwup. I've got a job at the hardware store, and then I see you talking to guys like . . . like Eddie, or that Damien. I see how men like that look at you. I see the way you smile at them. You could be with any man you wanted. You're that beautiful. We've been on this road a long time. We were young when we started. I'd understand if you want to leave me."

"I do want to leave you." She swept a tear from her face. "But don't you get it, Robbie? I don't care about those other men. All I ever wanted was to make a life with you, my husband, and you took that from me." She sighed. Paused. It was the longest moment of his life. "But the kids love you, and God help me, somewhere in my heart, I do, too. I'll give you one more chance. Just one more," she added vehemently. "Because if I see you so much as *looking* at a deck of cards,

I'll fix it so you're never alone with me or our children ever again."

"Thank you, Helen." He squeezed her hand and pressed it to his cheek. He knew not to try for more than that. "I'll show you. I'll prove to you how I can be a better man."

He would prove his worth to her every day for the rest of his life. He'd seen the edge of the precipice, and he wasn't going back, ever again.

Thirty-five

Laura shoved her suitcase into the back of her car. He'd told her to go. To stay gone. She slammed the trunk shut. He'd called her a robot.

Fine, then. She'd be the best, most successful damned robot Sierra Falls had ever seen. Only this time she wasn't going to come back until she was driving a damned Porsche. A red one.

"Do you have to leave *now*?" Sorrow came and leaned against her car. It was super early, and her sister had thrown on an ancient high school hoodie over her pajamas. Her hair was a messy, early-morning tangle.

Emotion clawed Laura's throat. All her posturing was just a lie. She'd be dying to come back home—would probably be home again by the end of the month. She'd just hide in the lodge next time, maybe park around back where people couldn't see she was there. Where nobody would think she'd returned with her tail between her legs. "Afraid so."

She needed to leave before the breakfast crowd showed at the tavern. Before she saw that red pickup driving down the road, where this time it wouldn't stop. She pasted a smile on her face. "I want to miss the Bay Bridge traffic."

Sorrow gave her a probing look, likely seeing what Laura had tried to hide, but all the mascara in the world couldn't mask a sleepless night of crying. "Come in and get some food at least."

"I'm not hungry." More like, she didn't think she could choke anything down. Her stomach was a knot.

"Toast," Sorrow said. "Coffee. Something." It was clear her sister wouldn't give up.

She peeked at her cell. She was checking the time but couldn't help but notice there were no calls. No texts. No Eddie.

"It's still so early," Sorrow said, guessing her concern. "We'll have the place to ourselves."

"Okay." She stopped trying to force the smile—her sister understood. "Just coffee. I don't think I can do anything else."

Sorrow unlocked the door, and Laura went to turn up the thermostat. She loved the quiet, chill feeling of the tavern in the morning. That feeling of solitude. The first *flick-flick* of the kitchen lights.

The sadness made her feel so heavy. She sagged into a booth away from the window. "I'll miss this."

"I still don't understand why you have to go."

She wasn't fully comprehending, either. It was happening fast, like a riptide sweeping her away. She hadn't reported the owls because she didn't want to ruin Eddie's business. He was a hero to those Reno kids, and she didn't have the heart to do something that might change that. But in not reporting the nesting ground to the authorities, she was letting the hotel construction continue, which could very well hurt her family business.

Her only choice was to help her family in another way.

And there was no greater help than money. Seeing Ellie's ordeal had brought back chilling memories of medical bills, insurance deductibles, all those fears for the future. But if she took her old job back, the practical fears would disappear.

Moving back to San Francisco. It'd been easy enough to go there in her head—she'd done it so many times. Had convinced herself so many times that leaving Sierra Falls was what she wanted. What was best for her family. Only now she feared she was going through the motions.

Sorrow tossed the tavern keys onto the table. "I know you want to get out of here, like, ten minutes ago, but sit. For one second. And *don't move.*"

God, she loved her baby sister. She raised her hand, promising. "Got it."

As she listened to Sorrow bustle in the kitchen, she checked her phone again. Since she'd given her CEO the thumbs-up, there'd been a flurry of e-mails from the human resources department. Benefits information. The contract for her to sign. Appointments she needed to make. The details about her stock grant.

Benefits, stock . . . It was the mantra she kept in her head. She had to keep repeating it. Had to keep reminding herself she was doing this for them. Whenever she stopped, too many doubts stabbed her.

She had all kinds of things to sign, but of course there wasn't a fax at the lodge. She clicked off the phone with a sigh. It was okay. She'd be back in the city by lunch. Maybe she'd head straight to the office.

She'd sign her contract, and then the decision would be made.

Sorrow reappeared with two mugs bearing the Thirsty Bear logo.

She breathed in deeply. "You made the good coffee."

"All my coffee is good coffee." Sorrow settled across from her with a smile. "But yes, I made your gross super-strong French press coffee."

Tears pricked her eyes, and she pursed her lips to stop them. She'd sworn to herself she wouldn't break down in front of anyone. Not even her sister.

"I'm going to throttle that man the next time I see him." Sorrow leaned forward and took her hand.

"It's not Eddie's fault." She pulled away. Too much contact, and she would lose it. "I was stupid to think there was anything there."

"You don't have to leave because of it."

"I'm not leaving because of Eddie," she insisted. Not really, anyway. "I've got a killer bonus package. I figure if I work even for two, three years, I can sock away enough to cover what Dad's IRA doesn't."

"Forget that." Sorrow squeezed her hand. "Dad has enough saved. We own the place outright. We *are* sitting on a gold mine, right?" she joked, referring to the veins of gold running deep through the rock, too deep for anyone to touch.

She laughed, and it was good to have a moment's respite from the intensity. "Don't tell Dad that. I'm sure he has dreams of being Prospector Pete."

The door jingled as Helen came in, and Sorrow checked the clock over the bar. "You're early."

Helen's eyes went from Sorrow in her jammies, to her, probably looking ready to crack. "Do you need me to come back?"

Laura tried her smile again, but she knew it was stiff. "Not at all. I'll be hitting the road soon. Just grabbing some fuel for the drive." She sipped her coffee—it was still too hot, but she needed something to burn away the emotion.

Helen tied on her apron. "I wanted to get out, grab some time to think."

"Work is good for that sometimes," Sorrow said, filling the uneasy silence. "Don't mind us."

"I'll get everything going in the kitchen, then." Helen disappeared into the back.

"Good." Her sister leaned forward. "Now I have even more time to convince you."

She gave her a rueful smile. "You're not going to convince me."

"You don't have to go back to work," Sorrow insisted. "The lodge and tavern will be fine. Mom and Dad will be fine. We've always gotten by. It's not up to you to shoulder everything."

"It's not just that. I don't know that I ever really belonged here."

"How can you say that? Sierra Falls is your home."

"I was fooling myself to think that I could be . . . I don't know . . . nature girl or something." She gave an embarrassed shrug. When she felt Helen emerge from the kitchen, going behind the bar to get the coffee started, she pitched her voice lower. "Here's the irony. That stupid ranch is on some sort of protected owl nesting ground. So, after all that, I actually *could* shut Eddie down."

"But you're not?"

"Of course I'm not. Why would I? The Jessups do good. They're a fixture in Sierra Falls. Scott the forest ranger. Mark the doctor. Jack's boy is off at boot camp. You don't get much more upstanding than all that. And then there's Eddie. He's practically a hero, using his own money to do stuff for needy kids. How many lives has he touched? How many kids' futures have changed because he's got the spare cash to buy gear and food? You pointed it out yourself; the Jessups aren't going to ruin us, so why should I put Jack and Eddie out of business? Especially now that I'll be going back to my old job. I've got great insurance, an IRA. Hell, with what my old boss is paying me, I could start a whole new hotel."

Sorrow gave her an evil grin. "You could do it to spite the Neanderthal."

"I guess . . ." She gave a halfhearted smile. "I don't know.

I was wrong about Eddie. He's a good guy. I think I'll just back away slowly, you know?"

They were speaking in hushed tones, but she could tell by Helen's pauses that the woman was catching dribs and drabs of the conversation. It hardly mattered, though. Not at this point. And besides, after all Helen had been through, she couldn't fault her anything. It was amazing she'd even let her husband back in the house. She guessed that was what marriage was about—commitment. And being a team for life sometimes meant forgiveness.

She'd thought she was ready for something like that, but maybe she'd been right about herself all along. *Business* was her strength. Not men. Spreadsheets in bed, just like Eddie had said.

She felt that ache again in her throat and took a last sip of coffee to burn it away. She checked the clock. "I should go, and you should get dressed." She gave her sister a sad smile. "You need to text me. And call. Anytime. If you take anyone else wedding dress shopping, I swear, I will kill you."

Sorrow walked her out. "Let us know when you get there."

"Next stop, San Francisco." She selected some music on her phone—an old Dixie Chicks CD, with songs about strong women walking away—plugged it in, and hit the road.

But the next stop wasn't San Francisco. She couldn't leave Sierra Falls without paying one last visit.

Thirty-six

∾

Eddie peeled into the tavern parking lot. He'd screwed up. Big-time.

He owed Laura a big apology. What he should've done was greet her news with congratulations. She'd apparently been offered some plum job, but instead of telling her he was proud, he'd acted pissy.

Sure, he could've asked questions, maybe raised doubts—hell, they could've had a little debate and resolved it back at his place. So why hadn't he? If he really thought about it—and there'd been little else he had thought about last night—it was jealousy that'd made him act like such a giant baby.

He loped up the steps. The real truth was, he'd follow Laura all the way to New York City, if that was what it took to be with her. He'd tell her so, immediately and in no uncertain terms.

"You just missed her," Helen said as he came in.

Still, he looked around, as if she might be mistaken.

"You came looking for Miss Thang, right?"

He finally focused on her. "Hey, Helen. Yeah, I'm looking for Laura." He needed to get himself together, act like a normal human being. "Sorry . . . you said she left?" He checked the clock—he'd barely slept and felt situated somewhere out of time—but it was still early, just past eight. And he thought *he'd* be too early. What time had she left to beat him out the door? "What time?"

Helen resumed clearing a table of its plates, cutlery, and empty cups. "I got in just after six. It was a little after that."

"Where'd she go? She's not *gone* gone, is she?" Maybe she'd run out and would be back in a minute. But at the crack of dawn? He couldn't wrap his mind around the notion that she'd simply disappear overnight. She'd need to say goodbye to people. She wouldn't just leave without a trace.

Helen shrugged. "She looked pretty gone to me."

He plopped into the nearest chair. He was numb. "Got it. Thanks, Helen."

Of course she was gone for good—it was Laura they were talking about. The great disappearing woman. Master of the getaway.

She came over with a carafe. "You look like you could use some coffee."

"Why not?" Maybe she'd hit him over the head with it—sure would hurt less.

"Sorry, Eddie." She filled up his cup and brought him creams and sugars.

"Me, too, Helen." He couldn't believe it. He'd spent his life bemoaning how elusive the pretty Bailey girl was, and this time, *he'd* been the one to send her packing. "Looks like I screwed up big-time." Every nasty thing she'd ever said about him—a Neanderthal . . . a delinquent . . . an unsophisticated, uncivilized brute—he'd proven it all true. In front of a crowd, no less.

He realized Helen was still standing there. Had she said something? He was like the walking dead. "Sorry, what?"

"I said, can I get you something to eat?"

"Sure." He scrubbed a hand through his hair, considering it. He had to eat—if he'd eaten something last night, he didn't remember it now, and neither did his stomach. "How about some eggs." He needed a plan, and food would help. "Three, scrambled hard. Side of bacon." He tore open a bunch of sugar packets and dumped them into his coffee. It was shaping up to be one hell of a morning, and he'd throw everything he could at it. "Maybe some home fries. Toast, too. What else . . ."

"Kitchen sink?"

"Huh?" He looked up and she was smiling down at him. He sighed. "Yeah, throw in the kitchen sink, too, would you?" He'd need to claw his way out of this hole if he was going to be any good to anyone.

When Helen came back with the first of several plates, he forced himself to make small talk, which was clearly what the woman wanted. He asked after Ellie. She asked after the ranch. They avoided talk of Laura and Rob and fistfights.

His eggs and toast were up, and as she brought him a bottle of ketchup and a little bowl filled with jellies, she asked, "So, you off to the ranch today, or is the project dead for good?"

He spread a big gob of strawberry jelly on a triangle of toast. "What do you mean?"

"The owls. I heard about Timber Creek having some nesting thing. I just assumed . . ." She began to look panicked.

What the hell? He made a split-second decision to play along. "Oh, that. Yeah." If she knew something she wasn't supposed to know, he didn't want to scare her off. Ever since Rob called the ranch project sketchy, it'd nagged him. "The nesting thing," he repeated. Whatever the hell *that* meant. Rob had overheard something—was this it? And had he discussed it with his wife? "Where'd you hear about it?"

"Laura and Sorrow were talking about it," she said. "I guess your ranger brother was the one who found the nests?"

"Something like that." His mind raced to put it all together. Had Laura discovered something about those owls? But it couldn't have been Scott who'd told her. His brother would flip his lid if he thought they were doing construction on some endangered habitat.

"I've never seen baby owls before," Helen went on. "Do you think I could bring Ellie by when she's better? It seems crazy that something like a few nests could stop a whole hotel from being built, but Laura knows, I guess. And, I tell you, I'd be pissed, too, if I were you."

"Pissed?"

"I assume that's why you two were fighting. She shut you down."

No, she didn't. She hadn't breathed a word of it. She could have shut his whole project down, but she'd obviously sacrifice everything and leave before hurting him.

What an ass he was.

"I gotta run." He wiped his mouth, tossed some bills down, and scooted away from the table.

"But your bacon hasn't come out yet."

"I'm not hungry anymore." He had a project to shut down.

And a woman to find.

* * *

Hunter Fox returned his call almost immediately, and Eddie pulled to the side of the road to take it. He wanted to give it his total focus. He wasn't generally a shark when it came to business, but he knew how to play ball, and how different could *this* be? Hell, this'd probably be easier than any ball game.

He didn't waste any time, telling the Fairview exec right off, "You're stopping construction."

Fox paused for a good ten seconds. "I am?"

He knew at once what the guy was up to. Fox would try

to unsettle him, using long silences, threats, whatever it took. But Eddie didn't scare easy.

He had only one thing to lose: Laura.

And the sooner he dealt with this bonehead, the sooner he could track her down. He'd apologize. He'd bring her home.

"You are. You're stopping construction. See, Hunter, I know what you're up to." He was officially done with *Mister Fox*.

"You do? You surprise me, Edward. What am I up to?"

Fox's voice reeked of amused disdain, but it didn't throw Eddie off his game one little bit. He had the ball and was going for the blitz.

"You wanted to bulldoze a protected habitat and cover it up." It was a leap to think Fairview knew about the nesting ground, but Rob had overheard *something* in that casino. If the guy was up to no good, hopefully he'd be quick to panic at anything. And sure, *bulldoze* was an exaggeration—they might've been on the same property, but those nests were nowhere near the ranch house itself—but he bet these monkey suits bluffed right and left. "You knew something like that would bring the government down on your ass, and yet you covered it up. There must be all kinds of laws protecting rare species."

Instead of answering, Fox was silent. *Bingo.*

He might not know business, but he knew all about sleazebags like this guy. He seized his advantage. "If you don't shut down your little boutique hotel, I'm calling every newspaper from here to the goddamn *New York Times* if I have to, telling them you were going to slaughter a bunch of endangered birds. How do you think your rich yuppie eco-tourists will like that?"

"Nicely done." Fox's voice was dangerously subdued. "Just one problem. Who'll believe you?"

"The whole town of Sierra Falls, for a start." He was freestyling now, but it felt right. Full-court press, for the win. "I've got witnesses. Your lackeys aren't the only ones who've heard about your *special projects*."

"Okay, Edward," Fox said genially, "Let's say I'm finding this two-bit town to be more trouble than it's worth. What would you say to that?"

"I'd say maybe it was time for you to get out of Dodge. Cut your losses. Except for one thing . . ."

Fox's voice hardened. "What do you want, Mister Jessup?"

Mister Jessup—how the tables turned. "I'll tell you my terms." He paused. "But first? The name's *Edwin*. Edwin Jessup."

He told Fox exactly what he wanted. And then he sped off, going after *who* he wanted.

Laura. She'd become his everything. She was all he really needed.

She was headed back to the city, but he had an idea where she'd go first. She'd told him once how special the falls were to her, and he knew in his gut she'd need to see them as part of her good-bye.

He drove straight to the trailhead, and sure enough, her shiny black Beemer was there.

He hit the trail, walking fast. But first he let himself take a moment to pick her a good pinecone.

Thirty-seven

⁓

Laura had dallied long enough. She'd said good-bye to the falls. She wondered what Grandpa would've had to say about her leaving—probably that she was a coward.

It was too late now. She'd accepted the job. Had chosen her path.

She got up and brushed herself off. It was time. She hadn't lied to Sorrow when she said she wanted to miss the Bay Area traffic. She hit the trail, heading back the way she came.

She'd made fun of herself for not being nature girl, but she did love these woods—she always had. It didn't hurt that it was an easy walk to and from the falls.

She took a good look around, memorizing the trees. Saying good-bye. Good-bye to the person she'd almost become.

Realistically, she wouldn't be back until autumn. The leaves would have turned by then. The quaking aspens—those were her favorites—they'd be yellow. There'd be some reds and oranges, too. But mostly it'd be the same pine trees, green and fresh, and feeling old as time.

She had to look away. Look down. She kicked rocks along the trail, thinking how lately she felt old as time, too. Would she ever really be happy? She was in love with Eddie, she knew that now. She'd probably been in love with him for years. All that sparring. All those sparks. Had she wanted him all along?

But she also knew that sparring, arguments, conflict . . . it was all she was good for. It was why she was so good at business. Why she thrived in a cold, big city.

"Penny for your thoughts, darlin'."

She looked up and her breath caught. "Eddie."

It was like she'd conjured him. For an instant, she had the fantasy that they hadn't fought. The fantasy that they were a couple, out for a hike. But she reminded herself it wasn't true. They were from two very different worlds, two travelers bearing different passports, with two very different destinations. So many differences never to be resolved. Seeing him, she mourned the person she wasn't.

"How did you find me?"

He walked right up to her. "Finding you was easy. It's catching you that's the hard part."

He didn't touch her, but he looked like he wanted to. She knew Eddie—the touching would be up to her. But she didn't have the guts.

He spoke of catching her . . . did that mean he wanted to keep her, too? She didn't trust it. What if she let him in, let him look deeper into her heart, and he decided he didn't like what he saw? The old fear and vulnerability began to slink back, and it sharpened her words. "Why are you here?"

"I told you," he said gently. "I love you. Why can't you believe that?"

Probably because she didn't feel particularly lovable at the moment. Last night's accusations came to her in a flood.

"I thought I was too controlling. A robot with intimacy issues."

"I didn't mean those things. I'm sorry—I was hurt and jealous. But I do love you, Laura, and I'll say it as many times as I need to until you believe it."

Then she saw what he had in his hands, and she burst into tears. "You brought me a pinecone?" Maybe he did recognize the real her. Maybe he had looked deep into her heart and still wanted what he saw.

"Yeah, goof." He gave her a loving smile, tipping her chin up to face him. "I can't hike to the falls without picking you a pinecone."

She'd held so much emotion dammed in for so long, but one pinecone, Eddie's smile, and—God help her—being called a goof when goof was the last thing she was, and she broke. Laughing, crying, smiling, sobbing . . . she stood in the middle of the woods and completely lost it. Lost it like she'd never lost it in front of anyone before.

Eddie panicked. "Oh, honey, no crying. I hate to see you cry." He finally crossed the divide, tucking her close, which made her only sob harder.

She let herself sink into him. "Oh, Eddie, I love you, too. I think I've probably always loved you, and now I screwed it all up."

"You didn't screw anything up." He squeezed her tight. "We'll figure it out. Just don't cry anymore—you're killing me."

"Are you kidding?" She sniffled. "I keep crying. I can't stop it. People think I'm a robot, but really I'm just a wreck."

"Nobody thinks you're a robot."

She couldn't catch her breath. She was a teary, shuddering mess. "You do."

"Well, you're going to rust yourself out," he said, and she laughed through her tears. He smoothed his hand along her head. "Really, it's time to come home, Laura."

"I can't. I told them I'd take this stupid job." She was stuck now. The riptide was tearing her away once again. "I've been jerking them around so much, if I don't take it, I'll never work in Silicon Valley again."

"I don't see the problem." He pulled away enough to meet her eyes. "How can I get it in your head that business success isn't life success?"

"But it's security." She'd spent her whole adult life building up the trappings of security, and she wasn't ready to part with the idea so easily. "What if something happens? You could go away tomorrow. My dad might get sick again. I need to think about those things."

"Nothing will happen. I'm not going anywhere. There's a whole town full of people who love you and will help you. Who want you *home*."

"But the business stuff . . . I can't lose that."

"So you keep managing the lodge," he said. "You rock at managing the lodge. Look how much it's turned around in just a short time."

She shrugged. She'd wanted respect for so many years, and here it was Eddie Jessup who'd been in her corner all along. "Sometimes I feel like it's all I'm good for."

"Hey"—he stroked a finger down her cheek—"you're good for *me*. Or you would be if you gave it a chance."

"I do want to give it a chance. But you said it yourself . . . I'm scared to let go." She stared off at the falls, crashing in the distance. "I've always felt so apart from all this. What if you were right about everything—that spreadsheets and numbers are all I am?"

"*Mine* is what you are," he said, and before she could come up with some other protest, he shut her up with a kiss.

It felt right. *He* felt right. He truly saw her and understood, and better, loved her for who she was. They kissed, and her blood sang as some essential part of her recognized that, city or country, being in Eddie's arms was the only place for her.

As he pulled away, she slumped with a curse. "Crap."

A startled, baffled laugh escaped him. "Not the usual response I get after kissing the ladies."

She curled a fist in his shirt. "You better be done kissing the ladies, Edwin Jessup."

"Oh, I am. I swear." He crossed his heart. "So then what's the trouble?"

"The trouble is, I've got to go back," she said. "I have this stupid job now."

"Well, now you have a stupid *new* job."

She peered up at him. "I do?"

He nodded, a wicked gleam lighting his eyes. "It's going to keep you here. And this new job has benefits unlike anything you'd get in the city." He cupped her bottom and gave it a suggestive squeeze.

She gave a little squeal, then swatted him. "Be serious. What are you talking about?"

"I'm completely serious. I'm taking over the ranch."

"What?" She pulled back to get a better look at his expression, because she wasn't getting it. "What about Fairview?"

"Screw Fairview. I found out about the owls. We've stopped the project."

She sighed. "Oh, Eddie. I didn't know what to do. I knew you'd scaled back, and so the nests would be fine, but what about your company? What about Jack?"

"Jack will be fine. I'm pulling out of Jessup Brothers. Having just one permanent employee will take the heat off, at least until this economy turns around. Meantime, my brother can rely on his usual subs on an as-needed basis."

She stepped away completely then. She trusted him—she was ready to make the leap, lose control, take a chance—but Eddie owning a ranch didn't register. "What are you going to do with a ranch?" She guessed she could learn to love . . . what . . . cattle? What did people do on ranches?

"I'm turning it into a camp for at-risk kids." He let the statement hang long enough for her to parse his meaning.

It took her a sec, but when she got it, she felt the grin burst across her face. "That's perfect!"

"Pretty good, huh?" He smiled. "And I want you with me. I hate all the business stuff, but I thought maybe you'd . . ."

"You thought maybe I'd . . . ?" She raised her brows, beaming, holding her breath to see how he'd finish.

"Help me."

She deflated the tiniest bit. Eddie's expression had turned so serious, she'd thought maybe their conversation was headed in another direction . . . of the relationship variety. "Oh. Sure I can help."

She went into autopilot and turned her mind to practical matters. "If I'm not taking back my other job, they'll still need me more than ever at the lodge. But I guess with Hope there, we can manage."

"Of course, of course. I assumed you'd need to spend most of your time managing the Big Bear. I just thought you could advise me on the business end of things, you know, as I get it all up and running. I'll need to establish it as an official nonprofit, all that."

A glimmer of sadness came and went. It was time to accept it—she was and always would be spreadsheet girl. And yet it was true consolation to feel how, more than anyone else, Eddie respected her. He valued her opinions and her help . . . valued *her.* "I'd love nothing more," she told him truly.

"You don't need to love it. You just need to love me."

"I do, Eddie. I do." Something deep down unclenched. She might've been all business, but Eddie loved her all the same.

"Then there's one other thing." He dropped to his knee.

"Oh!" She'd been right—he *had* been heading in a relationship direction. But still, she had trouble completely trusting what was happening. She had to be certain, because she

was having trouble believing what her eyes were telling her.
"So . . . you're not just offering me a job?"

"No, silly." He twined his hands with hers. "I am offering
you something else. *Me*."

She shook her head, speechless, the emotion threatening
to overwhelm her.

He knelt there for a second, teasing her. "What, no
crying?"

She felt her expression explode into a joyous smile—her
heart brimmed with it. As always, Eddie's easy good humor
sent a warm and happy calm spreading through her chest.
"Give it a second. The waterworks are on their way." Deciding it was her turn to get playful, she peered down at him.
"But I've yet to hear a question."

"I've known you all my life, Laura Bailey." He held
tightly to her hands, growing more serious than she'd ever
seen him. "And I do believe I've loved you from the start.
So what do you say? Make me an honest man? Marry me?"

"You're already an honest man, Eddie. The best I've ever
known. And yes, I'll marry you. I do believe I've been yours
all along."

Thirty-eight

❦

Laura pulled into the ranch driveway, and something in her shoulders released. Tension had a way of fading like that whenever her fiancé was nearby. It'd been a couple of months since she'd decided to stay—really stay—once and for all, and she was grateful every hour of every day that Eddie Jessup was the sort of man who didn't give up.

It was a gorgeous fall afternoon, the sort of day when the sky was wide and blue, but the air was crisp enough to cool the sun on her shoulders. When she turned off the car, she could hear the classic rock station blasting through her closed windows. She had to smile—it was just that sort of scene, the kind that gave an easy, grinning, sunshine feeling. Like a deep breath in.

Like her man.

The Fairview project might've been canceled, but the work hadn't stopped. Eddie continued to renovate the ranch house, only rather than turning it into a resort, it would host his camp for at-risk kids. That'd been his stipulation for not talking to the press about Fox and his antics. The man had known about the nesting area, but it'd been news to the Fairview board of directors, and they weren't too pleased about being associated with razing threatened wildlife.

Fox was fired, Fairview made a sizable donation to Eddie's new nonprofit, and as long as construction remained several hundred feet from the habitat, they were good to go.

Eddie had a whole crew of volunteers to help him, too. It seemed to her like the place was crawling with Jessups, but notably, Rob Haskell was also helping out, and he often brought Luke, his and Helen's eldest. They were at the stage in construction that was all final finish work, like painting and installing fixtures, and it was really any day now they'd be done.

She opened her car door, and their new puppy, Buck, sprang out. "Go get him," she called. After weeks of cajoling, Eddie had finally dragged her to the pound in Silver City, but she'd been the one who fell in love the moment she saw the rescue pup, a husky mix he liked to call a malamutt.

As Buck bounded toward Eddie's voice, she pulled their lunch from the trunk—a basket of cold fried chicken that Sorrow had helped her assemble from the day's tavern special. She'd stashed it in the back, having learned the hard way not to leave food unattended for longer than two seconds around the dog, and this would've been more temptation than the little guy could've handled.

At the sound of eager barking, Eddie came out onto the porch, and the instant he saw her, a smile burst onto his face. "Hey, gorgeous." He leaned down to scruff Buck's head but didn't take his eyes from her. "I'm happy winter's coming, but I swear, I miss seeing you tromp around here in your short shorts."

"Hey, are you saying you don't like my jeans?" She twisted backward to get a better look at herself.

"Not at all. I'm saying I like your legs." He came up to

her and stole a kiss that robbed her reply, which she quickly forgot, anyway.

She let herself snuggle into him instead, kissing him back, inhaling the scent of Eddie and fresh air and cut wood. "Mm-hm."

When they parted, he said, "Though I much prefer them naked."

"What?" she asked, a little dazed.

"Your legs. I prefer them naked. And this, too." He swept aside her hair to kiss her neck. "And this." He slid his hand up her shirt, and his hand was warm and strong on her belly. "All of it, actually. I can't get enough of you, but we need to do something about all these troublesome clothes." He tugged at her waistband.

"Hey," she scolded, "someone will see."

He walked backward, pulling her around the side of the house. "That's what wraparound porches are for, darlin'."

He began to kiss her neck, but as he shifted, she glimpsed a suspicious something over his shoulder. She slid a hand between them, planting it on his chest. "Eddie, what is that?" She nodded at a pile of lumber in the yard.

"That." He looked like a kid who'd just stolen some candy. "That . . . is a stack of two-by-fours."

She wandered to the edge of the porch to get a closer look. A shadow caught her eye, and she glanced up to find that the bones of a strange new structure had appeared in one of the trees. "And what is *that*?"

He raised his brows, giving her an innocent grin. "Tree house?" He wrapped an arm around her and gave her shoulder a little jiggle. "Aw, come on, Laura. Kids need tree houses."

"And you need money. We need more donations before you can be building deluxe tree houses." She peered closer at it. "Is that going to be two stories?" He really was too much.

"But you got us all that furniture," he said, referring to

a donation she'd solicited from a major chain store in Reno—enough metal bunk beds to sleep twenty kids. "It gave me the idea that maybe we could talk to Up Country about them paying the tax on the lumber."

"Okay," she conceded. "That is a good idea. I'll talk to Tom." She gave him a loving bump with her shoulder. "In the meantime, you need to stop being such a softie."

He took advantage and snagged her close. "And you need to stop being so irresistible."

She sank into him, and he was half a second away from convincing her that wraparound porches just might in fact be private enough, when a crinkling sound called their attention. It was Buck, trying to nose open their lunch basket.

Eddie groaned. "I'm thwarted at every turn."

"Hey"—she plucked up the basket—"get out of there, sneaky."

"I warned you, Buck Larsen probably doesn't make the best namesake for a dog. He wasn't exactly the most trustworthy guy."

She grinned. "Is this where you make a joke about saloon bitches?" Eddie burst out laughing, and she added, "I love when I can make you do that." She took his hand. "Come on. Let's go eat."

They made their way to their favorite picnic spot, beneath the old beech that housed all those owl nests. After they finished, she leaned against him, feeling sated.

Even Buck had gotten his fill of chicken scraps and was napping in a patch of sunlight. She watched as the pup twitched and yipped in his sleep, dreaming puppy dreams.

Eddie followed her line of sight. "Look at those giant paws. He's going to be a monster."

"You're going to need to build *us* a tree house just to fit him." She and Eddie were still moving the last of her stuff into his cabin, and even though she didn't own much, they were already running out of room.

"Hey, I cleared a spot for that treadmill of yours."

"Elliptical." She corrected him so much about the thing, it'd become a joke between them.

"It's jammed against the western window, but it fits." He sighed contentedly, leaning against a tree. "But you're right. We'll need to build another place soon. To fit all of our kids."

Laughing, she jostled him with an elbow. "Easy, cowboy. How about one construction project at a time?"

Then she sighed, too, looking up at the canopy of pine boughs overhead. Not too long ago, she'd thought she was saying good-bye to those trees, and yet here she was.

They sat for a while, just sharing the quiet, listening to the woods. Being there. Being together.

After a while, Eddie stretched and inhaled deeply. "I love how fall smells. Do you smell it?"

She nodded. "I love it, too. I was worried I wouldn't be back for it."

He turned to look at her, asking her earnestly, "Are you happy being here? Being back for good?"

"I'm with you, Eddie. It's the only place I want to be." She turned her gaze from him, taking in the land around them. Several yards down, the creek babbled happily, shaded by pines. Winter songbirds chirped and hopped among the branches. A copse of aspen stood out—they were well downstream on the far bank, but their golden autumn leaves popped from the landscape. She felt connected. Contented. Loved.

"I'm with you, Eddie. I love you. And it's *all* good."